Praise for Dark Woods

MW00617978

"DARK WOODS, DEEP WATER is an enthralling dark fantasy with a gritty, gothic heart. There are no heroes here: instead the characters' varying shades of villainy fit perfectly into this horror-laced tale. Nail-biting, grisly, and genuinely chilling."

— Jess Hyslop, author of *Miasma*

"Dark Woods, Deep Water drew me into its spell, weaving its beautiful threads around me until I looked up and realized I'd been reading long past the time I should have been asleep. From the first page, I knew I'd follow these characters into whatever dangers lay in wait. A gorgeous, layered, compelling tale in a world both familiar and strange."

— Kate Heartfield, bestselling author of *The Embroidered Book*

"An eerie, fascinating tale, which - like all great stories - retains its mystery even after the last page is turned. We meet characters of varying motives and complexity, each of whom is compelling and, above all, real. The liminal world Dunato has created, with its rich seams of Slavic folklore, makes Dark Woods, Deep Water an extraordinary novel and its author one to watch. I have a new favourite."

— Lucy Holland, author of *Sistersong*

"Dark Woods, Deep Water is a treasure buried on the bottom of a murky ocean--the sort of Slavic fantasy I've always searched for, but rarely found. Set in a world inspired by the Eastern Adriatic where vengeful gods trap lost travellers in crumbling, haunted castles hidden in snowy forests, this novel was atmospheric, creepy, both fast paced and intricately built."

— Genoveva Dimova, author of *Foul Days*

# DARK WOODS, DEEP WATER

Jelena Dunato

Dark Woods, Deep Water

Copyright © 2023 Jelena Dunato

First published in Great Britain 2023 by Ghost Orchid Press

This is a work of fiction. Names, characters, places, and incidents either are the product of the author's imagination or are used fictitiously. Any resemblance to actual persons, living or dead, events, or locales is entirely coincidental.

All rights reserved. No part of this production may be reproduced, stored in a retrieval system, or transmitted in any form or by any means, electronic, recording, mechanical, photocopying or otherwise without the prior written permission of the publisher and copyright owner.

ISBN (paperback): 978-1-7392348-3-6

ISBN (e-book): 978-1-7392348-4-3

Cover illustration © Līga Kļaviņa

Cover design by Jelena Dunato

Book formatting by Claire Saag

*To my family, who let me work in peace.*

# CHAPTER ONE

## IDA

### SUMMER 361 A.C.

How does a girl find herself in such trouble?

It all went downhill when Doctor Bellemus deceived me for the last time.

No, wait, I'm lying to you. It all went downhill long before that. I started tumbling down the moment I fell out of my mother's womb. Deeper and deeper, little Ida, sinking all the way to the bottom.

I'm a pretty girl with big eyes, so I am sure you want to hear my story. Which one do you want, the happy or the sad one?

We barely know each other, so let us start cheerfully.

I was born in a house of ill repute in Abia; my mother practiced the oldest profession in the world. She did well—I got this pretty face from her—and I cannot say that I ever wanted for anything in my childhood. I grew up in the streets near the harbour, with sailors' children and street cats. I learned the three-cup trick before my sixth birthday. I would set up a little stall near a ship that had just docked and catch the sailors before the whores emptied their pockets. "Find the ball," I would say. I relieved many of everything they had. They thought it easy to fleece a little girl. I was rich then—at least in comparison to other harbour rats.

Once, I spent a silver coin on fortune telling. The old witch we called Moray pricked my finger, sucked out a drop of blood and told me that one day I would be the greatest lady in Abia, living in the palace, all dressed in silks. "Do I look like a fool you can lie to?" I spat and kicked her in the shin.

My mother had an additional source of income. She practiced the sort of medicine that is not taught at the University: illnesses and injuries suffered by the girls who walked the streets and an occasional sailor with a complaint. Sometimes I would help her—I wasn't squeamish.

Eventually, my little three-cup trick stopped bringing me money. Not because I was bad at it, but because the sailors were interested in another game. "Time to change your trade," said my mother, and sold my innocence to a fish merchant who could not wash the stink off his hands. It wasn't exactly the life I had dreamed of, so I packed my things and moved on.

I tried acting for a while and was good at it, but the leader of our troupe had a favourite actress who didn't like me, so she hit me with a cudgel and broke my tooth. After that, I travelled the fairs selling herbal remedies. It wasn't a bad job, but a woman travelling alone always attracts trouble. I needed a partner. That is how I met Doctor Bellemus.

So far so good, right? You heard the cheerful story. Do you want the sad one, too? Here it is.

I was born in a village on the Elmar border. My father disappeared before I was born. My mother told me he went off to war, but as far as I am concerned, he might have wasted away his life on the streets of Abia. Mother and I barely survived. We had a flock of sheep and some land, but we would have starved without the coin from my mother's talents for healing and setting bones. We were getting by until the war reached us. One day, as I was coming home with our sheep, I saw a column of black smoke rising to the sky. I almost ran toward the village, but stopped at the last moment and hid among the olives and dry stone walls. I waited for night to fall and then crept into the village. All the villagers were there. None were alive.

I was saved by some travelling merchants who found me on the road. They left me on a farm near the White Mountains, where the mistress took me in as a scullery maid. I worked a lot and was paid only in food, which was scarce enough. I was so thin it was a wonder I grew at all. But grow I did. My clothes became too tight, and the master noticed it. He could not persuade me to yield to him with sweet words, but fists helped where tongue failed. I lost a tooth and my virtue at the same time. I figured it was time to move on, stole all the money I could find, and started travelling the fairs, selling herbal remedies. And that is how I met Doctor Bellemus.

Feel free to choose the story you like best; it is all the same to me.

I first met Doctor Bellemus at a harvest fair near Myrit. I had just arrived with my sachets and vials, ready to set up my stall. All my cures worked, more or less—against tooth-ache, painful joints, cramps—the usual stuff. I wasn't doing poorly; I knew what I was talking about, and I could make people believe me.

I saw a commotion out of the corner of my eye. A crowd was gathering around a man with no stall, no goods on display. A performer, a prophet? I pushed through the mass to get a better look. The speaker, a man of middling stature and indistinct age, stood on a wooden box, dressed in a tunic of fine black wool, such as the learned members of the University usually wore. He had a carefully groomed chestnut goatee and an impressive pair of bushy eyebrows.

"… and the secret of this tonic is known only to the royal physicians." He held one tiny vial above his head. "It is punishable by death to talk about it."

A royal physician? He spoke in an actor's voice, powerful and clear.

"You wonder how I learned about it?" His dark, piercing eyes searched the crowd, challenging the unbelievers. "I was one of them, but I could not bear the thought of keeping such an incredible potion away from the people. I left their ranks to come among you, because you deserve to know." The vial in his hand caught a ray of sunlight and sparkled. "This extraordinary concoction of thirty-seven rare herbs and eight precious minerals cures all diseases known to men. It restores your youth, health and …" A flicker of a slick smile in the corner of his mouth. "Virility."

I had no idea it was possible to work like that. Stupid Ida.

"How much?" shouted a voice from the back of the crowd.

"How much?" The outrage on his face was worthy of applause. "This amazing tonic cures all ailments, past, present and future, and you ask *how much*? Well, my good man, let me ask you a question in return: how much is a human life worth? Your old father, struggling to breathe? Your young wife, wasting away after childbirth? Your little daughter, burning with fever? How much would you pay to see them strong and flourishing again?"

"I want it," a woman shouted. "Please, doctor."

"I only have a few vials left." Regret in his voice was so sincere I shivered. "And I am quite unwilling to part with them. But if it's a question of life and death …"

People pushed coins into his hands, begging him to sell them the tonic. He kept the vials hidden in his bag, there was no telling how many he had. Desperate fools fought to reach him, bidding loudly.

His show ruined my trade for the day, and I didn't even bother to unpack my things. Who would want to buy a salve for blisters and cuts when they could get an elixir of youth? I bought a raisin bun and found a place in the shadows, waiting for the crowds to clear. When he sold the last of his vials, they were still clutching at his clothes, begging for more. It took considerable time and effort to get rid of them. Dragging my possessions with me, I followed him to an inn. He first went into the stable and, while he talked to the boy, I sneaked in. Was he doing so well that he could afford a horse? A sharp pang of envy pierced my chest.

It turned out he was not that wealthy. There was just a small grey donkey, patiently waiting for him. I watched as he took his clothes off, but if you think I saw something tempting, you are mistaken. He had a hairy body and skinny legs, and with that ridiculous beard of his, he looked like an old goat.

He folded his woollen tunic, wrapped it in a piece of sail-cloth and put it in his leather bag. He took out a shirt of rough linen, worn-out hose and a frayed tunic. In a heart-beat, he turned into a poor ragman. I only recognized him because I never let him out of my sight. The last detail was a greasy cap fit for a pig boy.

Doctor Bellemus was a doctor as much as I was.

He wasn't so stupid as to leave his bag with the donkey. He picked it up and sauntered into the tavern filled with thirsty fairgoers. I pushed through the crowd, ignoring the calls, avoiding the groping hands. Woe betide a woman travelling alone.

He sat in a corner with a group of drunkards. Although they were not too welcoming, when he paid for a round of wine, they became fast friends. I hoped I would be able to catch him when he left after a few cups, but my plan went belly up fast. He drank with a grim purpose: three cups, five, seven … Evening turned into night, the crowd cleared out, but he sat there still. I had to do something about it.

I gulped down my watery beer and ran my fingers through my hair. I straightened my dress, pinched my cheeks. He didn't see me coming, he was looking at his cup. I squeezed in beside him.

"Do you need company?" I whispered into his ear.

He lifted his head and eyed me.

"How much?" he asked, without offering me the wine.

I eyed him in return. "One vial of your tonic."

A flicker of surprise flashed across face before he turned away. "Leave me alone."

"I know you're a cheat," I whispered. "I've been watching you all day. You do it very well." I put my hand on his thigh. He stank of wine and old sweat.

"What do you want?" he growled, but my hand confused him, and his hostility was turning into interest.

"I think you need an assistant."

He was drunk, not senseless. "I don't need one."

I knew he would not warm up to it easily. He was doing just fine on his own. But I had a plan.

"You know what?" I whispered in his ear. "When you come to the fair tomorrow, I'll show you what I can do. If you like it, we can talk about working together."

"Don't you dare—" he started, but I was already heading for the door.

I slept in the hayloft that night with a group of puppeteers from the South, whose soft dialect reminded me of home. In the morning, they gave me some bread and cheese in return for a pot of my salve. I helped them set up their tiny stage and left my bag with them. After that, I had nothing to do but wait for Doctor Bellemus.

There was plenty of time to look around. The previous evening, he had drunk a considerable amount of wine and it wasn't likely he would appear early. I rarely had an opportunity to see the fairs. I usually worked from morning till night, trying to sell as much as I could. But that day, I was free. The weather was nice, I remember, late summer, a bright day without a cloud. The best goods for the richest town in the Amrian Kingdom were spread on a huge meadow under its walls. The previous year, when the fair ended, I'd found the courage to enter Myrit and see its wonders.

It was a city like no other, as white as snow, walled, paved, scrubbed and shiny like a new bride. There were shops on every corner: I had seen fabrics in colours I could not name, fruits from exotic lands, jewels fit for a princess. I would have stayed there gladly, but the shop girls were the blushing, pampered shop owners' daughters, the physicians and apothecaries were all men, and even the whores looked like ladies. Wherever I asked for a job, they looked me up and down, rolled their eyes, and threw me out.

That day, it seemed there was a whole other town built on the meadow, less orderly and more colourful than the real one, made of fabric and wood. You could buy whatever your heart desired: supple leather jackets, boots and gloves from Till, dyed jade green and blood red; silver fox furs from Virion; intricate amber and jade brooches and bracelets shining in the morning sun; smooth glazed pots and jugs with cloudy swirls of dark sand melted into their edges. And food, of course, delights that made my mouth water: walnut bread and soft rolls, sweet, moist blueberry cakes, fresh and dried fruit, tart blue cheese, cured meat. I could smell sausages and seriously considered buying one, but I didn't have enough money in my pocket.

And anyway, I had never eaten two breakfasts in one day.

The man selling silver jewellery told me I was beautiful and pinched my cheek. I tried on a necklace with blue opals, but it cost far more than I could afford. I consoled myself that a pretty girl's finest ornament was her smile.

I searched for entertainment. A juggler with six balls in the air, followed by three burning torches bored me quickly. Ten paces farther, my friends the puppeteers were performing the legend of the Drowned Prince. That was something new—the Southerners usually ignored the legends of the North. I paused to look, together with a small group of people and children in their best clothes.

"It was a time when the borders between the worlds were thin," a woman narrated. "The time when gods and heroes walked among the people and death was not final if you were brave enough to fight Morana in her dark kingdom."

The wooden stage was coloured in the blue and green shades of water, with see-through ribbons shot with silver in the background, like fish swimming in the depths of a lake. The puppeteers moved their puppets slowly, creating the illusion of moving through water. Morana, the Goddess of Death, was a fantastic creation: a fish-woman, with a moray's tail, pointed teeth, red gills and hair made of a hundred writhing eels.

Each time she lunged towards the golden-haired prince, the children squealed with terror, and when the eels wrapped themselves around his sword and snatched it out of his hand, one little girl burst into tears. Her mother whispered, "Prince Amron will win. Look, he broke his chains."

In the end, I clapped my hands as eagerly as the rest of the audience and awarded them with a few hard-earned coppers.

I moved on, passing by a group of musicians tuning their instruments, thinking about my plan. I was nervous, I admit. I didn't particularly like that crook. But my goods were not selling, autumn was approaching, and I had to survive the winter somehow. I could start looking for a job in some dirty tavern and hope to stay warm, or risk freezing to death in a ditch. I had no chance of doing business if he was around, and there were too few fairs left that year to risk him showing up and ruining me. It would be easier if we were together.

When he finally appeared, I waited for the crowd to gather and for him to get in character. I let him tell them everything about the well-kept secret and his vial's amazing properties. People started crowding around him, trying to see the vial he was holding. He followed his words with slow gestures, letting the light penetrate the green glass.

I took a deep breath and counted to ten. It was time for my performance.

"Move!" I shouted at the top of my voice. "Move, let me pass! I must reach him, move!" First, I had to elbow my way through the crowd, but as I pushed forward, people started turning in wonder and letting me pass. "I have to reach him! Move!"

The crowd parted before me, and there was a clear path leading to his box. He froze. Insecurity flashed in his eyes and then, when he recognized me, panic. But he was an experienced actor, he waited.

"Doctor Bellemus?" I called. The audience went quiet, their eyes on me. I walked toward him. On his box, he loomed over me like a statue. I fell to my knees and hugged his legs. "Thank you!" I sobbed, and tears started rolling down my cheeks. "You saved my father's life!"

"Your father?" His confusion was genuine now. He was still holding the vial in one hand, the other he put on my head. "Dear child, tell me what happened."

My face was wet. I let go of his legs and pressed my hands to my heart. "He was on his deathbed, Doctor. He was coughing out blood and could not get up and my little sisters were crying because they knew they would soon be orphans. No-one could save him. He took my hand and said to me:

'Daughter, there's some money hidden under my pillow, take care of your sisters when I'm gone.' So I … so I took the money," I sobbed, "and I went to the fair to see if I could find something that would ease his last days. And then I saw you …" I let the tears cut off my voice and looked at him with hope in my eyes.

He accepted my story. "Did you give him the tonic, child?"

"Yes, Doctor," I said. "And that same evening … that same evening he stopped coughing. By morning, he got out of bed. It was a miracle, nothing short of a miracle. My father … two days ago, he was dying, today he is a healthy man. You saved his life; you saved my family. Thank you, thank you!"

It was one of my best performances, I admit without false modesty. Doctor Bellemus sold his entire stock as fast as people could push the coins in his hand. Had his vials been filled with air, he would have sold them too.

I was greedy. Let that be a lesson to you.

# CHAPTER TWO

## TELANI

### AUTUMN 361 A.C.

It was a wretched autumn.

We descended to Myrit from the north in a foul mood, but the city cared nothing for our state of mind. It greeted us with banners and music and drunken joy spilling down the streets. Half the kingdom was already there, or so it seemed. The whole court, for sure, and every nobleman worthy of his name, celebrating the birth of a princess.

"I can't remember if I ever liked this," my lord said, wading through a sea of excessively perfumed people. "I think not."

We arrived looking like refugees after the long journey. Before entering the city, we'd dismissed most of our armed entourage, letting go of the unwelcome duty we had performed and its bitter aftertaste.

"I want to go to Abia," he said as we climbed the lavishly decorated streets. "I've been on the road for too long. I wish they could perform the naming ceremony without me."

"It's not just the ceremony, my lord. The king will want a report."

"Yes, Telani, I am aware of that," he said with a wry smile.

The moment we entered the palace, he threw himself into court protocol without missing a step. A wash, a shave, a change of clothes, and a grubby provincial knight turned once more into Prince Amron of Larion, the king's uncle and commander of his army.

"The priests are here," I informed him as the servants attached his ceremonial cloak.

He sighed. "There's no escaping them, is there?"

Still, he was gracious as he entered the throne room.

"Greetings, Your Royal Highness." Perun's archpriest, the representative of the Father-God dressed in grey and silver robes, stepped out of the crowd and bowed before him. He was careful not to touch my lord, not even with the hem of his sleeve. Other priests huddled behind him, the splendour of their robes in sharp contrast with their worried faces. They clucked like hens who could sense a fox creeping upon them.

He made them nervous. A man whom gods spoke to usually did that to priests. A man who had died and refused to stay dead, even more so.

And yet, he greeted them all with kind words and affable nods, gliding between the magnificent marble pillars of the throne room, aiming for the plump, dark-haired woman with a baby in her arms, who was standing on a dais under a blue canopy. He kissed her round, blushing cheeks.

"Congratulations, my dear," he whispered. "Ready?"

The queen nodded and he gave a sign. Perun's archpriest approached the black marble altar, holding a white dove in his hands. In one smooth, well-practiced movement, he cut the bird's breast with a sharp knife and collected the blood in a shallow silver bowl.

"We dedicate this death to you, oh Father, and call for your blessings," the archpriest chanted. "Turn your eyes to us and hear our prayers."

"It's time," my lord said.

The queen hesitated for a moment before handing the little princess over to him. The two of them liked each other well enough, but she was a sensible, down-to-earth woman and his presence unnerved her.

"It's all right," he said, taking his grandniece in his arms. The girl's cloudy blue eyes slid over his face, unimpressed, drawn by the colourful gems on his chest. "What did you name her?" he asked.

"Orsiana, if you permit," replied the queen.

"Welcome, Princess Orsiana of the House of Amris," he told the girl, while the priests and the noblemen crowded to see her. "I swear before the gods that I will protect you and defend your birthright."

A wave of cheers echoed around the hall, disturbing the child. When she opened her mouth to wail, he returned her to the queen, who snatched her a tad too quickly. The king appeared beside her and put a protective hand on his wife's shoulder, throwing a guarded glance at his uncle.

I wondered how much diplomacy, persuasion and force was needed for the subjects to accept those two dark-haired, unglamorous people, completely bereft of their predecessors' charm, as their king and queen.

While the priests performed their divinations, I followed my lord into the garden, where the three little princes waited for the commotion around their newborn sister to end.

"The boys have grown," he said, watching them as they raced around the bushes, waving their wooden swords. "I never thought I'd live to see that."

Neither did I. "We don't belong here anymore."

Myrit was shiny and new, slick and fat like a prized goose. Filled with young people who knew us not as persons, but as legends from another time, if they knew us at all. We were the relics of the past, remainders of a much darker age no-one wanted to remember. Our presence made them uncomfortable and staying at court, especially when it was crowded, made my lord melancholic. He yearned to retreat to Abia, to his roses and oranges, to his study with the windows facing the sea, where the only living things in sight were the seagulls on the horizon. I had hoped Gospa Liana might meet us in Myrit and lift his spirits, but she failed to appear.

The king caught up with us in the garden and seized my lord's elbow. "Uncle," he said, "we must talk."

He was a nice boy who had grown into an amiable young man. Almost too amiable to be true, deceptively simple. With his large body and unruly hair, his clothes that always looked dishevelled, even if he was freshly decked out, with his queen, sweet as pie, with dimples in her cheeks, he looked like a happy farmer. A man who understood his cows, made the best butter in the county, and begot a child with his chirpy wife every year.

He manoeuvred my lord into a wood-panelled study and got straight to the point. "Vairn, that stubborn old weasel, what did he do? I've read your report, but you were frugal with words." He sat down and motioned my lord to join him.

"There's not much to say."

"I sent you to deal with the treason in the north and you did. They all came down to Myrit, you know, one by one, just as you said they would, petitioning for pardon, swearing it was just a horrible mistake. And I've been lenient. Confiscation of property, heirs sent to court as hostages, and I was ready to forgive. They all came. All but Vairn." The king frowned. "So tell me, what happened?"

"Vairn of Virion refused to bend the knee."

"But why?" The king looked puzzled. "Vairn had always been loyal to the Crown, like all northerners. And now I find out that the greatest northern commander, your old comrade and a war hero, wanted to start a rebellion against me. I do not understand, I really don't."

"Vairn preferred death to your mercy," my lord said. "He was a shadow of his old self, bitter and grieving. I tried to reason with him, but ..." My lord closed his eyes. "It's done now."

"But ..." the king ran his fingers through his tangled curls, "they did not even come up with a name. That's impossible, a rebellion without a pretender. Did Vairn tell you whom they wanted? Did he tell you the name?"

"No."

There was a silence, and I knew he would say nothing of the words spoken in the depths of the black fortress in the heart of Virion. Nothing of the old warrior's despair and derision. *We fought for you, Amron,* he had said in his freezing hall filled with acrid smoke, *all of us, nobles and soldiers alike. You led us; you were the reason we were there, not that royal whelp. He may be the rightful heir, but we chose you for our king.*

*And I refused it, and would refuse it again. I've never wanted to be king,* said my lord.

*And yet you were, in deed if not in name. And your nephew will never forget that.*

No, my lord had no reason to mention that conversation.

"Well," said the king after an uncomfortable stretch of time, "Vairn is dead, and I suppose I should be satisfied. Is there anything else I need to know?"

My lord shrugged.

The king narrowed his eyes. "In that case, I have another task for you."

"Whatever you need, sire."

"But first, send your man out." The king's soft brown eyes turned towards me and dismissed me with a blink before returning to my lord. "This is for your ears only."

"Telani."

"Yes, my lord. Your Majesty."

They sent me to wait in the corridor, as if I were a provincial petitioner. His Majesty's chamberlain walked by, inspecting me with intense animosity. "Eavesdropping, are you?"

"Yes," I said cheerfully. "The best way to learn the news."

In truth, the door was too thick for that. I heard muffled conversation and raised voices, but I could not make out the words. I had a few dried apricots in my pocket, so I sat on the parapet and nibbled at them, watching the courtiers in the garden. The day was unusually mild. I thought of that peculiar angle at which sunbeams pierced the Bay of Abia in the autumn, turning the water from deep blue to perfectly transparent.

At the bloodiest of times, when Seragian troops raided the Amrian Kingdom, leaving a trail of scorched earth, when we were losing the war and none of us knew if we would live to see another day, my lord told me, *think of a place you want to get back to and keep it in your mind*. He did not say *person*. He was not so naive to mention women, men, lovers, friends, mothers, sisters and other human beings, mortal and fickle. He said *place* and I imagined it, a wharf in Abia, the sea calm as a mirror, autumn sun above my head. The first time I returned there after the war, I fell to my knees and kissed the stone.

My lord stormed out so suddenly that the door slammed into the wall. "We are not going to Abia." His mouth was a thin, sharp line of anger. "You are free tonight; I won't be needing you. We leave at dawn."

My eyes followed him as he descended to the garden. He greeted everyone who approached him, exchanged a few words and slipped out of their reach before they had time to elaborate. He crossed the flower beds in a complicated pattern and disappeared towards the practice yard. Some poor bastard was in for a beating he didn't deserve.

I wiped my hands and went my own way.

# CHAPTER THREE

## ELISYA

### SUMMER 320 A.C.

The road's persistent dust and heat, I feared, would darken my skin and I would reach Myrit looking like a peasant.

Riding beside me, Silya lifted her face towards the sun's blemishing rays, smiling like a buck-toothed rabbit. I cannot say she was a bad companion. She was chatty and helpful, and she always showed the appropriate amount of gratitude to my family for taking her in, though we knew she would probably never marry. Her prospects were grim: not only was she a poor relative without a dowry, but she was also much less beautiful than me.

However, there was no time for gloomy thoughts. A gleaming white city with red roofs appeared before us, sprawled on a gentle hill beside the silver river. Its stones reflected the sunlight as if dusted with glass shards: the walls, towers, palaces all radiated. It was a mirage, fairy magic made of vapour and light.

"Can it be real?" I asked Silya, not trusting my eyes.

When Father told me he would take Keldik and me to the tournament, I thought my heart would burst with joy. I'd never travelled anywhere. Silya and I had sat trapped in the castle like cursed princesses. This was my chance to shine like a jewel among the ladies.

I had a new gown, the colour of the summer sky, the colour of my eyes. I could already see the fluttering standards and crests, sunlight gleaming on polished armour. I could hear cheering. If my champion won the tournament, he would crown me the Queen of Love with a magnificent floral crown. All the knights would drink to my health and minstrels would compose songs about my beauty.

"Look at the size of the city, look at all those buildings, so many of them," Silya said, enchanted. "And ... oh, look at the tournament field!"

The huge meadow beneath the city walls was a bustling anthill of carpenters. Servants raised the silken pavilions, as colourful and delicate as the wings of a butterfly. The smell of roast meat, vegetable stew and sweet cakes wafted on the breeze. It was a terrible chaos and the most exciting scene I had ever witnessed, and it wasn't even complete yet.

Father wasn't interested in all that clamour, he barely glanced at the vibrant universe that sprouted from the ground like wild flowers. A wide road paved with stones led over a slender bridge spanning the river, towards the immense wooden doors built into walls that reached towards the sky. The entrance was wide enough for two wagons to pass, and as high as three men. We were swallowed by the crowds entering the city.

The streets were full of people, but there was no mud or rubbish. Goods were displayed in almost every window and doorstep. I didn't know where to look first. One shop had leather gloves, belts, purses in every colour, shape and size. Another displayed silver jewellery, cobweb filigree, shining gems and bright enamel. The third one sold toys: wooden ships; horses that could move their legs, with real manes; dolls with faces so pretty it would be a shame to give them to children.

The houses were all built of stone, even the top floors. Arched lintels framed the windows, resting on elegant columns with flowery capitals, balconies had balustrades overflowing with flowers. Gaudy little standards criss-crossed the streets, flapping in the wind.

Our horses moved slowly, restlessly shaking their heads. As we climbed, the streets became less crowded and there were fewer shops. I could see the white gables and red roofs of the palace on top of the hill but, instead of moving towards it, Father led us down a side street. We stopped in front of a massive wooden gate.

"We'll stay here," Father said. "This is my friend's house."

We entered a narrow courtyard behind a high wall and dismounted. Stable boys led our horses away, and while our servants carried our things inside, Father pushed Keldik and me towards the door where our host waited. He was the same age as Father, a little taller than him, with receding brown hair streaked with silver.

"Welcome," he said and hugged Father.

"This is Keldik, my eldest son," Father said, presenting my brother. "This is his first tournament, and he's very excited."

After Keldik managed to mutter his greeting, our host's eyes slid towards me. "And this charming girl is your daughter?" he asked.

Father looked at me, smiling. "Elisya, this is my old friend, Gospodar Bremir. He's a cousin of the Knez of Leven and one of the most important people in Myrit."

"I'm enchanted," he said, and I had a feeling he was making fun of me. I blushed and curtsied, not daring to look at his face, but noticing the exquisite green satin of his tunic and the supple leather of his boots.

Silya was not introduced.

As the lord led us into his house, I expected to be impressed, but I was disappointed. The house wasn't unkempt or messy, but everything in it—furniture, wall decorations, tapestries, carpets—was well-worn, despite the high quality. It seemed someone had richly furnished it from cellar to roof some twenty years before and then forgotten about it.

"This is not the brightest or the most elegant of houses," our host said. "Since my lady died, I'm afraid no-one has paid it any attention. But I will make sure you have everything you need."

Silya and I were shown to our room: it had a large, canopied bed with fresh, lavender-scented sheets and a vanity table with a mirror.

"I think the old lord is sweet on you," said Silya.

"He's ancient," I laughed.

Silya helped me change out of my travel clothes into my new blue gown. When I looked in the mirror, a lovely young woman looked back at me.

"You know," Silya reflected, brushing my hair, "when I was a girl, that's exactly how I imagined Alaina, Amris's rusalka-queen. That transparent skin and long, wavy hair. The young knights at the tournament will go wild when they see you."

A rusalka, indeed. Father always claimed our ancestors came in the first wave from the North, with Amris the Golden-Haired. Perhaps there was a rusalka in our family tree, too. Legends said that many strange things happened in those days.

As I stared at the mirror, its surface rippled like water. The rusalka smiled at me, her mouth filled with sharp teeth.

I gasped.

"Did I pull too hard?" Silya lifted the brush. "I'm sorry."

I blinked and the illusion disappeared. "No, no, it's fine." The mirror was still. It was just my face, nothing more. "I just though I saw something …"

"A vain, silly girl pretending to be a lady," a voice said at the door.

My brother entered the room.

"Keldik," I said, "we're busy. Go away."

I could not understand how we shared the same parents. He was blond like me, but all resemblance ended there. I was short and curvy; he was of middle height and prone to getting fat. His face was covered in angry boils and deep craters that put pockmarks to shame. And instead of compensating for those obvious failings with friendly nature and intelligence, he stubbornly remained a spoiled little boy, cruel and stupid.

"Don't worry, I didn't come to chat with you and your ugly friend," he said. "I just want you to return my book of heraldry you stole."

"I didn't steal it. I just wanted to read it."

He stopped in the middle of the room, a look of surprise on his face. "Why on earth would you do that?"

"Because I want to know who is who at the tournament."

He stared at me as if a pair of horns had suddenly sprouted from my forehead. "What use would that be to you?"

"How else am I going to choose my champion?"

"How else ..." He sniggered. "Your brain is so filled with those legends you read that you've become an idiot. What do you think is going to happen? Some handsome young knight is going to fall in love with you and ask Father for your hand?"

A hot surge of anger washed over me. "Well, I'm a lady. Whereas you are no knight. You're afraid of your own destrier!"

It was a pleasure to see his boils turn crimson.

"At least that horse is worth a lot of money," he said. "Unlike you."

Sunset burnt the sky red while I stood in our host's yard, in my blue silk, with a string of pearls around my neck, pretty as the goddess of love. I was ready for the best evening of my life, my moment to shine. I would gather the young men's hearts like roses from the garden.

Silya stood beside me in a lovely green dress that belonged to me once, with new lace added to her collar, and talked with our host about the noble families of Myrit.

Father and Keldik were late, and when they finally appeared, my brother looked as if he had swallowed a frog.

Earlier that afternoon, I had heard Father shouting at him behind closed doors about lances and horses and fear.

When they stepped out into the yard, the discord between them was still simmering, but then Father looked at me and smiled. I smiled back, enjoying the brief moment as his favourite child, shooting a triumphant look at that pimply toad in velvet beside him.

Servants came out with torches and a litter was prepared for Silya and me, to spare our delicate dancing slippers from walking outside. The men followed us on foot.

The entry to the palace was crowded. I was so excited I paid no attention to the space around us, until liveried servants drew the heavy curtains, and we entered a huge hall filled with music and laughter. When someone read Father's name and title aloud, he grabbed Keldik and me and dragged us towards the dais. Erimir, Knez of Leven and Lord of Myrit, the host of the tournament, stood beside the king's throne, whispering in his sovereign's ear.

Father bowed deeply and we followed him.

"Your Majesty," he said when the king nodded, "allow me to introduce my son and heir, Keldik, who will ride tomorrow for the first time. He is nineteen years old. And this is my daughter, Elisya."

While Father spoke, I dared to lift my head and get a closer look at the royal couple. Queen Orsiana had a magnificent cloth-of-silver gown: every time she moved, the fabric shone like fish darting through the clear water. It was far more impressive than the frail, flat-chested and wasp-waisted woman wearing it. She was probably three or four years older than me but looked like a mere girl. Her hands were two sparrows; one hard squeeze could have crushed them. Her light blonde hair framed her unsmiling face with cold grey eyes.

The king was another creature entirely. He took up far more space than his body required and radiated a nervous energy that reached all the way to where we stood. He had the legendary golden hair of Amris's heirs, a regular face with a straight nose and piercing blue eyes, wide shoulders, and long legs. His eyes slid indifferently over Keldik and Father and settled on me. Too late did I realize I was staring at him like an orphan stares at sweets.

"Elisya, am I right?" he asked. "How old are you?"

I opened my mouth to answer but no sound came out. Father's fingers dug into my arm, and I stammered, mortified, "Sixteen, Your Majesty."

"A real beauty," he said and lightly waved his left hand. A page rushed towards us and led us away. Someone was already calling out the names and titles of the next guests. Our audience with the king was over. I felt a cold knot in my stomach. Father was fuming.

"What came over you?" he hissed. "To stare in such a way … you stole the king's attention away from your brother. Be sure that the queen will remember you now, and not favourably."

I wished to reply that the king was free to choose whom he would look at and address, but Father dragged Keldik away and left me alone in the crowd. Silya was nowhere in sight. I was surrounded by people I didn't know, laughing, drinking and dancing. All the girls had wonderful dresses that made my long-desired and carefully tailored blue silk look like a rag. I wanted to burst into tears and run away into the darkness.

"How awkward," said a voice behind my back. "But he likes to do that to girls. Don't worry."

I whirled to face a tall, dark-haired young man. Blue eyes, nice smile. My heart fluttered in my chest.

"I've heard … I've heard the king likes girls and girls like him back," I blurted out.

He burst into laughter, revealing pearly-white teeth. "Fantastic! And to the point. But be quiet, don't let Orsiana hear you. He swore fidelity to her, *again*, and now he's been gritting his teeth for … oh, it must be six months already."

Orsiana? He called the queen *Orsiana*?

Swallowing down my embarrassment, I took a better look at him. His face was distractingly handsome, with smooth, pale skin, high cheekbones and full lips. I gathered myself with some effort and asked, "And who are you?"

"Vairn," he said, as if that were all one needed to know. I tried to recall what Keldik's book of heraldry said about the black wolf on a silver field and then it dawned on me. Vairn, of course, from the North, nephew to the Knez of Virion, and cousin to Queen Orsiana. The heir to the iron and gold mines and vast snowy lands. Rich beyond the dreams of avarice and good-looking to boot. "And you are Elisya," he said, interrupting my thoughts. "The king made sure to introduce you to us all. A real beauty, indeed."

I blushed. The king's disturbing praise became strangely captivating on his lips.

"It's an honour to meet you," I stammered, overwhelmed by his presence, unaccustomed to such attention, "but now I should really try to find my companion."

"Oh, come on," he cut me off. "After this, every buck in the hall will want to dance with you. Let me at least be the first." Not waiting for my answer, he took my hand and led me among the dancers. It seemed they parted to let us through. Bright golden light shone on the spot where he stopped and took me in his arms. Faces around us became a blur.

"Wonderful," he whispered in my ear. His hands were gentle, and he was light on his feet, but I had never been more aware that a male body was so close to mine. A whiff of sandalwood and bitter orange reached my nostrils, warm and intoxicating. "You are a real little dancer. But I think I must leave you to others now. Wait for me in the garden when the music stops. You'll see a fountain, there is a rosary there with a bench." He bowed and disappeared into the crowd.

I saw Father looking for me. "Elisya," he said, but his tone was no longer disapproving. Company and wine had obviously changed his mood. "I thought I'd lost you all. Silya has disappeared, Keldik is chasing some girl …"

I had no time to speak to him, because another young man invited me to dance. Vairn was right, everybody wanted to dance with me. While they were whirling me around, I looked for his face in the crowd, our conversation still echoing in my mind. When the music stopped, I tried to find the exit to the garden and saw Silya. I rushed towards her.

"Silya!" I called her.

"Elly! I couldn't reach you all evening, there's too many people—"

"I have to ask you something important," I interrupted. "You remember all the facts. Tell me, the young Gospodar Vairn of Virion, what do we know about him? Is he married? Engaged?"

"Neither, as far as I know," she said, "But why?"

I didn't wait for her to finish. I threw myself into the crowd, elbowing my way towards the garden. Many had the same idea: they wanted the fragrant night breeze to cool their hot skin and dry the damp silk that stuck to their bodies. Couples scurried to dark corners, their whispers and soft laughter filling the air. But Vairn's directions were imprecise, and I could not find my way. I stood there, feeling like a fool.

"Are you looking for someone?" he whispered in my ear.

I startled and tried to hide my relief. "This is becoming predictable," I teased him, but my heart leaped. In the moonlight, he looked like an enchanted prince.

Instead of replying, he bowed his head and placed a hot kiss on my lips.

"What? How dare—"

"This was not predictable, I hope," he laughed.

I wanted to slap him. I wanted to kiss him. I wanted to die of shame.

"Have you picked your tournament champion?" he asked. "Or do you perhaps hope your brother will win?"

"Him? Never."

"Then pick me," he said. "And I'll unhorse every knight reckless enough to challenge me."

I laughed. His words were terribly arrogant, but they were spoken in such a charming manner I couldn't stop myself from believing them. And yet, something bothered me.

"I thought that a hero such as yourself would already have a dozen ladies lined up. I would be terribly embarrassed to discover I have to share the Crown of Love with other girls."

"Oh, Elisya, you beautiful, suspicious girl!" He lifted a tress of my hair, curled it around his finger and touched it to his cheek. "Soft as silk," he said and lowered his head again to kiss me. This time I was ready, and the second kiss was far better: slow, gentle and long. When he moved away from me, I stood on my tiptoes and continued where he stopped. We kissed in the moonlight, breathing together, our bodies touching. I had never experienced anything like it. Somewhere in the background, the music started playing again, footsteps crunched on the gravel, but we didn't move from our hiding place among the roses.

"I could do this forever," I said at last. My lips were sore from kissing.

"Sweet words," he smiled. "Music to my ears."

We kissed some more, until the moon disappeared behind the palace.

"Where will I find you?" he asked. "Are you staying here?"

I explained that we lodged with my father's friend in the city.

"Gospodar Bremir," he repeated his name. "I know who he is. I will find a way to send you a message."

"There's a girl, her name is Etta," I remembered. "She is the daughter of the Lord's steward. She could be our secret messenger. If Father finds out someone is sending me messages, he'll be very angry."

"I'm glad he protects you, so I don't have to worry about other young men."

We parted with kisses and his promise we would meet soon. Before I returned to the hall, I stopped by the fountain and splashed my hot cheeks with cold water. I straightened my dress and tried to fix my hair in the dark. The hardest part was returning a calm demeanour to my face. My lips curved into a smile by themselves, my feet danced with joy.

I was certain that everyone who knew me would immediately notice.

The hall was less crowded when I entered, but the music was still playing and there was plenty of food and wine left on the tables. I was reaching for a drink when Silya caught my arm.

"You have no idea how lucky you are," she whispered. "Your father was already looking for you when he noticed the father of the girl he wants for Keldik. There they are, in the corner, chatting." She eyed me suspiciously. "And look at you! Did a wild cat just drag you through the bushes? What were you doing outside?"

"I was kissing a young man," I said, enjoying the astonishment on her face. I laughed happily. "Ask me how it was!"

"How was it?"

"Perfect. Once you begin, you cannot stop. I don't know why people don't do it all the time."

Silya lifted one eyebrow. "Really? All the time? Day and night?"

Of course she thought I was exaggerating. Who would kiss Silya the way Vairn kissed me?

"Oh, look, he's there, talking to the queen," I said. Vairn stood beside Queen Orsiana, motioning with his hands. She was looking at him with the palest little smile, leaning on one of her ladies. "Isn't he incredibly handsome?"

"Incredibly handsome, yes," said Silya. "And the queen's cousin, as well."

"The best catch in this hall." I was offended by her lack of enthusiasm. "He wants to be my champion."

"Oh, Elly," she sighed. "That's nice, but do not expect something more. Such deals are not made by two young people in the moonlight."

While she prattled on, Vairn caught my eyes from the other side of the hall and winked. I touched my lips with the tips of my fingers: a kiss only he could recognize.

# CHAPTER FOUR

## IDA

### AUTUMN 361 A.C.

His real name was Gair, or at least that was what he called himself when we were alone. We sat in a field under a tree with our spoils. The donkey grazed the yellowing grass and the hills of Leven stretched as far as our eyes could see. We had reached an agreement.

Looking back, it was a mistake, but I was just too tired to travel alone, at the mercy of every highwayman. I wanted to have more than a few coins in my pocket and a haystack for a bed. I had a feeling—and feel free to laugh at me because of it—that in his crooked game there was a grain of real chance of success.

I had developed a sixth sense when judging people. This low on the ladder, there was nothing to break my fall: I was constantly one wrong decision from floating face down in the harbour at dawn. One wrong man, one forced 'yes' or indecisive 'no', one fall in the dark. I had an uneasy feeling about Gair, but he looked like a rogue, not a murderer.

We were lovers, but I use that word in the broadest possible sense, for there was no love between us. You might think that, if an older man and a pretty young girl travelled together and shared the hardships of life on the road and the success of their venture, there should be at least some feeling of tenderness and friendship, if not love, between them.

It didn't happen. Gair treated me like a piece of wood, or another stubborn donkey he had to drag around. He stank of cheese, sour wine and sweat, his sharp bristles scratched my skin, and his fingers were hard and unkind. Though he wasn't intentionally rough or violent, he was horrible in his complete disinterest.

When I did my job well, he gave a satisfied grunt and greedily pocketed his share. All the other ways in which I made his life easier, from preparing the food, taking care of our possessions, to warming up the bed, were accepted without a hint of gratitude.

His only redeeming quality was his talent: for acting, cheating, trading—call it what you will. When he donned that tunic and combed his bushy eyebrows and beard, he truly became someone else. Doctor Bellemus—who knows how he came up with that character? Perhaps it started as a real man, or several real men, though I highly doubt anyone like him ever entered royal chambers. It was more probable that Gair had some contact with the University. I heard you could always find a bunch of wordy drunks dressed in black around there.

Gair's earnings were good, his investment negligible. The most expensive part of his amazing tonic was the glass vial. The liquid in it was void of any medicinal properties. A splash of spirit, a drop of honey, some herbs for taste, and that was all. In the beginning, I even offered to make something more effective, some concoction that could ease pain, calm down, wake up, do something but he declined it with indignation.

"There must be absolutely no real effects," he said, "because they could divert or weaken the power of the mind. And the human mind is, my dear girl, more powerful than any medicine you can make."

It was the most valuable piece of advice I got from him.

After the first two or three fairs we visited together, I realized my calculations were off. Money flowed into his pockets like a shiny waterfall, but he squandered almost everything he managed to earn. He gambled. He drank. The little that remained, I hid from him.

"I hope you do not think you will get rich with me," he said.

Cold tendrils of fear crept up my spine at night. I would check on our possessions. In the dark, I would search for the coins sewn into the hem of my skirt. I even considered relinquishing our venture, but if I had woken up one morning and said goodbye, he would have probably just shrugged. He was fine when I was with him, he was fine without me. I wasn't stupid enough to try such a theatrical gesture. After all, we both knew what bluffing was.

Working with him still brought me more money than I would be able to make alone. Even when I was spending it to cover our joint expenses, I was still comforted by the weight of my purse and the hope that the spring would soon come, with the fairs and the promise of income. What was it to me if he spent all his money? I would always be able to pay for our lodging and a bowl of watery stew. Without him, in mid-winter, I had no chance of earning anything, unless I wanted to wait tables and whore my way around dirty inns.

I travelled with a crook, I saw him perform: every live-stock-harvest-autumn fair at every town, village and shithole in the kingdom was our stage. I helped him cheat other people and still I believed he was fair to me. It turned out that swindling those fools at fairs was nothing compared to what he did to me.

I hope you do not think it was some kind of justice.

Trouble caught up with us in Haragov Dol, a filthy little place on the southern border of Leven. We had spent the night at the only inn in town and ate a hearty breakfast of rye bread, cheese and boiled eggs. Full and in a good mood for acting, we sauntered to a cobbled main square sur-rounded by half-timbered houses that had seen better days. Selling our wares in its middle, we managed to attract a de-cent crowd, although it wasn't a market day. Our perfor-mance transformed us into a travelling theatre company of two.

We had sold a dozen vials, when two uniformed guards and a dishevelled maid appeared round a corner and ran to-wards us.

"Shit," Gair muttered. "I hope this is not about market days, again."

I quenched my instinct to flee. Respectable doctors and their assistants didn't run from the authorities. Gair drew himself to his full height. The good townspeople moved to let the newcomers pass, thrilled that our show suddenly got a second act.

"Doctor, you must come with us immediately!" the maid cried. Her cap was all askew and her plump face red and sweaty from exertion. "It's a matter of life and death."

Gair didn't bat an eyelid, but I felt him stiffen. In every town there was a fool who wanted a home visit. But unlike other fools, this one had armed guards.

"What is the matter, good woman?" Gair asked.

"My lady, she needs your help. Her son is gravely ill, and my lord has gone to fetch a physician, but he hasn't returned yet, and the child ..." She paused to catch her breath. "You must come."

Two dozen curious eyes stared at us while the morning sun glinted off the guards' helmets. The money we had just earned was heavy in my purse, dragging me down like a millstone. There was no escape, and Gair knew it too.

"Take us to your mistress," he said. "And tell me what happened."

We gathered our things and started walking briskly away from the crowd, the woman hurrying before us and the guards following behind.

"We were travelling to Myrit. His lordship has been offered a position at court and we went with him. But as we were passing through this town yesterday, young master Teron got ill so suddenly he fell off his horse, shivering and unresponsive, right in the middle of the square.

"The mayor has been kind enough to offer us his house, but alas, the town has no physician. So my lord rode off at breakneck speed back home to bring the one we have there. All night, we tried to help the boy, warming him up, trying to feed him soup, waking him ... but to no avail. And then we heard there was a doctor in the town square and my lady sent me to fetch you and … here we are," she concluded, entering a small yard behind a house that didn't look much bigger or grander than its neighbours.

I exchanged looks with Gair as we walked into a dim hallway. A lord's son? If he lived, we would be rich. But if he died …

"Take me to see the patient," he said, and, to his credit, there was no panic in his voice.

The maid took us to a small room, where the lady kneeled down beside a bed. When she heard us enter, she rose with such a desperate look in her eyes that my heart felt heavy. Her young face, fair and freckled, looked haggard in the morning light.

"Doctor," she said, "my servants tell me you have a cure for all diseases."

"My lady." He bowed before her. "Indeed I do."

"Save my son, and I'll give you whatever you want."

He paused, sombre and dignified, like a raven among sparrows.

"It is not easy to cheat death, my lady, and therefore, I must prepare for the battle. Would your ladyship be so kind to leave me and my assistant to examine the patient alone? Any distraction at such a precarious time might be fatal for his weakened body. We must be left in complete peace until we decide on the best course."

She paled a little but then quickly nodded and kissed the child's forehead. "Do what you must to save him, Doctor," she said. "My maid will be in the hallway, call her if you need anything."

When the door closed behind her, he stepped to the window and looked down.

"Too high to jump," he whispered.

"Then we'd better do something to save our necks," I whispered back.

"Like what?"

"Like examining the patient? How about that?"

"What good will that do?" He walked to the bed, pinched the sheet between his thumb and index finger and pulled it off. The boy lay unconscious, his breathing quick and shallow. He was small, no older than seven or eight, and fair-haired like his mother.

"Hm." Gair scratched his beard. "Do you think he will get well by himself?"

"Move and let me see him."

I felt the heat as soon as I approached the bed. The boy was hot as a furnace. His shirt was soaked, his flaxen hair wet.

"The Elmar sweat," I said.

"What?"

"It's a sickness we have in the South." A flash of memory: shivering people, my mother trying to help.

"Some childhood disease?" he asked with a hint of hope in his voice.

"No. It kills you in a day." I bit my lip, trying to remember. "Unless … Open the window, quickly."

As the cold air rushed into the room, I stripped the boy, grabbed a wet rag and started washing him. His skin was so hot the water almost sizzled.

"Tell the maid to run to the kitchen and fill a tub with cold water."

"Are you mad?" he hissed. "What kind of peasant nonsense is that? No physician would ever—"

I let out an exasperated groan and opened the door.

"Hey, you," I called the maid. "There must be a tub or a big cauldron in the kitchen, fill it with cold water, quickly. We need to immerse the child."

She lifted her eyebrows and opened her mouth, but I screamed, "Run!" and she did.

Gair grabbed my shoulder. "What do you think you're doing?"

"Saving his life. Help me carry the child."

But he stepped back, his face distorted in contempt. "You fool. All we need to do is wait—"

"If you're not going to help me, move out of my way."

I took the limp little body in my arms, barely heavier than a lamb, and rushed down to the kitchen. He was so hot I thought my skin would blister. The maid and the cook were filling a wooden tub, while the lady wrung her hands in desperation.

I dunked the boy unceremoniously. "More water," I ordered. "He needs to be immersed completely."

"You'll drown him," the lady wailed, but the maid poured a bucket of icy water over his head. I held his head so that his nose and mouth remained above the surface.

"We need to bring down the fever, my lady," I explained in the most assured voice I could muster. "It will not break by itself."

"But he's ill, we must keep him warm."

My eyes met hers above the tub. She didn't believe me, but she dared not stop me. They had tried everything else, and it had not worked. Time was running out.

"Please," I whispered. To her, to the boy, to the gods above us.

She wept silently as we waited for what seemed an eternity. My calm assurance was just a mask hastily pulled over fear and anxiety, but I could not afford to show even a morsel of doubt. I held the boy's skinny limbs while his little body cooled down slowly. And then he shivered and opened his eyes.

"Mother?" he whispered.

"Teron. Oh …" She pushed me away and took him in her arms.

"Mother, I'm cold."

"Bring me the towels, quickly. We must get him back to bed."

"Keep him cool," I said, but no-one listened to me. Women took the boy, wrapped him up and carried him away, leaving me alone. As the commotion moved upstairs, a welcome silence fell on the kitchen.

I took a deep breath and rubbed my eyes with the heels of my hands, exhausted. Perhaps the boy would live, and we would get our reward. But at that moment, I only wished for a soft bed in a dark room.

"You," a voice said.

I startled.

A woman in black stood in the tub, in the icy water that reached up to her knees. I didn't hear her enter; I didn't hear the water splash.

"You took something that belongs to me."

She was an arm's length away, but her shape was hazy, like something seen from a distance, in a fog. An illusion. White, expressionless face, two black holes for eyes, a gaping mouth. Behind it, a wet, writhing black mass, like a coil of snakes moving under her skin, and sharp white teeth.

"Ida." The Goddess of Death reached towards me. The tip of her finger touched my forehead and I screamed.

# CHAPTER FIVE

## TELANI

### AUTUMN 361 A.C.

The morning light pierced my head like an ice pick. I tasted blood and realized I had acquired a deep cut on my lip sometime during the night. My lord looked me up and down in silence when he came into the stable, and his stern face warned me it was best to mutter a *good morning* and move away as fast as possible.

Dawn dyed the sky pink, but as soon as we rode out of Myrit, dark clouds gathered, and a light drizzle turned into a cold downpour. A portion of the retinue who had followed us on our previous journey joined us again on the road: six men who knew our pace, talked little, and gambled with me at night around the fire.

I removed my hood and lifted my head towards the sky, letting the rain wash away my fatigue and hangover. I breathed in deeply, wiping the drops off my face.

"Like the old times." Those were the first words my lord had uttered since we passed through the city gates. Perhaps it was just a trick of the light, but I saw a faint smile tug at the corner of his mouth.

Like the old times … I feared I had become soft, that I had lost my edge, and not only because of my age. The idea that I was my lord's secretary used to be a hilarious joke. Oh, I could write a letter and add two columns of numbers, but that was not my true purpose. I was his last line of defence, his eyes, ears and knife in the dark, a physical barrier preventing attack. Somebody who didn't have to play by the rules.

And I still was, in some ways. I went where he could not go and did what he could not do. The peace in the kingdom was not as firm as it looked, nor did everyone accept things as they were. The old Knez of Virion was not the only noble who thought my lord should have taken the throne. At one point, it looked like the most logical solution. He was a prince of the blood, he had won the war, he was a competent regent who understood the needs of the kingdom. But the order of succession was clear, and my lord said we had not spilled all that blood just to steal the crown from the rightful heir.

I wondered how the king felt, knowing that he wore the crown just because Prince Amron refused it.

Nevertheless, times had changed. No longer did I wake up in the morning wondering if I would survive the day. I spent most of my time in the palace in Abia, holding a quill instead of a knife. I slept in a featherbed; servants took care of my needs. If I wanted money, or land, or a young bride, I only had to ask.

"Who wouldn't miss this?" I asked. "Open road, bad weather, days spent in the saddle ..."

"The best years," he said, and I knew the dark cloud that engulfed him in Myrit had lifted.

Time barely touched him, although he complained he was getting old. The blond hair of Amris's descendants was unmarred by grey, the sharp face perhaps a bit sharper, his tall, wiry figure the same as twenty years ago.

"What task did His Majesty give us?" I asked. "If it's not a secret?"

"It's not a secret," my lord said, his good mood evaporating. "And it's not a task, not officially."

"It never is."

If I were a fly on the wall in the Small Council meetings, how many times would I hear: *Send His Royal Highness, Prince Amron?*

"His Majesty asked me to visit a woman I haven't seen for almost twenty years. She was my mother's lady-in-waiting."

I nodded in silence. He looked at the rain, at the trees that lined the horizon. The sky was a silver mirror, dividing the realm of men from the realm of gods.

"She has a son. The king wants me to take him to Abia as my ward."

Fostering noble youngsters was a common practice. But a king asking a prince to take some minor noble's offshoot? I frowned, curious to know what made the youth so special.

"They live in the north-east of Leven," my lord carried on. "The journey shouldn't take more than twelve days, if we don't go through Myrit on our way back, but cut directly to the south. It's still early in the year for snow, and we might be lucky enough to return without problems. I thought—twelve days, that much I can give to my king. And then I will remain burrowed in Abia until the spring."

"We have to be fast," I said.

"Aren't we always?"

The rain followed us all day, as if it wanted to make clear the journey north was a bad idea. By evening, we were cold, hungry and tired.

An inn with a fox's head on its sign looked as though it might have dry stables and hot food. Rooms, too, perhaps even clean sheets, without bedbugs and lice. The days when I had made do with some straw in the corner were far behind me.

The inn was empty but for a small group of merchants travelling south, chatting by the fire. Nobody familiar. I took a room, checked if the horses and the men were happy with their quarters and ordered dinner.

"Hot food and a girl to warm your bed?" asked the inn-keeper, winking.

"Yes, and no," I said.

My lord ate alone upstairs, and I remained with the soldiers. They stuffed themselves with roast pork and crusty bread while their cloaks dried by the fire. Someone produced a deck of cards. We spoke little as I graciously lost a handful of coins and bid them good night.

I knocked on my lord's door. At roadside inns, he would find a desk, a table, or any hard, straight surface, and get his quills and papers. He never kept a diary, but wrote to his wife every day, even when he had no means of sending the letters. I wasn't even sure she read them; she wasn't the reading type. Gospa Liana preferred fast horses, archery, dancing, filling her days with sweaty exercise and reckless laughter. She could hardly sit still, even for the time it took to read a letter.

He lifted his eyes off the page. "Is everything all right?"

"Yes. Our men will stand guard till morning. That other group, they really are merchants, I checked their baggage while they were eating. Beautiful samples of wool, if you're interested."

"Perhaps some other time," he laughed.

I shut the door and leaned on it.

"My lord, this task the king has given you." I cleared my throat. "Is it going to be as hard as defeating the Knez of Virion?"

"I don't know." He pinched the bridge of his nose. "Maintaining the peace is supposed to be a noble duty, but sometimes I wonder."

I waited for him to explain, but instead he picked up his quill.

"Do you need anything else, my lord?"

Two candles illuminated his face above the small desk beside the window. I thought he would not reply, but then he said, "They gave her my mother's name, imagine that."

"They wanted to pay tribute to Queen Orsiana. I believe they thought no further." I sighed. "Does it bother you?"

"No, no, it doesn't. I just wish they were wiser. Why provoke?"

"They are not afraid, obviously."

"No. Nor should they be. But if I had a daughter, I'd wish her to be happy, not magnificent."

At dawn, we went downstairs for porridge and small beer before continuing our journey. Outside, the sky was clear, and a northern wind was rising. The cold nipped my face as I mounted my horse. We had left Abia in the early autumn, on a mild, sunny day, but long years on the road had taught me to always take my fur-lined cloak with me.

My lord looked at the sky, sniffed the wind. "It won't snow today," he said.

We travelled fast. Two days later we were already in the rolling, rich fields of North Leven, stunning in autumnal colours. I rested my eyes on the red and gold opulence of the trees, on neat little villages and great estates beside the road. The quality of the food improved, and the inns became more comfortable and welcoming.

We reached our destination on the afternoon of the third day. A hunting lodge nestled in a pretty valley under a steep, wooded hill. It looked like a small castle, built of wood and yellow stone, old, but well-kept. A place created solely for amusement.

As we dismounted, a group of servants surrounded us, leading our horses away, bringing refreshments. Their mistress was close on their heels. She greeted my lord with a formal curtsy and proceeded with informal kisses on both cheeks.

"Your Highness! How long has it been?"

"Lenka," he smiled. "A hundred years, or so it seems."

She wrapped her little hands around his. I had never had the chance to see the late Queen Orsiana's court, but the stories about her ladies-in-waiting, the prettiest, smartest, richest, most cunning girls in the kingdom, could inspire generations of minstrels. The golden years, before the war had destroyed every joy, every frivolity, every quest for beauty.

When I asked him about life at court, my lord once told me: "I remember clearly a deep feeling of uneasiness. I remember quarrels, jealousy, deception, hostility, isolation and unfounded self-confidence. And yet, when I think of it now, it seems my whole life there was one long summer afternoon, spent on the grass, with a glass of cold wine in my hand and my head in some pretty girl's lap."

Gospa Lenka certainly fit that description, with her oval face, large brown eyes and hair still almost completely dark. She had married in the meantime, had children, left the court, buried one husband and then another, and added their wealth to her already substantial estate.

"You came," she said.

"His Majesty insisted," he replied.

She paused, the welcoming smile fixed on her face, hiding something darker beneath it. Caution? Fear?

"We haven't seen each other in a very long time," she said guardedly, "but I see you haven't changed at all."

Although she had lost the freshness of youth, she was light and swift on her feet. She took care of accommodating our men, stabling our horses and stirring the kitchens to get the preparations for the feast going.

Our soldiers retired, but I followed my lord. I never assumed I was free to leave until he released me. Our hostess shot me several furtive glances before she lost patience and asked, "And what shall we do with you? I don't believe I know you. Are you a part of the retinue, or …?"

"This is Telani, my secretary."

"Secretary?"

I straightened up, tried to smile, and bowed to her.

"Pleased to meet you, my lady."

She examined me closely, with a slight frown. I was used to such reactions: even at my best, I wasn't an attractive sight, let alone in situations like this, when I was tired and dirty. Women, especially this breed of women, never cared for me. Fortunately, the feeling was mutual.

"Secretary, yes," confirmed my lord.

She was not fooled by the thin varnish of my politeness. "But he looks like …"

She didn't finish her sentence, yet it was clear what she meant. Rat, rascal, southern scoundrel. Prince Amron should have hanged me on the spot when we met, but he took me into his service instead. Her look of distaste tempted me to tell her that.

My lord shrugged. "There's nothing he can do about it. I keep him close because he makes me look better, and he also writes in a beautiful hand." He winked at me over her head. "You're free to go. Make yourself presentable, you're scaring the lady."

I wandered off, hoping someone would direct me to my room and tell me where I could wash and shave. I walked the corridors of the lodge, built in the shape of a horseshoe around a paved courtyard. A covered passage stretched around the entire length of the first floor. I stopped to watch grooms entering the stables, huntsmen at the kennels on the other side of the yard, serving girls and little pages in livery running from one end to the other. The place was teeming with life.

I turned away and passed through several connected rooms that reminded me of the stories of Myrit before the war, when you could cross from one side of the palace to the other on woollen carpets, without your feet ever touching the bare floor. Chamber after chamber, all filled with hunting trophies, well-crafted weapons, carved furniture, lavish tapestries and colourful carpets. A fire was lit in every fireplace, as if a huge company were expected to walk in at any moment.

I sat in one of the chairs by the fire, just to rest my feet, but I must have dozed off because a soft sound awoke me. A skinny youth eyed me from a safe distance, rolling on the balls of his feet. The fire behind his back turned him into a dark silhouette.

"So. You are the prince's assassin," he said. "Did you come to kill me?"

My eyes were unfocused, my neck stiff. "I am the prince's secretary," I said. "And I have no idea who you are."

But the youth was already gone, swallowed by the darkness. Perhaps I only dreamt him, for the next thing I remembered was someone gently touching my hand: a little page trying to wake me up.

"I apologize, sir," he said. "I was sent to find you."

Once again, I had the opportunity to enjoy the blessings of civilization, like a spoiled young lady: hot water, richly foaming soap and soft towels. Where were the times when real men simply scraped off the top layer of dirt from their faces and carried on?

Clean, groomed and shaven, I drew the line at scented oil. I chose the formal clothes I wore at the ceremony in Myrit, judging that in this case too much was better than too little.

At the long table in the brightly lit great hall, there were so many people that I quietly found a free spot at the end, looking for our men. When I saw them seated comfortably, with full plates and cups, I sat to dinner with a light heart. My lord was at the high table, our hostess beside him, wearing a gown the colour of marigolds, her hair pinned up with bright gems, her hand touching his elbow too often, her gaze resting on his face. *Another one.* Like moths to a flame, but who was I to judge? I had spent my whole life watching men, I could see him just as well as any woman did.

Later, when the food disappeared from the plates and only the wine remained, when the moon set and midnight had long passed, I followed my lord to his chambers.

"Do you want me to guard your door tonight?" I asked.

"No," he said. "The page sleeping outside will be enough, and I have some unfinished business I've been carrying with me since Abia. I could squeeze an hour or two of work from this night. I need you here."

We wrote letters for a while, enjoying the silence disturbed only by the scratching of the quill and crackling of the fire. A knock on the door interrupted us and my lord smiled, eyes still on the document before him. Suddenly, I knew why he wanted me to stay.

"It's just me," a hushed voice said. Gospa Lenka entered the room in a simple dress, her hair already plaited for the night. "I saw the light so I thought we might talk." Her eyes slipped over me. If my presence surprised her, she didn't show it.

He put down the quill and motioned to an empty chair.

"Little night talks," she said, sitting down. "Just like the old times."

He gave her a neutral smile, letting the veneer of politeness cover the sharp edges. People pursued him mercilessly, tugged at his sleeve, lay in wait for him in corridors, broke into his room at night. On countless occasions, I served as a barrier between him and people who lacked common decency—usually rich, powerful, and accustomed to getting their way. And in all that time, I had never heard him raise his voice or utter an angry word.

I believe he kept me by his side all those years because I never asked him for anything. I had no family, no land, I had paid my debts long ago, and picked my lovers according to their insignificance. I knew he had full confidence in only two people: me, who would be a dead man without him; and his wife, who could have had the whole world but chose him instead.

Gospa Lenka straightened her dress over her knees and accepted a glass of wine. She shot me a dark look under her lashes: washing, shaving and changing clothes had made me no more acceptable to her. I returned her look with a smile and found a more comfortable position in my chair, burning with curiosity. Old times? Night talks?

A king's son and a queen's lady-in-waiting, how predictable.

"I'd like to talk about His Majesty's letter," she said, glaring at me. She could not complain of my presence directly, but she made her displeasure very clear.

"Does he bother you?" my lord asked, following her gaze. "Telani, please, pretend you're not here." And then to her, "He's just a secretary, Lenka. Anyway, it is late, it wouldn't be proper."

There was a moment of tension before she said, "No, no, it wouldn't." She bit her lip.

"So," he said, "my royal nephew asked me to come here and solve that … problem that's been dragging on for months. This was not my idea, but I cannot refuse the king, can I?"

She was polite enough to blush. "Of course you can't. I got a letter, too. His instructions are very clear." Her fingers crumpled the fabric in her lap. "I understand why His Majesty is interested in Raden. But his plan terrifies me." She met my lord's eyes, pleading silently.

I rushed through the gallery of faces we had met that day. Raden. A gangling blond youth with serious eyes and a sharp nose. Eighteen or so. Too uncoordinated to lift a spoon to his mouth without spilling. He had stuck in my memory: there was something odd about him.

"Surely you don't think the king would hurt him?" my lord said.

"You know the king far better than I do." A shadow of fear crossed her face. "But no, I fear Raden might hurt himself. My son has many qualities: he is talented, brighter than his brothers, diligent. And yet he does himself a disservice. He makes no friends. He is hard to love."

My lord nodded but said nothing.

"When he was a boy, he showed a talent for divination. I don't understand it, but the priests confirmed he was a natural. The University invited him, and I thought that at fourteen he was too young to go on his own, but Raden wanted it, fascinated by all that knowledge, all those books. It turned out he was miserable there. The other students envied his talent, they tortured him for it. And then he read some books he shouldn't have, and the priests accused him of being a—" she stopped and looked at my lord.

The word she couldn't utter was probably *heretic* or some similar rubbish the University loved to flaunt. He motioned her to continue.

"After they expelled him, he returned home crestfallen, but I thought, he's alive and that's all that matters, he'll find some other interest eventually. But Raden sits in his room surrounded by books, or rides alone through the countryside, and shows no will to set his life in order."

She was creasing and then straightening her dress. Words eluded her. She shot me a quick look before she continued.

"The king invited him to Myrit. Offered him a place at court. Imagine the honour. But Raden refused. If I had known, I would have stopped him, and told him to accept. Gods, it was such a friendly gesture!"

"I almost find such honesty more appealing than relentless fighting for the king's favour," said my lord with a shrug.

"Almost but not quite, yes?" she retorted. "That would simplify many things. Although, in truth, Raden is ill-suited for Myrit and smart enough to know it. Dangerous beasts lurk in the shadows. They would tear him apart."

My lord drummed his fingers on the desk. "And the king understands that, obviously. That's why he suggested Abia."

She took a sip of wine and looked at my lord with her head cocked to one side. "Give him a chance. I know he's not very likable, and his talent is scary, but he is a good boy and in the right surroundings …" Her eyes teared up, she wiped them with the back of her hand. "You're leaving for Abia in the morning?"

"Yes, but not through Myrit. We're taking a shortcut, straight to the south-east. The roads are worse, but the journey is shorter and I'm in a hurry. We'll need nine days of fast riding, if the weather permits."

She nodded. "And what if I asked you to leave Raden here for a while longer? To spend the winter with me? I promise I'll send him to you in the spring."

My lord shook his head.

"I know I ask much of you," she added quickly. "But it would be easier for you and him both. He will be a burden to you, trust me, if that boy is good at one thing, it's complaining. And I will make sure he does nothing stupid this winter, I swear. And as soon as the snow melts, you'll see him in Abia."

"I don't doubt it would be good for all of us," my lord said. "However, it is not my decision, but the king's. And the king wants him to leave now." Seeing the expression on her face, he added, "I promise Raden will be safe. He will have to endure nine days of uncomfortable journey and that is all." He lifted an eyebrow. "Come on, you can't claim the boy has no taste for adventure. He had to inherit at least a little bit."

"I'm afraid not." She scowled. "Looking at him, you'd think he was preparing for an execution. He locked himself in his room yesterday and refused to come out. He calmed down tonight, after talking to you. Whatever you told him, it helped. But I still think it is not the right time to travel."

"He made no mention that he didn't want to go. Actually, I got the impression he wanted to see Abia," my lord said. "From one closed room filled with books to another, is that so bad?"

She blushed. "Raden would never dare tell you he didn't want to go. You are his … I don't even know how to say it and not make it seem absurd … hero? He keeps asking me questions about you, about Queen Orsiana …"

The name fell like a lead weight, followed by a heavy silence. I gritted my teeth: I abhorred turning real people into legends and heroes. It glossed over the pain and loss; it ignored the price they paid. My lord's fingers glided over the surface of the table, drawing invisible letters.

"I hope you remember her fondly," he said at last.

"Your mother was the kindest woman I've ever met," she said. "I hope she had forgiven me."

"If she had found the strength to forgive my father, I am quite sure she forgave everyone else," he said softly. "I have never heard her say *all my ladies were good save for Lenka.*"

I thought she laughed, but then I realized she was sobbing.

"I'm sorry," she said, trying to dry the tears that kept running from her eyes. "I'm crying and I have no right."

My lord shot me a quick pleading look. I produced a clean handkerchief and poured more wine into her glass.

"Here, dry your tears, please," he said. "If we are remembering the old days, let's remember the light-heartedness."

"Oh, yes." She sniffed, and a smile lit her face. "Your brother and the ladies, or that commander of the guard we were all in love with." She shook her head. "I wish someone had warned us those were the best years. We wouldn't have listened, but still … Afterwards, all the colour was drained from the world, and not just because of the war. Everything was worse: the wine was sour, the men ugly, the parties boring and all we could do was scurry off to our mouse holes and feed on our memories. All this," she waved her hand, "is a futile attempt to recreate a time that is lost forever."

"Lost indeed." He smiled sadly. "Preserved only in our memories. And yet, I would not go back, even if I could. If I compared what I had then with what I have now, I would not exchange Abia for anything."

"Then you are lucky," she said.

"Oh, I think I had quite a bit of luck. I was no better than the others, nor did I have greater merit. I never wanted to be a hero."

"You fought the Goddess of Death and won."

"I escaped, barely." He turned his head to avoid her curious gaze. The cold that seeped out of his words made me shiver. "But Morana is never far. I avoid waters that belong to her, do you know that? I never touch moats or ponds; I never disturb abandoned wells." He lowered his voice so that we could barely hear him. "Sometimes at night, when I cannot sleep, I try to convince myself she forgot all about me, that I died once, and it was enough."

"I think one death is enough for everyone," Gospa Lenka said. "You men, you can at least kill yourselves in some brave adventure. You snatched all the good deaths. All those messy, slow, demeaning ones, you left to us."

I thought she would cry again, but she just bit her lip and raised her chin.

"Raden," she said. "I beg you to reconsider. For me, for old times' sake." She clasped her hands together. "Please."

"I cannot disobey the king, Lenka."

Her mouth twisted in contempt. "Of course you can. Everybody says that Prince Amron orders the king and not the other way round. This is such a small, insignificant matter."

"You of all people should know how important it is."

She rose with an angry flash in her eyes.

"Now I remember something else about you," she said. "You've always been the coldest one of them all. The stone-hearted prince." Tears spilled from the corners of her eyes. "I hope one day you'll find out what it feels like to have it ripped out of your chest."

She left in a swish of skirts. My lord remained seated, with an unreadable expression on his face.

I tiptoed to the door, checking that we were alone.

"That was quite a performance," I said. "She's used to getting what she wants, isn't she?"

He shook his head. "She is right."

"She is unfair."

He waved my words away.

"Go to sleep, we have a hard day before us." And then he added, "This is the last thing I do for the king. The last thing."

# CHAPTER SIX

# ELISYA

## SUMMER 320 A.C.

The first morning of the tournament arrived, sunny and bright. When we woke up, Father and Keldik were already gone to prepare for the joust, and I had no reason to hide my smile. Gospodar Bremir waited for us to get ready.

"Elisya, you were dazzling yesterday," he told me. Perhaps Silya was right when she said he liked me.

We went down to the meadow outside the city walls, where that half-built chaos of the previous days had turned into a brilliant jigsaw with pieces that fit perfectly. We bought cinnamon cakes and ate them as we looked around the fair: the things I would never think of buying, such as pots, clogs, candles, wooden chests—and the things I could barely resist buying, like colourful handkerchiefs, perfumes and love potions.

"It's time to go," our host warned us, "or they will begin without us."

The tournament lists and the stands covered almost as much space as the fair. The stands with a separate royal box faced away from the sun, while the common folk gathered on the other side. Most spectators were already in their seats, and we barely had time to sit before trumpets and cheering announced the arrival of the royal couple.

"I thought the king was competing," I whispered.

"Not today," our host said, "today is the day for challengers only. After they've ridden, the best ones will have the chance to ride against the champions. There are no famous names, and you probably won't see great skill. However, sometimes you'll see a great fighter emerge from the crowd. Once or twice per season, perhaps. Later you'll be able to say you've seen the Lord Famous while he was still just a challenger."

"They move too fast," I complained when the first two knights clashed.

"Patience," said Gospodar Bremir. "In time, you will learn to notice the details."

Heralds announced Vairn's name. My heart lurched when I saw he was the first knight that day who grabbed the attention of the audience: the shining steel of his armour, black shield and black plume on his helmet. And his manner: he looked like a winner. He entered the lists like he owned the world, he waved to the crowd, charming them into cheering, caught the lance his squire threw him and got ready for the attack while his opponent was still trying to turn his horse in the right direction.

"What do you think of this one?" Silya asked Gospodar Bremir, poking me secretly.

"Great armour, good posture, but I have never seen him before. Queen's cousin, isn't he? I think he's very young."

The herald gave a sign and they started, riding fast towards the middle. Vairn controlled his horse well, held his shield firmly and pointed the lance at the right moment, striking his opponent in the middle of his chest. The other knight's lance missed the mark, the upper part of his body flew backwards, the horse barely managed to stop, struggling against the reins, but the saddle held, and he did not fall. While he was still trying to catch his balance, Vairn threw away the remains of his broken lance, ripped his helmet off and blew kisses to the audience. His handsome face was radiant, his dark hair plastered with sweat.

"Well," Silya said, "I think we have the people's champion."

I said nothing; my nails were dug into my palms to prevent me from jumping to my feet and shouting at the top of my voice.

After that, the rest of the day was even duller. At one point, heralds called Keldik's name, and we dutifully cheered him. He was lucky. The knight who rode against him was a clumsy, inexperienced youth. Keldik managed to point his lance at the right moment to touch him and win. Father would be happy.

When the jousting finished, we were ravenous, and the afternoon sun was uncomfortably hot on our faces. We went back to our host's home to freshen up and rest.

"Elisya, you received an invitation for tonight," said Gospodar Bremir.

"What invitation?" A surge of excitement tightened my throat, although I knew there was no way Vairn could have directly invited me anywhere.

"The queen has invited girls from the best houses to gather today at the palace."

"Oh," I said, guessing who it was. "Father will be glad."

I was wrong. He arrived in a good mood, because of Keldik, but frowned when he saw the invitation. "Where did that come from?" he grumbled.

"I am sure they want to honour you," I said. "After all, our family is old and important. Why should your daughter be overlooked?"

He gave me a doubtful look and I wondered if he saw how everybody wheedled him incessantly: Keldik, my step-mother, me. But then he nodded and said, "All right, go, but be careful. I don't see what the queen might want from you."

When I arrived at the palace, there were dozens of girls scattered around, most of them from bigger and more prom-inent families. I studied their faces and outfits closely and decided I was pleased with myself. My dress, although not as opulent as some, was elegant enough, and my face pret-tier than most. Socializing with them, however, was more difficult, as I didn't know anyone, and I couldn't join the little cliques that formed in the corners. A few inquisitive looks followed me around and there was a whiff of animos-ity, as if they smelled an intruder.

I could barely see the queen. There was no formal intro-duction. Instead, we were led in as we came. She was sitting by an open window. Once more, her dress was amazing, a deep, lustrous shade of purple that emphasized her alabaster complexion. And once more, she looked tired and listless.

A tray of perfect sweets was brought to her, and she waved them away indifferently. Now and then, one of her ladies would introduce a new girl, who would curtsy and answer a few questions. I had no-one to introduce me.

While I struggled to keep smiling, a little page touched my sleeve. "Gospa Elisya?"

"Yes. What is it?"

"Follow me, please."

We went out of the hall, through a corridor to an arcade that led to the garden, where he left me. I turned around, looking for my sweetheart, but he managed to surprise me again.

"You are even more beautiful in the daylight," he said. He was hiding behind a column, and when he stepped into the light, he was so perfectly groomed and fresh that no-one could have guessed he had jousted that morning.

"You got me invited here, didn't you?"

"Of course," he smiled and kissed me. "Would I miss a chance to see you?"

"Will you introduce me to the queen then, please? Perhaps she does not blame me for what happened yesterday."

"I doubt she remembers you at all. She has more urgent problems," he grinned.

"I do not understand why she is in such a bad mood," I dared to comment. "If I were in her place, a guest of honour at a tournament in this beautiful city, surrounded by people who strive to please me in every possible way, I think I would try to smile once in a while."

He rolled his eyes. "She is pregnant again, and she hasn't had the time to recover from the previous one. She has been terribly sick, vomiting day and night on our way here."

"I see," I said though I didn't see it at all. My elder sisters were far away, and I only found out about my stepmother's pregnancies when her belly could no longer be hidden behind a loose dress. I didn't know if women felt wonderful or terrible when they were pregnant. I didn't know if they vomited or ate for two. I had a vague idea they should be happy about it.

"Let's go for a walk in the garden." He took my hand. "This palace is packed to the rafters. There's no other corner where we can be alone."

The garden was not completely abandoned, either, but it was huge and filled with lush greenery. We sat on a shady bench and Vairn touched my cheek with the tips of his fingers: no one had ever caressed me that gently. I closed my eyes, absorbing the warmth that radiated off his skin. When he kissed me, warm honey spread through my veins as the whole world finally clicked into place. His lips were two rose petals on mine, his eyes deep pools which reflected the image of the luckiest girl in Myrit. Our beating hearts and our swift breathing measured the sweet moments of that enchanted afternoon.

I was in love, for the very first time. "You were magnificent at the tournament today."

"It's nothing, wait until the champions show up tomorrow." He ran the tip of his thumb across my lips. "I think it's time you gave me a token."

I untied a blue ribbon that was wrapped around my plaits and gave it to him. He kissed it. "It smells like you."

"I hope it will bring you victory."

"And then I'll crown you with the Crown of Love. It would fit you perfectly."

"Everybody would be stunned! Unknown girl from no-where, the Queen of Love."

I thought of all those conceited rich girls gathered around the queen and realized I didn't envy them. I had something a thousand times better.

"I want to be alone with you," Vairn said.

"We are alone," I said, confused.

"No, not like this, in the palace, where someone might interrupt us at any moment. I want to be with you where we won't be bothered." He gave me a look so intense I blushed. "Is there such a place in the house where you're staying?"

"Gospodar Bremir's house?" I thought about it. "Perhaps. When Keldik and Father go out, our host follows them. But someone would have to sneak you into the house."

"How about that girl you mentioned?" he said. "Etta, the steward's daughter."

"She's very clever," I said. Etta was a brisk, practical girl who showed Silya and me around the city while the men were busy with the tournament.

"I'll find her, then." He smiled. "I think I have a plan."

The second day of the tournament was just as sunny as the first. The fair on the meadow still attracted us, but we were no longer enchanted by its size, nor did we wish to pick every single thing up. Instead, we glided elegantly among the stalls.

"So, have you picked your champions yet?" asked Gospodar Bremir.

I kept my mouth shut, but Silya said, "It is clear that the queen's cousin was everybody's champion yesterday."

There were two rounds of jousting. First, the challengers against each other, and then the remaining challengers against the champions. When Vairn rode out in the first round, with my ribbon tied around his arm, my heart fluttered.

"Look, our knight received a token," Silya said, and I gave her a sharp nudge.

"That doesn't surprise me," Gospodar Bremir said. "By the end of the tournament, he'll have a dozen if he goes on like this."

I bit my lip, suppressing a rush of jealousy. Vairn rode well, easily beating his opponent, to the cheering of the crowd.

Keldik, who managed to survive the first day with a bit of luck, showed some skill in the first round. Father's shouting paid off, apparently. If I had to choose, I too would rather have ridden against a heavily armoured knight than suffer Father's anger and contempt.

In the second round that day, the twelve champions rode against the remaining challengers. The real show had finally begun, as heralds started announcing the famous names. Their equipment was marvellous: armour that fit them perfectly, vivid colours on beautifully painted shields. And skill, of course. I soon saw why they were the champions. The challengers flew out of their saddles one by one, my brother among them. The tournament was over for him.

"Keldik was good," Gospodar Bremir said soothingly.

"It will never be enough for my father."

He looked at me as if he wanted to add something, but decided against it. His politeness baffled me. His brown eyes looked mild, and I could not imagine him uttering the harsh words that were in Father's everyday vocabulary. And yet, he was a good friend of his. I wanted to ask him if Father had ever been a kinder man, but I thought he would be too loyal to discuss it with me.

Vairn was the last knight to ride that day.

"I think he has a good chance of winning," said our host. "He has beaten all his opponents with ease so far."

I took Silya's hand and squeezed it so hard I left red marks. I held my breath as the horses sped up, and then there was a sudden loud crash. When I dared to open my eyes again, both knights were still in their saddles, holding broken lances.

"What happened?" I asked.

"They hit the shields, both of them. They will ride again."

Three times they rode against one another, and three times each met his equal. Judging by the noise, that was exactly the kind of spectacle the audience was waiting for. Bets were placed all around us, Vairn's odds grew more favourable. The fourth time they rode, Vairn's opponent grazed his shoulder, but Vairn managed to hit him in the chest. His straps tore and he flew out of his saddle, to the cheering of the crowd. Although he had as many victories as the others, Vairn was clearly the champion of the day.

When I returned to the house, Etta was waiting for me in the corridor. "Go to my room and I'll take Silya out for a walk." She handed me the key. "Someone's waiting for you."

Father and Keldik were still out; they would not return before dinner. I went to the room I shared with Silya and told her my stomach hurt. She frowned and opened her mouth to say something, but at that moment, Etta barged in and grabbed her hand.

"Let Elly rest," Etta said, "and come with me. I want to show you that shop with Seragian silks."

When they left, I slid like a thief down the corridors and climbed to the attic. Etta had told me she preferred privacy to luxury when she first showed me her room, a loft more suitable for spiders than for girls. My heart was beating like a starling in a cage. I paused before a low wooden door, wondering what I was doing, and more importantly, why no-one was trying to stop me. But Father was occupied with Keldik, Gospodar Bremir was with them, Silya left with Etta without a backwards glance. Everything was so impossible and unreal I felt I was watching some other girl unlock the door, enter the shadowy, sweet-smelling loft, and turn the key in the lock.

The room was small, with a slanting ceiling. The wooden shutters were half-closed, making it comfortably dim. Someone had left a jug of wine, two cups and some dried figs on the low table.

"My lady arrives on time," Vairn said, getting up to greet me. "You have good friends, with a sound attitude towards money."

I didn't understand what he was trying to say, but was unwilling to ask him to explain. And also, the moment I saw his smile, everything else became irrelevant.

"You were incredible today," I said.

"I was, wasn't I?" He laughed. Again, I couldn't see any traces of fighting, any signs he had spent the whole morning jousting. He was wearing a clean white shirt and a perfectly tidy tunic of olive-green silk with silver embroidery, like he was going to court. I wished I had my blue gown on instead of an ordinary dress, but he had already seen me in it, and I was afraid he would think I only had the one.

"You must be thirsty," he said, pouring me a cup of wine.

I took a sip, and then another one, because I didn't know what to say. Conversation, which had been so easy and exciting in the palace, now dwindled in this close space.

"We are finally alone," he said, filling his cup and raising it. "To beautiful ladies and their champions."

I raised my cup, holding it too tightly, worrying I would spill the wine.

"We don't have much time; this could be our only chance," he said.

I nodded again, unsure of what he was trying to say. The tournament wasn't over yet; we were planning to stay for a few more days in Myrit, surely we would meet again. Especially considering that he had so far arranged our encounters so well.

He approached me, pried the cup out of my fingers and put it on the table. And then, in a move so suave it looked rehearsed, he removed the clip from my hair. Golden waves spilt down my back and a strange surge of excitement marched like ants down my spine.

"That's better," he commented.

I gathered the courage to touch his black locks, smooth and cold like silk. I ran my fingers down his cheek and felt the stubble on his jaw. It was an entirely new sensation. Then, in a surprisingly bold move, I touched his lower lip, pulling it lightly until I revealed the pink flesh, and then I kissed him so suddenly that his knees buckled, and he pulled us both down on the heap of pillows on the floor. His hands were all over my body and mine all over his. We were as close as we could be, our lips touching, our limbs entwined, in an irresistible need to become one.

The warmth of the afternoon and the bulky folds of our clothes forced us to break free. His tunic and shirt went easily, my dress was more difficult: there were ribbons and clasps that needed to be conquered, but our fingers managed it somehow. The touch of his bare skin on mine was surprisingly intense and I was aware of every part of my body.

I didn't know what we were doing, but I knew I was enjoying it. And yes, I was aware it was prohibited. To lie down with a man, to take one's clothes off, to kiss—all of that was on the list of forbidden things, but I didn't know why it was forbidden nor where it led to. No-one had explained to me the details of love-making: Silya was just as uninformed as I was, my stepmother refused to talk about it, the maids would sometimes whisper and then roar with laughter at our confused looks. And so I reached my seventeenth year without ever being told what men and women did together once they took their clothes off.

Perhaps I should have stopped when I entered that unfamiliar territory. And I would have stopped, had I been afraid or uncomfortable, but I felt wonderful, light and hot and dizzy. Vairn knew what he was doing, every touch was better than the previous one and it didn't occur to me to ask for explanations or instructions. I let go completely.

I dared not move my eyes off his face while he touched me where no-one had ever touched me before. I was afraid I would see something embarrassing.

"Tell me if it hurts," he whispered in my ear, but I had no idea why he was saying that, nothing hurt. Our bodies merged, but it didn't feel like something terrible or crucial, it was just a new sensation in a day filled with new sensations.

"It feels good," I said, thinking, *it feels great, don't stop*.

He was so close to me, he was a part of me. After such closeness, what could keep us apart?

My fingers touched tiny beads of sweat on his back when he moaned, "Oh, Elisya." I wrapped my arms around him, listening to his gasps, and then he froze. I opened my eyes, thinking something was wrong, but he was looking at me, smiling.

"Oh gods," he said, "what a day for victories!"

He lay beside me, trying to catch his breath in the stuffy room. I was bemused by the shocking whiteness of my naked body on the dark pillows. He put his hand on my collar bone, stroked my breasts, paused on my belly. Mapping his territory.

"I love you," I said, out of nowhere.

"You are the most beautiful girl I have ever seen," he said, still following the soft lines of my body with his fingers.

It occurred to me that I should ask him what we should do, but the movements of his hands and lips didn't allow for serious conversation.

He stood up, naked, and walked to the window unabashed. I watched him from the corner of my eye, too shy to stare. Every part of him was beautiful. Although we had just separated, a sudden rush of desire lit my whole body.

"Come back," I said.

He turned with a surprise that bloomed into a brilliant grin. When he touched me again, my skin began to tingle.

"Please …" I moaned, not knowing what I was begging for. I didn't know what to do, but he did. He touched me with his fingers, then his tongue, then entered me again. This time, I was ready. This time, I wasn't ashamed.

I heard myself breathing hard, but I was also somewhere else, outside that room, climbing higher and higher up to the point where I thought I would faint with pleasure. I must have shouted; his hand covered my mouth.

When I came to, I just said, "Why was I not told this was so good?"

"It is the worst kept secret in the world," he whispered.

I wanted more. I wanted never to get up from those pillows, I wanted to do it every day and night. But he got up and peeked through the shutters, looking for the sun travelling pitilessly across the sky.

"Time to dress," he sighed. "Everybody will return to the city soon."

I moved in a haze; my hands were heavy, my thoughts confused. I managed to pull my dress back on, but if he had not tied my laces, I think I would have gone out all askew.

"I'll see you soon." He kissed me. "Now you're mine, just mine."

"Tomorrow you will win the tournament for me, with my token on your arm," I whispered in his ear. "And then the whole kingdom will know."

He slipped out like a cat, leaving his scent behind him. I drank some wine, plaited my hair and tiptoed back to my room. I laughed to myself softly until Etta and Silya came back.

"Do you feel better?" Silya asked.

"Oh, much better."

For the first time in my life, I had to keep my mouth shut before Silya. I was burning with desire to tell her everything. After all, it was the love we had discussed in detail since we were little girls. But it wasn't the right moment, not yet. There would be enough time to talk about Vairn. This was just the beginning.

The day had more news in store. We sat at our host's table eating our dinner, Keldik beaten and ill-tempered, Father ominously quiet. Gospodar Bremir, however, decided we had to celebrate.

"Come on," he told my father, "remember how many times we lost, and much worse. Keldik was good for the first time. Great, really." He turned to my brother, who received his words with a sour smile. "There's no shame in being beaten. Next time you will be better."

"I doubt there will be money for the next time," Father said through gritted teeth.

"Of course there will," laughed the lord, "especially if we become family."

Those words roused me from my daydreaming over the food. Family? But Gospodar Bremir had no daughter he could give to Keldik. What was he thinking of?

"I haven't mentioned anything to her," Father said.

"Well, mention it now. You've been here long enough."

With those words, they both turned to me. The spoon fell out of my hand, and I gasped. "Oh." It was all suddenly clear.

"Elisya," Father said, "before coming to Myrit, Bremir and I discussed the possibility of joining our families. We agreed I would bring you here, but wouldn't say anything in advance so that you could be … unburdened by expectations." Father cleared his throat. "Now that you've met each other—"

"Now that we've met," the lord cut in, "and I've seen your beauty, obedience and good manners, it is my honour to ask you to become my wife."

My stomach dropped into an abyss. I looked at him, really looked at him closely, his greying hair, his yellowing teeth, the lines on his face. He was almost thrice my age; it never occurred to me he could so much as consider … Even if it were not for Vairn, I would have hated the plan. The idea of kissing that old man made my skin crawl.

Father's look nailed me to the chair.

"I …" I stammered, "I'm afraid I cannot accept."

"Elisya," Father growled, with a clear threat in his voice. Somewhere in the background, Keldik looked relieved that the title of biggest disappointment of the day had suddenly switched to me.

Gospodar Bremir raised his arm, quenching Father's fury. "Easy, Tolmir, she didn't see it coming. She'll get used to the news and then we'll talk again."

Silya hid in the shadows, quiet as a mouse. My only possible ally in that room was my suitor, so I turned to him.

"Thank you for understanding I cannot accept your offer right away," I said in a shaky voice. "I did not expect such an honour. Allow me to think about it."

My words caused a silence so absolute we heard birds chirping in the garden. Gospodar Bremir shrugged, but Father was livid. I dared not breathe.

Father turned his eyes on me. "Elisya, I hope you understand your duty. I hope you don't have some silly notions in your head!"

I didn't know what to say. Of course I had romantic ideas. Although I was sure Vairn and I felt the same, he had not formally asked me anything. There was no understanding, no promise I could depend on.

"Perhaps the girl likes one of those young tournament knights, as all girls do," Gospodar Bremir said, lightening the atmosphere.

"Yes, Elly, tell us which champion stole your heart," Keldik teased.

I blushed and bit my tongue. They had no idea how close to the truth they were. All three of them were laughing now and the tension was gone.

"I heard the king praise her beauty," the lord said to Father. "I wouldn't be surprised if the others noticed it."

But after the first wave of laughter and disbelief, Father turned to Silya. "You were with her at all times. Tell me, does Elisya fancy some other man, or he her?"

Silya was looking at them through half-closed lids, with her head down. Had my father even the slightest hunch she helped me in my deceit, that she allowed me to do something stupid without warning him, he would have thrown her out immediately.

"I don't know, my lord," she answered. "Not when I was with her."

"I thought you told each other everything," said Keldik.

Silya gave him a cold look and remained silent.

"Tolmir," Gospodar Bremir said mildly, "Elisya grew up sheltered, far from places like this one. Perhaps she did speak with a young man, perhaps he courted her a little, perhaps there was some affinity, and now she thinks she is bound in some way."

Those were considerate words and offered a reasonable excuse. Looking at his kind eyes, I was seriously tempted to tell him my heart was already bound, although there was no formal agreement. If Father and Keldik were not present, I might have done it, but years of experience with my family taught me to be careful.

"Please," I said in the sweetest voice, "just allow me to think about it."

Gospodar Bremir nodded, and Father said coldly, "You have one day."

That was all I needed. The moment we entered our room, I said to Silya, "Find Etta."

She nodded and rushed away. I sat down and picked up a quill. I wanted to write that I was afraid, and that I loved him and believed in him, but in the end, I wrote just a few words. *Father wants to marry me off. I have to give my answer tomorrow. Help me, please. E.*

When Etta showed up at the door, I shoved the note and a couple of coins in her hand. "Please be quick," I said. "And wait for the answer."

The answer came a little before midnight. *You will run away with me*, he wrote. *I will let you know when and how.*

It was summer, so there was no fire in the hearth. I tore the paper to shreds and let the night wind carry them over the city.

# CHAPTER SEVEN

## IDA

### AUTUMN 361 A.C.

I woke with a start, sprawled across a chair. I must have been so exhausted that I dozed off and dreamt that the Goddess of Death spoke to me. Damn those puppeteers, their monstrous Morana was so vivid it had stuck in some dark corner of my memory.

Horses neighed in the yard and shouting broke into the corridor. Harsh male voices, heavy footsteps. I creaked the door open and peeked out. A large, bearded, sweaty man in riding clothes was pushing the lady away.

"I want to see my son. What have you done, woman?"

"There was no time," the lady squealed. "We asked for help …"

The maid was saying, "… in cold water, can you imagine?" to a tall, gaunt man in a long black robe who trailed behind his lord. A real physician, obviously.

"The boy needs to be bled, quickly," he proclaimed as they climbed the stairs to the boy's room. And then, aghast, "Who let this charlatan in?"

More shouting. *Poor boy, he needs to rest.* Then Gair came tumbling down the stairs, a black avalanche of rage and wounded pride.

"If you ever come near my son again, I'll have you flogged," the lord shouted.

I grabbed Gair and pulled him into the kitchen.

"This way," I said, "before he sets his guards on us."

Through the kitchen, out to the back yard and into the street. We walked away as fast as we could without drawing attention to ourselves.

"I left my bag in there, damn it."

"We'll get you a new one," I said.

It was a strange, dark day. Grey clouds sucked away the afternoon light, and it looked like dusk was already setting in. The inn's sign was swinging in the wind, creaking unpleasantly as we approached. I shivered; my dress was still damp.

"It's all your fault," he said.

"What?" I froze in the middle of the street, staring at him.

"It is all your fault, you stupid bitch," he repeated in a thick, nasty voice. "Bathing? Who's ever heard of that? You gave them proof that I was no physician."

"I saved the boy's life!"

"Sure you did," he snarled. "And look how well that turned out for us." His eyes were two black dots of fury. "You should've listened to me. We should've waited."

"But the boy would be dead now."

"Or not. We should've kept the pretence. They would've paid us." He grabbed me and dug his fingers into the soft flesh of my arm. "Did you think they'd see you saved him? Did you think they'd be grateful to you? You fool! People see only what they expect to see. You know that."

I wanted to punch him in his ugly face, but instead I took a deep breath and said, "I'm going to check on the donkey. You order dinner."

As I slipped into the stable, three large chestnut coursers lifted their heads. It seemed that this cursed shithole of a town was overrun by fancy folk.

"Do they feed you well?" I asked the donkey, scratching him behind his ears. The animal brayed, startling the horses. "You're better than Gair, you know," I whispered. "I wish I could leave him and keep you."

When I entered the inn, I was greeted by warmth and the smell of roast meat. For a heartbeat, it felt like coming home. The place was clean, tidy and well-lit. The floor was not beaten earth, but good, hard stone, the tables were well-scrubbed, the hearth packed with wood. Bundles of herbs hung from the rafters. Three young men sat at one table. They were obviously the owners of the pretty horses in the stable, as they were equally well-fed and groomed. Shiny hair, fur collars, silver brooches, fine woollen clothes—deep blue, moss green, plum purple. Swords and daggers in decorated scabbards. Loud, self-assured laughter. Noblemen.

Poor travellers like Gair and me rarely met their kind on the road, but that day in Haragov Dol it seemed there was no escaping them. I remembered the scenes of war from my childhood, the images of knights in armour, on their enormous destriers. Gospodar This, Gospodar That, it mattered little as they all had the same job, and that job was killing. Always with weapons in their hands, always surrounded by soldiers.

To be fair, the men at the inn didn't look like they had fought in the war. They were perhaps a few years older than me, barely grown to their full size. One of them threw a glance at me when I entered. He was good-looking: dark-haired with shiny eyes that paused at my face with interest and slipped with disgust over the rest of me. I was a sorry sight: tired, wet and crummy like an alley cat.

The handsome one said something to his friends, and they turned to stare at me, too. Anger rose in my chest. I shot a dirty look at Gair, who had found a warm spot by the fire and was following my interaction with the young men with some amusement.

One young noble whispered something that made the others burst out laughing. I walked by their table, ignoring them.

"I told the innkeeper we'll stay one more night," Gair said when I sat beside him. "And I ordered some food. They have roast pork and cabbage." The mere idea made my mouth water. "The witch made me pay in advance."

"Really?" I said. "A fine gentleman such as yourself?"

He shrugged and took a swig of ale. I stared blankly into the fire, trying not to worry about the future. When the food arrived, I wolfed it down. By that time, Gair was already on his third or fourth mug.

"I'm going upstairs," I said.

He caught my hand and stopped me.

"Ida." He didn't look angry, not anymore. Just drunk and mean. "You can sleep here tonight, since I've already paid for it. But tomorrow morning, I want you to gather your things and disappear. Our partnership is done. I've had enough of you."

I wanted to smash a mug over his head, but the three nobles were still sitting there, drinking and playing cards. No use making a scene.

"Fine," I said. "I've had enough of you, too. You squander every coin you earn and you're not as great an actor as you think you are. It was you who ruined our chances today, not me."

It felt good to see my arrow penetrate his drunken haze.

"I played my part perfectly—"

"No you didn't, you miserable sot. You had to improvise, and you failed. I did the hard bit; I saved the boy's life. All you had to do was come up with some fancy explanation and stay in character. Instead, you let them call you a cheat and throw you out like trash. You're the one who botched it up, not me."

My hands shook as I walked away from him, too angry to remain in that warm, bright room filled with men's voices and laughter. I never expected life to be fair or people to be grateful, but if he had backed me up, if he had just recited his pompous, learned monologue while I did all the work, they might have believed we had performed a miracle.

I got a jug of hot water from the innkeeper and went upstairs, knowing it could be my last chance to wash beside a fire in a long time. I undressed and rubbed the dirt off with a rag. I disliked the bones protruding under my skin; they were a warning I might be too weak to survive the winter. Many years ago, an expensive whore in Abia told me that highborn ladies sometimes starved themselves to look more frail and delicate. Judging by my thinness, I could have been a princess.

I washed my hair and combed it. It was dark and long and heavy, my plait as thick as my arm. There was no mirror in that little room, and I wondered if I were still pretty, after all the troubles that had befallen me. For how long would my skin remain smooth, my hair black, my teeth in my mouth? I thought I had a few more years, but if we continued to rough it, I would not last that long.

What was I going to do?

Gair was drunk and angry and humiliated. If he stayed downstairs, he would get even more drunk, gamble away all the money in his pockets, fall asleep under the table and wake up in the morning with a headache and a hazy recollection of the night before. I could probably lie and flatter my way into the partnership with him again. Or I could pack my things and try my luck elsewhere, before winter caught up with me.

It was too hard a decision after a long, horrible day.

While my hair was drying, I rinsed out my clothes and stretched them to dry overnight. I added two logs on the fire and slipped between the sheets, tired like a farmer after a day in the field, but my food lay heavily in my stomach and I tossed and turned, unable to find a comfortable position. Half the night trickled away before I finally drifted off.

I awoke to the sound of footsteps on a creaky floor. I thought it was Gair and moved out of habit to make room for him in bed. Then I heard another pair of feet and some disturbance. Someone was rummaging through my things.

"He said the girl kept the money under the pillow," an unfamiliar voice said.

I froze. I opened my eyes just a tiny bit, peering through my eyelashes. Pale dawn light seeped in through the cracks in the shutters. There were two of them: the handsome, dark-haired one and his shorter, stockier friend. Their eyes were bloodshot, their cheeks covered in stubble. And they were armed.

I was being robbed by two noblemen?

"Come on, girl," said the fat one. "Wake up."

With a quick flick of his hand, he yanked the cover off the bed. I screamed in terror and coiled up, trying to hide from them. When they saw I was naked, they started to chuckle.

"Help!" I cried. "Help me, I'm being robbed!"

The handsome one cuffed me across the mouth, lightly, as a warning.

"Don't waste your breath," he said. "The innkeeper knows we're here. We just came to collect what is rightfully ours."

"What is rightfully ... what?" I repeated like an idiot. Then it dawned on me. "Where is Gair?"

"Far away from here, if he's got any brains. He did not have much luck tonight."

"How much did he lose?" I asked cautiously. "Perhaps I can pay you back."

They looked at one another and started chuckling again.

"Will you tell her, or will you let me do it?" asked the fat one.

"Well," the handsome one said, "your sweetheart—"

"He's not my sweetheart," I spat.

"I don't care. Your … Gair, as you call him, joined us at our table last night, playing cards. He did well for a while, but Krasil," he motioned towards his friend, "and I are very, very good players." They sniggered again. "So when he started to lose, we decided to see how far he would go. We took all his money, of course. Then there was a certain donkey, still in the stable downstairs. Then one tunic of fine black wool, a hunting knife, some sundries …"

His donkey, his tunic? There was no Doctor Bellemus without them. What madness was that?

"We were ready to stop there," he continued. "Donkey and the rest—what are we to do with that, we don't need it. But then he mentioned there was more money upstairs."

While he was talking, the fat one pushed his hand under my pillow and pulled out my purse. I tried to grab it, but he pointed his dagger at me.

"But that's my money," I said. For the first time in years, real, sincere tears filled my eyes. I did not have to pretend I was desperate. "My money, all of it. I've earned it."

"That's not what he told us, girl. He said you were just a wench who followed him and the money in the room was his."

"And if he told you the money in the royal treasury in Myrit was his, would you believe him?" I cried. "He lied, he is a bloody gambler, he would say anything just to remain at the table. Please, you have to believe me!" I tried to catch their eyes: a greedy, swinish, blue pair and a hard, chestnut one. I had no friends there.

"Whatever," the handsome one shrugged. "He lost that money at cards, it's gone. You can try and force him to give it back to you, together with the other things."

"What things?"

The handsome one made a little circle with his index finger. "Everything. When he lost the money and all his possessions, he switched to yours. Two gowns, a pair of boots, a woollen cloak …"

"No," I said. "What is wrong with you? Those things are mine; they were not his to offer, are you too stupid to see that?"

He laughed while his friend took my clothes. "You settle that with your sweetheart, when you catch him."

They were having great fun; I could see it in their faces. They didn't need any of those things, not even my meagre savings. Any one of their horses was worth more than everything Gair and I had. They just liked the idea of taking every last thing. Especially if they took it from a naked girl.

There was nothing I could do. I have seen worse injustice in my life, this was just a disgusting little joke I accidentally walked into. Who could I ask for help? The innkeeper, who collected her bribe and hid in a mouse hole? Some local sheriff, if there was one? Why would such a man even agree to see me, let alone believe me? Justice was for those who could afford it.

The handsome one reached for the dress drying on the chair.

"No," I said, "not that dress, I beg you! I have nothing else to wear."

"I see," he said.

"You don't even need it. Just look at it, it's old and mended many times. What use could you have for it?"

"None," he said, shaking it and lifting it up. "I have no use for that rag, I'll throw it in the first ditch I come to. But in the meantime …" he looked at me over the frayed hem, and his eyes shone, "I'll see you running around the inn wrapped in a sheet, and that will be amusing."

"And that's not even the best part," the fat one added. "Do you want to hear the best part?" I didn't want to hear the best part, but the glint in his eyes told me I was going to hear it regardless. "He lost *you* at cards. My lucky friend got you!"

I knew it was coming. They were no better than brigands. My first impulse was to rage, to scratch their eyes out, screaming I was nobody's slave and that no-one could win me at cards and that they should bugger off before I awoke the whole inn. I took a deep breath …

*Think, girl!*

… and breathed out. Whatever had overcome Gair the previous night, it had made him destroy everything. Our partnership was over, Doctor Bellemus had vanished into thin air. I had nothing but those two men in my room. They thought they had me, but that was their mistake.

I locked eyes with the handsome one and held them for a few heartbeats.

"So you won me?" I said slowly.

I lay back down on the bed. He looked at me, confused. My anger entertained him, my docility less so. The fat one burst into laughter at the door.

"Get out of here," his handsome friend ordered, when he finally realized I was serious. "I want to talk to her in private." He shut the door in his fat companion's face and cut off his laughter. He unbuckled his sword belt, wasting no time.

"If you make me happy, I might give you back your things," he said.

"You don't have to give them back to me, they are yours," I said. "I am yours, too, you've won me. Take me with you."

He paused, half-undressed.

"What would we do with you?"

"I've played ladies on stage," I said. "Imagine what you could do if you had a young lady in your company. You wouldn't look like young ruffians, but like dutiful nobles protecting a helpless woman."

I was aiming blindly. They had the arrogance and the attitude of true nobles, but they travelled alone, slept at an inn and gambled with beggars. Their garb was garish, but up close I could see it was frayed from too much wear. They looked like people who had been on the road for too long. They were crooks like me, only with better clothes. I saw the thoughts rushing behind his eyes as he took the rest of his lavish garments off.

"Smile," he ordered, "and I'll think about it."

Business first, talk later. I curved my lips and brought some ardour to it. I looked him up and down and liked what I saw. Much better than that old goat, Gair. I could even do this willingly, I thought. I was curious.

When we finished, I was still smiling. And he was in a much better mood.

"My name is Criscer," he said, pulling his clothes back on.

"Ida."

"Your idea could work; we could use a woman in our company. There is a castle nearby, the innkeeper told us.

We decided yesterday to try our luck there. I'll ask the boys what they think. Get dressed and follow me."

When he left, I washed my face and rubbed my body with a wet rag. I pulled my old dress on and plaited my hair. I straightened my back and lifted my head up high. The doctor's apprentice was gone. Now I was a young noblewoman travelling with her cousin.

For two seasons, I had travelled with actors. I learned to read, speak and act like a lady. It seemed ridiculous and pointless at the time, a cheap trick for the hastily built stages in villages and fairs. I had quarrelled with the leader of the troupe when he insisted on the correct posture and walk. I had said, "What do these stupid villagers know? If I wear a dress with fake golden embroidery and fake pearls, they will see I am a lady."

He had replied, "If you don't learn to walk properly in that dress, you will fall flat on your face after two steps, and they will throw rotten cabbages at you."

I learnt to walk, sing and pretend I was eating a chicken made of coloured wood from a silvered plate. My speech became loud and clear, so that even the drunks in the last row could hear me.

I walked into the room where the three of them sat like I owned it. My stomach was cramped with fear: they could still take my money, clothes, boots, they could rape me and leave, and nobody would stop them. But showing fear would mean I had already lost.

"Where are my clothes?" I said in the most arrogant tone I could muster. "Do you expect me to walk around in these rags?"

The red-headed one just stared at me, while the fat one flushed in anger.

"What's this whore—" he stammered, but didn't have the time to finish because Criscer burst out laughing.

"Guys, meet Gospa Ida," he said. "These are Krasil," he pointed at the fat one, "and Edon." The ginger.

I nodded haughtily. And then looked at Criscer. "Clothes. I'm waiting."

"You're right," he said. He dug through the pile on the floor and pulled out Doctor Bellemus's black tunic. "Use this, the fabric is good. In the meantime, we'll think of a new plan."

The fat Krasil sullenly returned all my things.

"Tell the innkeeper I want breakfast in my room. And a sewing kit."

Krasil shot me a glance so poisonous it singed my skin, but Edon was already on his feet.

"Certainly, my lady." He learnt fast.

# CHAPTER EIGHT

## TELANI

### AUTUMN 361 A.C.

When the first light appeared on the horizon, Raden was already waiting for us in the stable. I quickly examined his horse, saddle and equipment and found them lacking. He had invested more in beauty than in quality. I rummaged through his saddlebags and threw out unnecessary clothes, books, pots and other nonsense that overburdened the horse.

"What are you doing?" the pup whined. "Those are my things."

"Your mother can send them to you when you settle in Abia. You don't need them now."

"I do!"

We were about to start our journey with a quarrel, when my lord swept in. Instead of keeping his mouth shut, the pup went over to him. "He threw half the things out of my saddlebags," he complained.

"You're lucky he left you the other half," my lord replied cheerfully. "He takes my clothes all the time, better keep an eye on him."

The boy opened his mouth, but he wasn't sure if my lord was teasing him or giving serious advice. In the end, he flashed me a sullen look.

Our soldiers joined us, and my lord sent a flask of brandy around. The boy took a swig and choked on it immediately.

"How … how can you ride when you drink this?" he stammered, eliciting sniggers from the other men.

It was only when I saw him up in the saddle, beside the prince, that I realized what had bothered me the previous evening. The boy was tall and golden-haired, with a face that almost, almost reminded me of … well, all of them, really. The descendants of Amris's line.

It was not obvious at first glance. The height and the hair were a good sign, but they were not conclusive, otherwise half the men in the North would be candidates for royal blood. The boy had different eyes, meek and light blue, and his mother's oval face. But there was something about his clean profile and his smile, baffled on the surface, but with a subtle note of sharpness underneath. I tried to think away the traces of boyish softness from his face, I turned the scant flesh on his bones to muscle, straightened his back, lifted his chin towards the sky. The likeness was there, yes.

I wondered: *is it possible?* And more important: *is it likely?*

I could but guess, of course. Any question in that direction would be unthinkable. Who was I to ask my lord such things?

I sometimes wondered what my life would look like if I served a merrier prince. Gods knew there were more of those who sought love and wine than swords and order. My lord's late brother, in his wild years, or his nephew, the current king: they had left a trail of weeping wenches and angry fathers, gambling debts and unpaid bills. They had brawled, whored, duelled and made life difficult for the people who protected them. It had made for a spectacular mess.

On the other hand, when my lord complained of disorder, he usually meant that documents needed to be filed and letters arranged. I was stuck with probably the only tidy, meticulous prince in the history of the dynasty. The one who worked hard to turn chaos into order. The one who hid his private life from the public, even when it was discussed on every street corner.

I introduced Raden to our soldiers. He muttered a greeting, looking at the ground, prickly and distant, making no friends. The men who rode with us would never openly belittle Prince Amron's ward, no matter how feeble he appeared. But they were experienced travellers and fighters, and you could earn their respect only by being tougher than them. In their sentimental soldiers' hearts they had room only for bastards worse than themselves.

We started our long ride in the cold drizzle with sharp gusts of northern wind. The light was grey, and the day promised to be frosty and bleak. Raden was excited at first, almost feverish with the sudden freedom of an open road.

"Your Highness, how many miles can your horses travel in a day?" he asked. And then, "How far is Abia from here? Is it a difficult road?" Also, "Are inns on the road any good? I don't like stews with meat I can't recognize, and I hate lice, they are so hard to get rid of."

He badgered my lord like a puppy jumping around an old hound. He fussed over his horse every time we stopped for a break, he dug through his saddlebags, he searched for food, water and additional clothing.

By afternoon, his mood had plummeted, smothered by my lord's reticence and the speed we were travelling.

"My feet are cold," he said to no-one in particular. "My thighs hurt." He wiped his runny nose on his sleeve. "It's freezing. I thought we'd have some hot food today."

When nobody offered him comfort, he retreated into a sullen silence interrupted only by sniffing.

I hoped the inn would lift his spirits, for we were all tired of his dour face. They had a huge fireplace, hot food, comfortable beds. At dinner, my lord took pity on him.

"Abia is not as pretty as Myrit, but it grows on you," he said. "You'll love its narrow streets, teeming docks, colourful sails and ancient palaces. It's more alive than any town I've seen, bristling with pride and insolence. It doesn't reveal its beauty easily, but there are autumn afternoons when the light is soft and golden, and the walled gardens smell of oranges and jasmine. There are shadowy squares with fountains, where young men fence out of boredom, houses with heavy wooden shutters and light curtains lifted by the summer wind, there's salt in the air, and the constant, faraway sound of the waves."

He was probably the only man who loved it more than I did.

Raden took a gulp of ale, rolled his eyes and said sourly, "Let's not pretend I was sent to Abia because of its beauty."

Instead of slapping him, my lord just shrugged.

Raden sulked for the rest of the evening. I followed my lord to his room and made sure that he was comfortable.

Then I returned downstairs, where our soldiers waited with cards and ale beside a warm fireplace. They didn't invite Raden to join them, so he hovered in the shadows, waiting for me. When he reached for my sleeve, I thought he would beg for a place at the table.

Instead, he whispered urgently, licking his lips, "Tell me, in Abia, I am to live at the palace, right?"

"I suppose so."

"With the prince and his wife?"

"No, I don't think you will live with—"

He prattled on, "Is it true that Gospa Liana is stunning?"

I slapped him. Not hard. Like a mother would slap a naughty child.

"Go to bed, you idiot."

Next morning, Raden found his boots in the yard, filled with frozen piss.

"Who did this?" he moaned. "Why would anyone—"

"Be quiet," I told him. "They're testing you."

"But why?"

"Quiet."

He shut up, but the pained expression on his face when he mounted his horse told me there was more trouble ahead. He could not keep up with our pace. He was a fair rider, but he had no stamina.

"Make it a bit easier for him," my lord whispered when we were out of earshot. "None of us were born in the saddle. Remember how you felt the first time you rode for a hundred miles without rest."

"I was twelve," I replied, irked by Raden's behaviour. "And he's a grown man acting like a sullen boy."

My lord shot me a long look. His blue-grey eyes were weary and cold, and I bit my tongue, ashamed of my words.

When we stopped to water the horses, I padded Raden's saddle, which helped a little, but in the afternoon he started to cough.

For the following three days, I felt like we had been given a small child to take care of. He whimpered about his saddle sores, mewling like a kitten. My only consolation was that he found us as difficult as we found him.

But then the fifth day of our journey came, and everything went wrong.

Snow started falling from the leaden sky in the middle of nowhere. It was around noon, and we'd been riding since dawn without seeing anything resembling a village. The road curved along the edge of a forest. On the other side, a windswept plain stretched to the foot of the distant mountains. My lord surveyed the barren land, calculating where we were.

"Get the map," he told me. "I'm sure there is nothing on this road until Haragov Dol, and we won't get there before dark, not at this pace." He paused and looked at the clouds. "The snow is coming harder now."

The sky had gone dark, and the wind started howling. A blizzard was coming.

"Can you hear it?" Raden asked. "The voice in the wind, calling?"

I thought the pup was imagining it, but my lord said, "Yes. Don't listen to it, it's the blizzard and it will lure you to your death." He reached for the map. "Let me see. I think there's something in the woods."

We hunched over the piece of parchment while the wind tried to rip it out of our hands. Raden slid beside us, too curious for his own good. My lord's finger followed the line of the road winding through the wilderness.

"Ah, here it is," he pointed.

I bent down to get a better look.

"It looks like an ink stain to me," I said. "It has no name."

"Look again," Raden cut in. "There's a trail."

He was right. About a quarter of a mile farther east, a thin line separated from the road. Just a forest trail leading to a tiny spot, a fort or a homestead, that looked like a mouse dropping. I should have recognized shit when I saw it.

Our eyes met above the map. I was against it and so was my lord. If we had to sleep under a roof on our journeys, we chose road inns where we could blend in. A provincial nobleman with a small retinue and modest belongings, nothing unusual. It was unlikely any of the common drunkards would recognize the quiet stranger for what he really was.

Noblemen's lairs, even the poorest ones, were dangerous. You never knew if they had attended ceremonies, feasts, negotiations, campaigns. Perhaps they had relatives at court, perhaps they were ambitious or just curious for the worst possible reasons. War had created unexpected enemies and unreliable allies. My lord's entourage was always small, for speed and discretion, and we were aware you could get killed in a miserable hole in the middle of nowhere just as easily as in the marble halls of a royal palace.

"Is it worth the risk?" I whispered.

He looked at the sky once more; he knew snow like sailors knew the winds. We could choose between an unknown, badly marked, but closer place in the woods and a small town at the end of a long, open road. As if it was hurrying us, the blizzard struck in full force. Our soldiers' dark cloaks turned white.

"No," said my lord. "We ride for Haragov Dol!" he called to the retinue.

We moved on through the whiteness. I counted the people out of habit. One was missing. I stood up in my stirrups, looking around.

"Where's Raden?" I shouted.

One of the soldiers, a sharp-eyed fellow, spotted a dark, barely discernible shape in the vortex of snowflakes. Raden was riding straight for the forest. Alone, through snowdrifts, blinded by the squall.

When I spurred my horse, the wind tried to lift me from the saddle. The obedient animal broke into a gallop on uneven ground, risking a fall. I was bewildered by the weather. I had seen winter on the slopes of the Frostpeaks and houses buried so deep only their chimneys were visible. I had seen a girl who had a white bear as a pet, but I had never seen snow coming horizontally, lashing mercilessly in white curtains. I could neither see nor hear, blind and deaf like a man under a waterfall.

I rushed into the forest, where the trees provided some shelter from the onslaught of snow, but the path became more difficult. The woods looked dark and neglected, like a relic of an ancient age when the earth was covered in forests and ice, and the gods still walked it. The snow covered the trees, not just the tops, but the trunks, the leaves on the ground, the stones and the potholes. Every uneven bit of ground became a trap.

Onwards, onwards, after the youth who still managed to elude me, pulled by some unknown force. Over the roots, under the branches, through blinding whiteness. A dark spot in front of me. I thought I had seen a red flash of fox's fur through the trees. A blood-curdling scream rang through the storm. The voice was high, female, and filled with mortal dread.

My horse recoiled and tripped, throwing me out of the saddle. My head slammed into something hard, and I sank into darkness.

# CHAPTER NINE

# ELISYA

## SUMMER 320 A.C.

The next day, Vairn rode out with my ribbon tied around his arm. Surrounded by Father, Gospodar Bremir, Keldik and Silya, I willed my heart to be still.

"The remaining twelve will be divided into two groups now," Gospodar Bremir said, still acting as our guide, "and the knights will first ride against those on the opposite side. But it will soon turn into a melee, where they'll fight whoever they want. The last man standing is the winner."

"Sounds very harsh," said Silya.

"It can be ugly, yes. Perhaps it is good Keldik is not down there, this being his first tournament."

"I heard it looks like a real battle," Keldik said, looking quite happy to be in the stalls.

Only three challengers and nine champions, the king among them, were left. They all greeted the audience, but with less flourish than on the previous days, armed to the teeth and followed by their frowning squires.

At the sound of trumpets, the knights rushed forward in a cloud of dust. The noise was unbearable. Heavy thuds, the loud crash of metal, the breaking of wood, the neighing of horses and men screaming at the top of their voices. When the dust cleared, three knights were dragged away by their squires. Vairn was not among them.

My eyes found him. He was still in his saddle, his sword drawn, fighting a tall knight in black armour. I tried to follow him, but other fighters were blocking my view, charging at each other, trying to oust as many opponents as possible. If there were any rules at all, I couldn't recognize them. The sand soon turned red. Armour prevented us from seeing the injuries, but we still heard the cries of the wounded men. I could no longer understand why tournaments were so popular. I wanted to close my eyes, cover my ears and wait for the whole mess to end.

But Vairn was somewhere out there. He pushed one knight away, attacked another. Father must have liked that: that courage and nerve.

The horses were gone, injured or led away. The king, in his beautiful armour, was the most popular target. His ransom must have been enormous, as well as the fame going with such a victory. When Vairn went after him, I risked taking my eyes off them for a moment to look at the queen. Her face was serious, but she didn't seem worried or tense. She sipped from her cup and whispered something to her ladies-in-waiting.

"This young challenger is an excellent fighter," Father said, the first comment he uttered that day, "but he's getting tired."

I wanted to disagree, but the scene below us proved him right. Vairn's reactions became slower, he was giving ground as the sword grew heavy in his hands. He refused to surrender, though. In a desperate attempt to turn his luck, he lifted his blade and lunged with an angry roar. The king's sword moved in an arc so fast it was blurry, blocking Vairn's attack and then hitting his upper arm right in the spot where my ribbon was tied, cutting through the steel. Vairn screamed, falling on his knees, and the king held the blade to his neck. The tournament was over.

I wanted to get up and run to Vairn as soon as he was carried out, but I had to stay and see the end. The king took off his helmet and threw it to his squire, revealing golden hair plastered with sweat above a beaming face. People were clapping their hands, stomping their feet and shouting fervently. Two lovely girls crossed the stained sand and brought him a crown of summer flowers. The queen descended from the royal box and walked towards him, unconcerned about the train of her white dress. He put the crown on her small head and kissed her in front of everyone.

They stood in the sun looking so perfect, like characters from a legend. Larger than life, invincible … and fake. As if all this, the tournament, the parade, the celebrations, the guests, was just a big set up so that they could show themselves like Amris the Golden-Haired, the son of Perun, and his rusalka. I should have believed in that picture, I know. It was a scene I had imagined so many times. But the king's golden beauty was marred by the blood on his armour and the screams of the wounded still echoed in my head.

Before we left for the last celebration in the palace that evening, Etta brought another message.

"Your sweetheart can't write at the moment, but he wants you to know his arm is all right," she whispered. "Tonight, when the fireworks start, you have to sneak out through the garden. When you come to the orange trees, turn left and enter a passage. He'll wait for you at its end. Do you understand?"

I nodded. "Thank you."

Silya watched us in silence. When Etta closed the door behind her, leaving us alone, she said softly, "Are you really going to do that?"

"What else can I do?" I retorted. "If I don't run, Father will force me to marry Gospodar Bremir."

Silya's stern face softened for a moment. "Perhaps it is a better destiny than eloping with a boy who's never made any serious promises."

I tried to imagine how I would feel if I was forced to do with my father's friend what I had done with Vairn willingly, and I shuddered.

"I'd rather die than lie with Gospodar Bremir," I said.

I thought she would accuse me of being overly dramatic, but she just gave me a pitying look.

When we got ready, Father and Keldik were already gone.

"They had to go to the palace early for some business with the knez," said our host. "But I will accompany you."

The gathering was less formal and merrier now. The blood and chaos of the tournament had been forgotten, and men chatted as if they hadn't tried to kill each other a few hours earlier.

"You look so worried," Gospodar Bremir said, taking my hand gently. "Let's dance."

I could not refuse him. He danced well and focusing on my steps helped me relax. When the music stopped, he brought me a cup of watered wine.

"Have you thought about your answer?" he asked.

I blushed. Honestly, I had not even considered it since I thought I wouldn't have to give it. "I …" I hesitated, "I don't know what to say."

"Tolmir is rash, I understand," he said, "but he is not here now. Listen, I believe you are confused. But look around. If you say yes, this will be your life, instead of that sad little castle. With your beauty, you won't just be the mistress of my house, but of the whole city."

Those were perhaps the best words a girl could hear, yet they left me cold. I had no desire to be paraded like a prize heifer and share my life with an old man. "I do not love you," I whispered.

I saw that he almost laughed but stopped himself in the nick of time. He squeezed my hand. "I can still save you, Elisya," he said seriously. "It's not too late."

"No, thank you," I replied.

He looked at me and shrugged. And then he disappeared in the crowd.

Around midnight, the fireworks started, and everybody went out into the garden. All heads turned towards the sky, all eyes watched the colourful flowers exploding above us. It was easy to slip away.

I found the orange trees and the dark passage behind them. Explosions echoed in the narrow space and smouldering rushlights barely alleviated the darkness. I shivered with cold and excitement, grateful to Silya for making me take the cloak. I expected the passage to end at some yard, or at an exit out of the palace, where Vairn would wait for me. Instead, I came to a door left ajar, with a uniformed guard before it.

"Please, come in," he said.

I entered a well-lit room and froze. Father was there, together with Keldik, Knez Erimir of Leven and, far in the corner, Vairn, flushed with anger.

"Time to deal with this," Father said. To someone who didn't know him well, he would appear dignified and sensible. To me, he looked like a volcano about to explode.

Knez Erimir of Leven, a tall, portly man a few years younger than Father, with dark hair and restless eyes, said curtly, "Not yet. We're still waiting for someone."

"But we agreed this would be a secret. Who else—" Father tried to object, but the knez cut him off with a flick of a hand. Silence fell over the small room. I tried to catch Vairn's eye, but he would not look at me.

We heard steps echoing in the passage and the guard greeted someone. A woman entered the room. I didn't recognize her at first, she was wearing a hood, but when all men in the room bowed their heads, I realized who she was.

"Good evening, my lords," Queen Orsiana said, waving away their greetings. "Vairn, what have you done now?" She sounded like my old nurse when I tore my dress or botched my embroidery.

Vairn lifted his head defiantly. "I asked Gospa Elisya to run away with me," he said, ignoring the angry men in the room.

The queen sighed. "Well, that is quite romantic." She turned to look at me. "Oh." She was surprised. "I remember you."

I blushed. From this distance, she looked prettier and gentler than she seemed before. She had clear, bright grey eyes and an exceptionally beautiful complexion, very fair and glowing. In some other situation, we might have held hands and walked into the garden, laughing at the boys and their stupidity, but not that evening. That evening the only stupidity to laugh at was my own.

She turned back to Vairn, frowning. "What did you promise her?"

"Nothing," he said, and it was his turn to blush.

Father was rigid with rage. Keldik, for once in his life touched by wisdom, held his arm firmly, keeping him in the corner.

"What did you plan to do with her, then?" asked the queen.

He shrugged, looking down.

"Your Majesty!" Father exclaimed, unable to control himself. "I demand—"

He didn't end the sentence because the knez's open palm hit him in the chest, not very gently. "Calm down," Erimir said. He turned to the queen. "Perhaps this is just a folly. Perhaps we are not too late."

It took one look for her to read me. "No," she said calmly. "We are too late."

No man dared contradict her or ask how she knew. Hot tears spilled from my eyes and rushed down my cheeks. I looked at Father for the first time that evening.

"If you weren't forcing me to marry, I would never have thought of running away," I said through my tears. "Perhaps

Vairn and I wouldn't have to hide then, and perhaps ..." my voice faltered.

The queen put her hand on my shoulder. "I'm sorry, but Vairn forgot to tell you he is already promised. And even if he weren't, an heir to one-third of the North cannot choose his wife as he wishes." She was polite and she did not add: especially if the lady in question is a daughter of an irrelevant noble with a small dowry.

I looked in his direction, gasping for air while dismay gripped my throat. He would not look at me.

"But we have already ... we are ..." I whispered just for the queen's ears, thinking that I would die of shame. She shook her head slowly.

"He has dishonoured my daughter," Father growled. "I demand that he marry her or fight me to the death!"

"Don't be a fool," said Erimir. "You've seen him fight. And as for marrying her ... he cannot do that, and you know it."

"He will compensate you," said the queen, "although you don't deserve it." She took her hand off my shoulder and walked up to my father. She was half a head shorter and yet he, burning with rage, took a step backwards. "You should be ashamed of yourself," she said. "My cousin acted deplorably, but you have betrayed your daughter in the worst possible way. You brought her here among these people and did nothing to protect her. You taught her nothing."

Father was boiling with fury but couldn't say anything.

"Elisya, come with me while they come to an agreement," the queen told me. "Erimir will see to it that they don't kill each other." And then she spoke to the others in the room. "Take a good look at yourselves," she said, with fresh anger in her voice. "Shame on you all." And with those words, she dragged me out of that terrible room. Vairn did not give me a single look, let alone a goodbye.

I wailed all the way to the queen's chambers.

"Bring some wine for the girl," she ordered her ladies. "And a handkerchief, she will ruin her dress with tears."

But I cared nothing for the dress. I pulled my knees to my head and curled into a small ball of misery in the chair. Instead of the well-lit, scented, comfortably furnished Queen's apartment, I wanted to be in the darkest corner of the basement, where I could die of grief and shame in peace. From the corner of my eye, I noticed the Queen of Love's floral crown, left on a table and, it seemed, already forgotten. The flowers were wilting.

She let me cry myself dry. She sent her ladies out and, at one point, went out herself, leaving me alone. I thought she would send someone to take me away, but instead, she returned after a time and sat beside me.

"Here," she gave me her handkerchief when the tears finally stopped, "wipe your eyes and nose." After I did that, she handed me a piece of cloth dipped in cold water. "Put this on your face, it's swollen."

"My father will be looking for me," I mumbled under the cloth.

"No, he won't. I told him I'd send you home when you calmed down."

"And what if you never sent me to him?" I whispered without much hope.

I didn't see her face because mine was still covered, but she touched my hand lightly.

"I cannot do that, I'm sorry. I saw him a few moments ago and asked him what he wanted to do with you. He told me he had plans. I have no right to interfere."

I thought perhaps he had not given up on the idea to marry me to Gospodar Bremir. After all, my shame was not public, yet. I removed the cloth from my eyes.

"What am I to do now?" I said, more out of despair than looking for advice. "Vairn, he won't …" I started, feeling a flicker of hope at the sound of his name, but had no courage to continue.

"Vairn won't do anything because he's already on his way north with an armed escort to prevent him from acting stupidly." There was something like empathy in her eyes. "He doesn't deserve my defence, but you should know that he didn't plan to be so callous. He is simply rash and spoiled, in love with himself, with his achievements at the tournament and beyond. He saw you, liked you—and why wouldn't he, when you're so pretty—and went as far as he could."

"And I didn't say 'no' because I thought …" I was not sure what I thought, not anymore.

"You thought he loved you as much as you loved him."

"I thought we didn't need formalities."

She lifted her eyebrows, looking sideways at me. "That was very naive of you. But I've seen dozens of petty nobles like your father, stiff and stern, who keep their daughters uninformed about men and the ways of the world. They bring them to an event like this, hoping their provincial in-nocence is attractive enough to overshadow a bad dowry and hook some rich old suitor."

I gaped at her. She was right to the last detail.

"Your father thinks your ignorance is good as long as it works in his favour. I bet he lectured you about duties and obligations, all the while denying you any opportunity for real knowledge. He let you fill your head with legends and stories that shaped your idea of the world. Amris the Golden-Haired and Alaina, something like that?"

I nodded, my mouth hanging open.

"Amris was one heartless bastard, did you know that?" she added casually.

I shook my head.

"No, of course not. Who doesn't want to dream of great love? Of something brilliant, strong enough to change your destiny?" Her voice was sad. "Your mother is dead, isn't she?"

"Yes, she died when I was little."

"That explains a lot. A mother would not send you into the world so unprepared."

I bowed my head, looking at my entwined fingers. "You must think my behaviour was terribly naive and irresponsible. But … It's not that I didn't know anything. My friend, who was wiser than me, warned me to be careful with men." I laughed at myself. "But I truly believed we were something special from the first moment. I thought something so strong and pure had to be real. What are rules to those chosen by destiny?" I bit my lip.

"I understand," she said tenderly. "And when the first pain abates, you will wonder why fate let you two meet if nothing can come of it. A love like a forest fire that consumes everything cannot be a mistake, can it? It cannot be an illusion, a one-sided deception, where the other side is just a hollow shell." She clasped her hands. "You will feel the world should tremble when gods make such a mistake." Her eyes were fixed on some faraway spot behind my shoulder. "But gods don't care for such things, and the world goes on, the sun rises and sets, the days go by. And you realize your sorrow is ridiculous."

Then she did something unexpected: she opened her arms and hugged me.

"I am sorry," she whispered in my ear.

"So am I."

Under the layers of silk, I felt the frail bones of her ribcage, her ragged breathing. She smelt of jasmine.

"There," she said, with a smile, when we separated, "sometimes it is easier to cry in front of a total stranger. A broken heart is not so very rare."

She spoke sense, but I hardly followed her. I hazily thought no-one had ever been as badly let down as me.

"Will it heal?" I asked.

"No. But you will learn to live with it."

"Thank you for everything," I said.

She took my hand. "Sometimes, when you think no-one is your friend, it's nice to have someone listen to you, even if it's just for a few hours. I believe we won't see each other again," she added with a strange certainty, squeezing my hand so hard it was painful. "Beware of your own wishes and … oh …" She put my hand on her belly, still perfectly flat. "We won't meet again, but you two will. Give him this." She took a thin gold ring from her finger and put it in my hand. Then she straightened up, pale and serious, and smoothed her dress. "Good night." She left, trailing a faint scent of jasmine.

Consoled and confused in equal measure, I slipped the ring on my little finger: I had small hands, but hers were smaller. It didn't look particularly important: just a little gold band, several threads intertwined into an endless knot. It was even more modest than those few pieces of jewellery I owned, and I thought I would never be able to brag it was given to me by the queen. I wondered what she was trying to tell me, but as I was thinking about our conversation, tiredness overcame me, and I slept until they came to wake me up.

In the morning, I felt I had dreamt the nocturnal conversation. There was no trace of the queen. Two silent ladies brought warm water and helped me put on the same blue dress I had been wearing the previous night, so inappropriate for the morning, and plaited my hair. I acted as though I were clumsy and sleepy, delaying the beginning of the day as much as I could. The comfort I received the previous night and the feeling that all would be well evaporated in the harsh light of day. There was only sorrow and anxiety that gutted me.

I could not remember if I had ever been too small to fear Father. Had he ever been just a parent who took me in his arms, whirled me around and laughed with me? Perhaps he had, when mother was alive, but my earliest memories were filled with my dread of him: a man who rarely showed up. When he did, he turned the female quarters upside down. He shouted at nurses and maids, he inspected and upset things, he measured, interrogated and judged, and always found fault with me and my sisters. He never beat me like he beat Keldik, but neither did he caress me or speak kindly to me. He believed in severity; he thought gentleness was for women and weaklings.

When he arrived at the palace, his face was twisted in disgust. The moment I joined him in the courtyard, he turned on his heel and marched out without adressing me, and I scurried behind him, head bent in disgrace. As we approached Gospodar Bremir's house, Father stopped and forced me to look at him. "We will walk in now and pretend nothing happened. You spent the night at the palace at the queen's invitation. Keldik will remain silent. That little snake, Etta, will be punished. Bremir knows she helped you get in contact with some boy, but nothing more than that. Whatever he asks you, your answer will be *yes*. Do you understand?" He shook me till my teeth chattered.

"Yes," I stammered.

"Clean yourself up, dress modestly and then we'll talk."

When I entered the room I shared with Silya, it was empty. Hot water came and I undressed, washed myself, combed my hair and chose a simple morning dress. The decision I had been avoiding for days was now before me again. I hardly had a choice: I was disgraced and abandoned. Staying in Myrit seemed like a better destiny than living with my father and brother for many years to come. At least Gospodar Bremir had never intentionally hurt me.

When I was ready, a servant took me to the Lord's study, a comfortable room I had never seen before. It had tall, arched windows overlooking the garden and the red roofs of the city. Clear sunlight danced on rich tapestries and furniture made of dark, skilfully carved wood. Father, Silya and Gospodar Bremir were waiting for me. I glanced at her, checking whether she was all right, worrying that Father blamed her for my escape. She looked perfectly composed and greeted me with a smile.

"Did you have a good time last night?" our host asked.

"Yes," I said. "I talked to the queen, and she was …" I tried to find the word to describe her, but in the end, I just said, "kind."

He nodded. "I've heard that before. She doesn't look it, but if you say so … She did you a great honour, truly."

Father wasn't in the mood for chatting. "Elisya came to answer your question."

Gospodar Bremir gave me a surprised look. "But she did answer my question," he said. "Yesterday evening. I thought you knew."

Father glared at me. I had forgotten that conversation and shook my head mutely.

"Elisya was too excited yesterday to give a rational answer," he said. "She has thought about your offer."

"Stop," said his friend.

And, amazingly, for once in his life, my father stopped.

"I asked her, and she gave me an honest answer. I don't believe she changed her opinion in the meantime." He looked at me carefully but continued addressing Father. "Tolmir, I'm sure your daughter is obedient enough to marry me if you order it, but I am too old for such games. It was a good idea, and if Elisya had agreed to it, I would have been happy. But as it is now, I would be stuck with an unhappy girl who doesn't love me and is not wise enough to see the advantages of living here. It is the last thing I need at my age."

"But Elisya will get used—" Father started.

"Please, don't force her. I found a better solution."

Father stared at him, uncomprehending, but I saw everything right away. I glanced at Silya, serene in the morning sun.

"Come, dear Silya," Gospodar Bremir said, and she approached him and caught his hand. "I found a young, smart woman who will be happy and grateful to marry me," he concluded, brutally honest.

"But …" Father managed to utter before all words escaped him.

"She has no dowry, I know. And she is not as beautiful as Elisya. But when you choose a woman to share your life with, some other things are more important. Such as compliance, gentleness, gratitude, wisdom."

My father, who could hardly find any of those qualities in my stepmother, except for superficial compliance maybe, seemed baffled by his words. . But I understood everything. While I had been committing one foolish act after another, dreaming of eternal love, Silya had taken care of herself.

"I am glad for you, Silya, I really am," I said.

Father turned and struck me hard across the mouth. I tasted blood on my lips. He raised his hand again, but Gospodar Bremir caught it in mid-air. "Enough," he said sharply. "There's no point. Let's part as friends."

Father didn't answer. He shook his hand off and stormed out. An awkward silence fell, and then Gospodar Bremir cleared his throat and said, "I'll leave you two alone to say goodbye."

I touched the tips of my fingers to my mouth: when I removed them, they were stained with blood. My lower lip was hot, and it throbbed painfully. The Silya I had known would have rushed to me with a wet handkerchief to stop the bleeding, but this new Silya kept still.

"There's clean water in the bowl," she said. "Rinse the blood before it dries."

I did as she said. What else could I do? While I was wiping my mouth, I studied her rabbit face, her flat figure. She was still wearing my old, remade dress, but I was certain that would change soon. Finest taffeta and satin were waiting to be cut for her, gold jewellery was ready to glow on her skin. It would not matter that she had crooked teeth and mousy hair. She would smile, leaning on her husband's arm, and do everything that was necessary to live a good life. She had learned that lesson well.

"That evening when Gospodar Bremir proposed to you, when you sent me to find Etta quickly, Keldik saw us in the corridor," she said, looking through the window. "You know how he always meddles ... He caught me and interrogated me, but I said nothing, I swear, even when he threatened me. However, when I realized later you would run away and leave me at the mercy of your father, I knew I had to take care of myself."

"You betrayed us? You?" I wanted to jump at her and scratch that smiling face. I thought it was Etta, I thought she told Keldik and Father.

"Keldik knew something was going on. Trust me, they would've caught you one way or another," she continued. "But I didn't go to your father, I was too afraid. I went to Gospodar Bremir, who appreciated my honesty and good sense. One thing led to another and so—"

"So he knows of me and Vairn. That's why he doesn't want me anymore. How clever of you, Silya."

"No, that's not it." She smiled. "If I am not mistaken, he offered you a way out, up in the palace, before you went to Vairn. Even then, he was ready to marry you and take care of me in some other manner. But you refused, and he had no choice but to go to your father and confirm Keldik's suspicions. They caught Etta and made her reveal the time and place. You know the rest."

I saw how it all happened behind my back, while I was dancing in the hall, waiting for the fireworks. Everyone I was close to betrayed me that night. Father, Keldik, Silya, Etta, Vairn. All of them.

"I can understand everyone else," I said angrily, "but I don't understand you. I thought you were my friend."

Silya inspected the frayed fabric of her skirt in the sunlight. Some of the dresses she wore were kept together only by her sewing skill.

"Your friend?" She sounded incredulous. "No, Elisya, we have never been friends. I was your companion, seamstress, maid, messenger and many other things. But your friend? No. You wanted to elope with Vairn without sparing me a single thought, without wondering what would happen to me. And you know very well what kind of man your father is."

"But Gospodar Bremir would—" I tried to interrupt her.

"Really?" she cut me off. "Will you attribute that to yourself as well? Do you think he's kind to me because of you? If you managed to elope, causing complete chaos here, do you think Gospodar Bremir would have time for me? Do you think anyone would? Do you think I could ask for mercy or understanding? They would assume, correctly, that I knew and didn't tell. What do you think they would do to me?"

I didn't want to answer her question. "You ruined my life," I said.

"You ruined it yourself," she said. "You had a perfect chance here in Myrit. A rich, generous suitor who would treat you like a princess. But no, you wanted a tournament champion, the handsomest, richest, noblest boy you could find. What did you think this was, some kind of romance? You fall in love with someone, elope with him and live happily ever after?"

"Yes!" I cried out. "Yes! Perhaps that makes me stupid, but at least I'm honest. I love Vairn and will love him forever. I would do anything to be with him. I don't care what others think. I may be disgraced, but at least I haven't sold myself to an old man I don't love for some jewellery and a house in the city."

Silya blinked.

"Well …" she said slowly, "I wish you luck with your honesty."

"And I you, with your transaction."

# CHAPTER TEN

## IDA

### AUTUMN 361 A.C.

We spent that day at the inn. I couldn't travel in my old rags—even the best stories about young ladies needed a good costume. Gair's fine black wool came in handy. It allowed me to present myself as a young noblewoman in mourning—that would explain the lack of jewellery and lavish undergarments. Luckily, my experience with the acting troupe included sewing and mending, so I had some skill with the needle. It took me an entire day, though, and the result was more like a costume made for the stage than a real lady's gown. Criscer eyed me suspiciously, but when Edon appeared with a pair of handsome boots in far better shape than my old ones, and Krasil threw a fur-lined cloak over my shoulders, the impression was much better.

"It will do," Criscer said. "You are pretty, men will look at your face, not your clothes."

I wanted to tell him that men were never the problem, but I kept my mouth shut.

Krasil and Edon sold Gair's donkey that afternoon and, when they subtracted the cost of my boots and cloak, they were left with enough money to have a bit of fun. I hoped for one night of peace and solitude, but it was not to be. In the middle of the night, Criscer slipped into my bed without a word, marking his territory. For a girl who had slept on the floor beside a hearth, there were worse things than sharing a bed with a warm, young body.

He woke me up before dawn.

"You must leave before the innkeeper sees you, she mustn't know that you left with us, or she'll tell someone that you're just a ragged crook's apprentice. Get out of the town, follow the road west and we'll catch up with you. Leave your things here, I'll take them."

It crossed my mind that there was nothing to prevent them from heading in the opposite direction. "I would rather have my things with me," I said.

He guessed what I was thinking. "We've spent a fair sum on your boots and cloak. We'll come, don't worry." He pushed a small loaf of bread into my hands. "Wait for us."

He helped me jump down to the back yard. I passed the stable and climbed over the wall. As soon as I moved away from the houses, I found myself in the empty fields where ice cracked beneath my feet and wild birds flew over my head. The town was a tiny settlement surrounded by a vast, desolate landscape.

I wondered about the castle Criscer mentioned, since Gair and I had seen nothing fitting that description on our arrival. My new boots felt strange, supple and snug, as I walked carefully across the frozen mud. I didn't want my clothes to get dirtier than necessary, so I returned to the road as soon as I left the last houses behind me.

The weak winter sun was slowly rising. My new cloak kept me warm in the freezing air. The sky above my head was clear, but black clouds rolled over the distant mountains to the north. I was neither cold nor hungry and it wasn't raining. It occurred to me that I could simply walk away from the events of the past two days.

But being a young lady on the road, with no horse or escort, was worse than being a poor beggar. I needed the protection of those three crooks, at least until the first town, the first opportunity to hide from the winter. I walked through the bleak countryside, with empty fields on the one side and thick forest on the other, looking for a dry place where I could rest until Criscer and his friends arrived. There were no travellers on the road at such an early hour and my attention faltered. That is why he managed to surprise me.

He jumped from behind a tree like a hungry mongrel, blocking my path. I didn't recognize him at first: a night in the forest had turned him into a scruffy vagrant. He was dressed in a tattered shirt and old trousers, his only possessions now. Which was more than he had left me.

"Ida!" he exclaimed. "Thank the gods! Nobody ever comes down this damned road, but I knew you would come looking for me!"

Gair was glad to see me, can you believe it? Was he so drunk the night he gambled me away that he forgot everything? Or did he think it was nothing unusual, insulting me, breaking up our partnership and leaving me for the three rascals to do as they pleased? Just another successful day in the life of the great Gair.

"I was worried about you when I heard what happened. I know they cheated," I lied smoothly. "I waited for the chance to steal back some of our stuff and run away from those bastards."

He looked apprehensively down the road towards Hara-gov Dol. "Are you sure they won't follow you?"

"I am. They said they were heading for Syr. Also, I had to leave the donkey behind. They can get good money for it."

He puffed angrily. I wrapped the cloak more tightly around my skinny body to hide my new dress.

"So, you left them the donkey and the tunic. Doctor Bellemus is gone, we have to think of something else." He checked out my new cloak and boots. "You did steal something useful, I see, although you were thinking only about yourself. Let's get off the road, just in case. Do you have something to eat?"

"I have some bread. You must be very hungry."

His eyes gleamed at the mention of food. He took my arm and led me into the forest, not very far, just enough to hide behind the first row of trees. I tripped while he was pulling me and fell to the ground.

"I'm coming," I said. "You don't have to be so rough."

When I stood up again, I gave him the bread and he wolfed it down.

"Where do you plan to go now?" I asked.

"To Abia," he said. "It's smaller than Myrit, but there are better chances for me to find a job. Perhaps I'll become a sailor ..."

Gair on a ship? Not bloody likely. But just in case, I asked, "What will happen to me?"

He stared at my new cloak more greedily than he had ogled the bread.

"I will take care of you," he said, and did what he had never done before: he lifted his hand and stroked my face. Then he lifted the other hand, too, and wrapped his fingers around my neck. "I will take care of you right now."

I let my eyes widen in surprise while he strangled me and I gasped for air, but my hands didn't fly to my neck to break his hold. I swung my right fist, clutching the stone I'd picked up when I fell to the ground, and hit the side of his head. Once, twice. Warm blood spilled over my fingers, and Gair's grip loosened. I broke away from him as he fell to his knees, holding his head.

I have survived this long because I could always guess what people wanted to do to me.

I almost ran towards the road, as far away from him as possible, when I heard a voice in my head. A soft hiss, a whiff of decay, something writhing in the darkness. It said, *no, not yet.* I looked at my bloody fingers, still wrapped around a stone. I looked at Gair, who was in no shape to run after me. If I had left him there, perhaps he would have died of his wounds, or he would have frozen to death, or wild beasts would have found him. But I didn't leave him there.

I went back quickly and hit him in the head once more. He fell to the ground and tried to say something. I smashed his teeth and turned his mouth into a bleeding wound. Then I brought down my hand for the last time and the stone met his temple with a sickening crunch. Gair stopped moving. I let the stone fall to the ground and wiped my hands on his shirt. My new cloak was sprayed with blood, but on dark brown wool, it looked like ordinary mud.

I stood up and shook my head, as if I were waking from a trance. I had never killed a man before. I waited for something to hit me, anything: a wave of guilt, fear, sorrow. But I felt only rage towards Gair, damn his bones, who wanted to kill me for a cloak and a pair of boots too small for him.

I heard the sound of hoofbeats. Without a backward glance, I ran between the trees. Criscer and his mates were coming. I grabbed some wet forest soil and rubbed it between my fingers, to remove the smell of blood. Now my hands were just dirty.

"It's good to see you again, my lady." Criscer smirked, reining his horse. "We don't have a mount for you, so you'll have to ride with me." He lifted me up into his saddle.

I waited to see if they would notice something odd in my face, strange stains on my cloak, if they would ask me what I was doing in the forest. But no, they were in a good mood and paid no attention to me. Criscer put his hand on my breasts and pulled me closer.

"The innkeeper gave us directions," he said cheerfully. "She herself suggested we might visit them, she told us guests were always welcome there."

"Visit whom?" I asked.

"Gospodar … what is his name?"

"Selern," said Edon.

"Gospodar Selern, yes. He has a castle in these woods. He owns everything around here. He likes guests." He chuckled.

"Are you sure that's a good idea?" I dared to ask. "A castle has guards, armed soldiers."

"Don't worry, girl, it's not the first time we've done this." Krasil laughed.

They didn't tell me the details and I didn't ask. I found out they had been together for over two years. Criscer and Krasil were indeed nobles, and Edon a banker's son, but none of them had a home to go back to.

"They renounced us, we renounced them, and so ..." Edon explained and shrugged.

"Why did they renounce you?" I asked.

"I was losing too much money gambling before these two taught me a trick or two. Krasil tried to get his inheritance early. And Criscer ..."

"I was too irresistible to pretty ladies, so I had to run away."

"He's lying." Edon winked.

"Shut up."

I was a stranger among them, I didn't know their stories or understand their jokes. But while Criscer's hand rested on my chest, I was certain the others wouldn't touch me.

We were returning by the same road Gair and I had travelled two days earlier, and it felt like years had passed since then. From the horse's back, the landscape moved by so much faster. The morning sunlight soon disappeared behind the clouds. Southern mountains were at our backs, while on one side lay empty, frozen fields, a solitary tree in the distance, and on the other, the woods. It was a bleak, unwelcoming landscape, and the grey sky above it did nothing to make it more inviting.

"Where do you come from, Ida?" asked Edon, the kindest of the three.

"Oh," I said casually, "here and there. I don't have a permanent place, I travel the kingdom, following the fairs."

"Where were you born?"

"Down south, in a small village you won't be familiar with."

"We've ridden across the whole of Elmar. What's the name of the village?"

"It's gone, destroyed in the war," I retorted.

I hoped we might ride in silence for a while, but the empty landscape put them in the mood for talking.

"How old are you?" Krasil asked.

"Seventeen," I said. It was probably true.

"Criscer, isn't she a bit too old for you?" he laughed.

"Perhaps she's too old for me, but she is definitely too smart for you," he replied.

"If you could sleep with that crook you travelled with, you could be kind to us, too." Krasil winked at me. "Criscer, did we not agree that we would share everything?"

"No," he replied.

"Oh, come on," pushed Krasil, "be a true friend and share her with us."

"Enough!" Teasing suddenly turned into tension that vibrated in the air. Criscer glowered at Krasil, who was still grinning. I thought they would fight over me, but Edon slipped between them.

"Stop it, both of you," he said. "We need to decide who she is and why she rides with us."

"I will introduce you as a poor cousin from the South," said Criscer. "You grew up in isolation, in your family home, you've never travelled before, and you know nothing about the world. You're just a simple country girl. Your mother died and you are in mourning. I am taking you to Leven to be my dear mother's companion."

"Your dear mother," laughed Krasil. "Gods, that's a good one."

"My dear old mother," continued Criscer, "who has been alone since my father died." He wiped an imaginary tear from his cheek.

"Keep your eyes down and speak little, with the strongest southern accent you can muster," said Edon. "And we will take care of the rest."

"Grab the lord's attention. You have big eyes, let them fill up with tears when you talk about yourself," added Krasil. "Criscer will take care of the lady, those stupid women locked inside castles adore him. And Edon and I …" he didn't continue, he just laughed.

We stayed on the main road for some time. The sun hid behind the clouds, but my stomach told me it was time for lunch. No matter how light I was, I still slowed the horse down. In the end, we had to stop, so that the horses could drink and rest. Edon took some dried meat and a loaf of bread from the bag. We ate sitting on the roots of a giant oak, shielded from the sharp mountain wind.

"Shall we arrive before dark?" I asked. "Did the innkeeper give you precise directions?"

"We should soon find a forest trail," said Criscer. "She said we couldn't miss it."

We mounted our horses again and rode on. Criscer was right: we followed the main road for just a little longer and then came to the point where a narrow trail branched off, winding between the trees. If I had seen it two days earlier, I must have thought it was a local hunters' footpath. The horses trotted slowly, avoiding potholes and sharp stones. Heavy branches hung low above our heads, threatening to knock us out of our saddles.

"What a forest!" said Krasil. "There must be bears and wild boars here."

I had no desire to meet them. Something scared me about that forest, and it was not just the deep shadows of the bare branches. I had a feeling it was more than a labyrinth of entangled trees, a live organism: very old and aware of our presence.

"This place feels wrong," I whispered. "Have you heard any stories about it?"

"Oh yes," said Krasil, "there is one about a girl who travelled with three friends, and she was very generous ..." I didn't listen to the rest.

And then Edon said, "I think you are right, Ida. I can almost believe that deep in its heart, gods still walk the earth."

A cold shiver went through me as I remembered the vision in the bathtub, the freezing, inhuman touch of the Goddess. I had persuaded myself it was just a dream, but now I wasn't so sure.

"Did you have any strange encounters on your journeys?" I asked.

"With the gods, you mean?" said Criscer. "Oh no, but many people got on their knees and prayed before we were finished with them."

"There have been no gods on the road for a long time," said Krasil. "There's just us."

Their words sank like stones in the deaf silence of the forest. I felt a strong aversion towards my new companions.

I had no illusions about the castle, either. It would be nice to imagine I could find a friend in such a place, but my experience had taught me otherwise. I had no mother, cousins or childhood friends, and the women I met travelling never included me in their company. They would take one look at me and decide I was too pretty, too slutty, too ragged or simply too strange to earn their friendship. Men had never been so picky.

Once you were on the road, the return to a normal life was almost impossible. Wherever I went, I was a stranger, and nothing could change that. Most village and farm folk lived their whole lives surrounded only by their family and the people they knew from childhood. Most of them never travelled more than a few miles from their homes, rarely beyond the next town or fair. Soldiers were an exception, but when the war ended, they too returned to their villages, married their cousins and inherited their fathers' land. Everything that came from the outside world made them suspicious and afraid.

Rich people travelled, of course. Nobles and merchants had armed attendants, horses, wagons, whole caravans. They didn't depend on the hospitality of common folk: they had enough money to afford to stay where they wanted. They had houses, castles and palaces that waited for them with doors wide open.

The rest of us—common travellers, vagabonds and wanderers—we were dubious. We brought the news, sold goods from faraway places, did the jobs that our hosts could not or would not do—and still they looked upon us as a threat. They thought we were thieves, beggars, or that we spread diseases. Women on the road were everybody's loot. If they could not defend themselves, they were left at the mercy of every man they met.

My only comfort was the idea that I had learnt more on my travels than any miserable peasant would learn in a lifetime, but, as comforts go, it was a cold one.

"We're almost there," announced Criscer.

I lifted my gaze. The evening was upon us, the sun set behind the trees, and the first stars appeared in the east. The moon showed its round, yellow face among the clouds. The curve in the road brought us into full view of the castle. The men stopped their horses, staring at it.

"The innkeeper said the lord was rich," said Krasil, "but this …"

"This is too much for a fort in the woods," added Edon with suspicion.

We gawked at the high walls and slim towers, the deep moat with a drawbridge, the smooth grey stone and colourful standards fluttering in the wind.

"We'll leave this place rich," laughed Criscer.

He was wrong.

# CHAPTER ELEVEN

## TELANI

### AUTUMN 361 A.C.

"Telani, Telani, wake up, damn you." My lord crouched above me like a ghoul emerging from the storm. "We have to press on."

My head was slow and my tongue even slower.

"What—" I stammered.

"You fell off your horse and hit your head. Thank the gods you have a stone-hard skull, otherwise you'd be dead. How many fingers do you see?"

"Four, my lord …" I blinked and my vision cleared. "Two. I see two fingers. I think I heard a scream before I fell."

"Yes, I heard it too. But first, let's see if you can get up. Come, take my hand."

"How long have I …?"

"Too long. Come on, grab it."

I stood up slowly. My head felt like it was going to burst. A wave of nausea hit me, and I doubled over and vomited. He held me until the dizziness subsided. Then I cleaned my mouth with fresh snow.

"Raden is somewhere in the woods," he said. "I must find him. Do you feel well enough to ride with me, or do you want to go back to the road?"

"I'm going with you. If you help me up, I'll be able to ride alone."

We followed Raden's tracks to a small clearing among the trees. There was blood in the snow and signs of fighting. We dismounted and approached carefully, loosening our swords in their scabbards. A barefoot man in ragged clothes lay under a tree. His throat was cut, and his head was split like a watermelon. I did not know his face.

"Poor ugly sod," I said. "Beggar? Robber?"

"Bit of both, probably," said my lord. "But these injuries … This man's head was smashed, that's an old injury, look at the crusted blood … and then someone cut his throat." He showed the wound on his neck. "Why kill somebody twice, with two different weapons?"

"There was another person here," I said, pointing at the bloody footsteps in the snow. "Injured as well. Perhaps the woman we heard?"

We paused for a moment, while the blizzard raged around us.

"I don't understand." My lord wiped his forehead with the back of his hand.

Neither did I. I could not explain a single detail, starting with the question of why Raden had decided to throw himself blindly into the snowstorm. Clouds swarmed over the grey sky, like an endless army of darkness.

We were alone.

"We must keep moving," my lord said, looking around us. Fresh snow was already covering the traces of the fight. "Before the storm covers his tracks."

"Are we going to wait for our soldiers?"

"I ordered them to ride to Haragov Dol. We don't have enough time to catch them now. We need to get to Raden. This looks bad." He pointed at the trail of blood leading deeper into the forest. "Let's go."

We rode on as fast as we could, forcing our way through the woods. Hoofprints led us to a forest trail. It was just a narrow strip of snow meandering through the tall trees, but it was better than nothing. The cold was as sharp as the breath of an iceberg.

"Take the map out," said my lord, looking into the distance. There was no living soul in sight. "This has to be the trail."

Once again, we bent over the creased bit of parchment, trying to see the lines in the weak light.

"This is the road. And this is the only trail through the forest," he said. "There's nothing else."

Bloody hoofprints in the snow led toward the heart of the woods: the castle drawn on the map.

"We could still go back to the road and find help," I suggested carefully. "Or at least send one of the men for reinforcements. They will need a few days, but they will arrive. Otherwise we'll be completely alone."

He nodded. My task was to protect his precious head. His task was to do what had to be done.

"You are right. We should go back," he said. "But we won't. We don't have the time."

And that was all we said about it.

We plodded toward the castle, not much faster on the trail than we were among the trees. My legs turned to ice and my hands froze inside the fur-lined gloves. At one point, the traces vanished, covered by the snow. I didn't know how long we were riding. It was dark and we were surrounded by wilderness.

"This trail looked shorter on the map." Fatigue engulfed me like a heavy cloak. "Can we stop for a bit?" I slurred, the reins slipping out of my clumsy hands.

"If we stop, we'll freeze," said my lord. "Hang on. We'll soon be there."

I thought nothing could be further from the truth. The snow was knee-deep and still falling as the winter night caught us. We moved on by sheer force of will, in the vain hope that our quarry was somewhere before us, that we had to press on just a little bit more. But the woods, the snow, the night and the merciless cold sought to end all movement. Sooner or later, I knew, we would have to stop. And when we stopped, we would die.

Even my lord, who was usually impervious to cold, started shivering so violently I could hear his bones clatter. A frozen branch broke somewhere nearby and caused my horse to start. I barely managed to stay in the saddle. Had I fallen, I would not have had the strength to mount again. The water in our flasks froze, the cured meat was inedible. Only the brandy remained.

There was no shelter in sight, no cave where we could rest and light a fire, just the endless white woods. Onwards through the night we rode, hoping our horses wouldn't give in and seal our fate. Was it possible, I thought, that we had come so far to perish in a random blizzard, lost in the woods because of a stupid boy? What kind of destiny was that?

Deep in thought, my head started nodding and I could barely keep my eyes open. I wasn't so cold anymore. We could dig a shelter in the snow and sleep for a bit.

"Telani!" My lord's voice startled me. "Look!"

I thought it was an apparition in the dark. There was a clearing with something that resembled a village buried in the drifts. My heart gave a hopeful jump and I started to shiver immediately. And then my eyes focused, and I took a better look at the scene before us. Two dozen wooden houses, dilapidated. Black holes instead of doors and shutters, caved-in roofs, gardens overtaken by the forest. Snow covered the whole scene and hid its ugliness.

There were no signs of life, neither light nor smoke. The village was empty and dead. I am no weakling, but I swear that tears welled up in my eyes at that moment, freezing on my lashes.

"Shall we take shelter here?" I asked, though I knew it was in vain. None of those hovels could shelter us enough to get warm and rest.

"The castle should be close now," said my lord hesitantly. All the years I had known him, he had never lost his way, but this forest was something else. "This trail defies all attempts at orientation, but if it brought us here, it will bring us to the castle, I think."

Looking at the abandoned village, I said, "And what if everyone is dead there, as well?"

He shot me a long look through the darkness. "We do not have to fear the dead," he said softly, "but those who use them."

We passed the abandoned houses in silence and the trail soon became wider. The snow eased and the night wind dispersed the heavy clouds above our heads. The whole world was frozen still.

We rode for another half-mile, when the trail broke out of the forest into a wide clearing. The castle stood alone on a snowy field, under the night sky. We stopped in our tracks and stared at it.

I expected some miserable forest fort, a mass of mossy stones, forgotten by gods and men. What else could stand in this wilderness, at the end of this winding trail, behind a decaying village?

I was wrong.

An impressive structure stood before us, with high, smooth walls, four towers, high crenelations, all surrounded by a moat. Ice covered it with frozen lace that gleamed in the pale moonlight. No light poured from the arrow slits and no guards patrolled the walls, but the drawbridge was lowered. We stopped in front of it, reluctant to enter before we announced our arrival.

"Damn it, you got a blow to the head, but I'm the one who sees double," muttered my lord.

"What do you mean?" I squinted, but the outlines of the castle remained sharp and clear.

"I can see darkness and light, ruins and walls, two castles, one over the other." He rubbed his eyes. "What illusion is this?"

"My lord, if there is something wrong with this place …"

But he wasn't listening to me. "Raden is in there," he said with an uncanny certainty.

I urged my horse forward onto the drawbridge. "Hey!" I called. "Can you hear us?"

One dog howled in reply, followed by the whole pack. But still, there was no guard in sight. We spurred our horses reluctantly over the bridge, through the gate, and entered the paved courtyard covered in fresh snow. We saw a stable in one corner and an arched corridor on the first floor. Flickering torchlight poured down.

"What on earth is this?" whispered my lord.

I was looking around furiously, trying to see what he saw, trying to find the guards, servants or any inhabitants of that strange place.

"Hey," I called again. "Is anyone here?"

Silence.

And then soft creaking that grew louder. I recognized that sound in a heartbeat and turned quickly towards the gate, just in time to see the iron grid thunder down behind us.

# CHAPTER TWELVE

## ELISYA

### SUMMER 320 A.C.

We started our journey home at dawn, in the rain, with only the servants to see us off. Silya sent me a chest with all the things I had given her. All the dresses, veils, cloaks, jewellery, even the presents, new things that never belonged to me, she returned it all with a message, "You'll need them more than I do." She wanted to hurt me, but my heart was so tired I barely felt the sting.

No-one talked to me. I was held like a prisoner, almost expecting Father to order that my hands should be tied to the saddle. Riding through the wet, empty streets, I felt I would never see Myrit again and was glad. The tournament meadow was no more than a muddy field now, the stands were a heap of wood, the colourful flags just wet, dirty rags.

I was thinking of Vairn. He must have travelled that same road north the previous day, watched the same fields and villages, perhaps even stopped at the same inns. When we sat down for our evening meal, I imagined him sitting on that same bench. Perhaps, if he travelled slowly enough, there was a chance we could catch up with him and then … Or he could pretend to be sick, wait for me and then abduct me, like a robber knight in a story.

My head was still full of impossible plans.

So what if he had not said a single word in my defence, asked my father for my hand, or fought for me? If he'd materialized in front of me and told me to run away with him, I wouldn't have hesitated for a moment. I imagined us together, leaving everything behind us: our names, our inheritances, relatives, everything we owned. We could be fugitives and live on love.

The weather improved after a few days. It was still high summer, blooming and fragrant. We travelled quickly, without unnecessary stops, sleeping at the roadside inns. I expected to feel Father's rage as soon as we left Myrit, but he remained silent and distant. He refused to look at me: I was nothing but a dark shadow on a sunny day. If he wanted me to do something, he would address Keldik: "Please, tell your sister …" My guess was that the punishment he designed for me couldn't be administered on the road, and so he waited for us to come home to discipline me properly.

Keldik wasn't that patient. "I will tell Father the money for your dowry should be given to me," he said, happy as a toad with a belly full of flies. "You are just an unnecessary expense now; there will never be a return. He will have to feed you, of course, but everything else is pointless. You don't even have any skills we could use at home."

I didn't deign to reply. Instead, I asked him, "Tell me, what happened to the girl Father intended for you? How did the talks end? She found your festering face too repulsive?"

He paled and the boils on his face turned crimson.

"Were it up to me, I'd leave you in a ditch beside the road."

"And I would prefer that."

I considered running away. At night, Father would lock my door, but it never crossed his mind that I could slip through a window. I spent a few nights looking at moonlit back yards, thinking about the sheets I could use for descending, the horses I could steal from the stables and the gates I could unlock … and I knew it was never going to happen. Even with a horse, I wouldn't get very far. I didn't know the road, I had no map, and I had no idea how to travel alone. I was utterly helpless.

We soon left the main road that led north and turned towards the east. One morning, Father divided us into two groups. One comprised me, him and a small group of guards, and the other Keldik and the rest of our large escort, with the baggage and animals.

"Hurry home," Father ordered Keldik. "Tell my wife I will follow in a few days. I must pay an urgent visit to our neighbour. Do not tell her what your sister did in Myrit, even if she asks about her. Do you understand me? I will tell her everything when I get back."

Keldik nodded mutely.

We went on, much faster than them, and rode for hours through a dismal landscape: empty, barren fields on the one side and forest on the other. The sun reached its zenith and started descending. When we left the road, which at least looked like travellers occasionally used it, and took a narrow forest path, winding between the trees, the icy claws of fear gripped me. There was no telling where we were going; the afternoon sun did little to dispel the deep shadows and it was like walking through eternal dusk. The woods should have been teeming with life, but no birdsong reached our ears, no animals crossed our path. It was eerily quiet. Our guards became silent and turned around in their saddles more often than was necessary.

"My lord, the evening draws near," one of them said. "Are we close to our destination?"

"Yes," Father replied. "I know the way."

It didn't sound very comforting. The forest knew we were there; a group of strangers riding through an unknown territory.

"Father," I said, fighting the fear and doubt growing in me, "where are you taking us?"

He shot me a long, cold look from the saddle of his large courser, but I knew him well enough to know that the mask of arrogance hid uncertainty.

"We are going to visit one of our neighbours, Elisya. We have been invited and we have put it off for too long."

Many things crossed my mind when he said that. The path didn't look like it led to a nobleman's home. In Myrit he had never mentioned any visit he planned on the way back. If he had wanted to visit his neighbour, it was strange that he had sent Keldik and most of our escort home, leaving the rest of us looking like a band of poor travellers. But I didn't have the courage to say any of that aloud.

We progressed slowly, for the path was full of potholes and roots and it was a challenging task for our horses. Was it possible that Father had made a mistake, taking us in the wrong direction? The guards were whispering in the background; they might have come to the same conclusion. What nobleman would live like a charcoal burner?

After a long ride, we came to a clearing with a village so miserable I had never seen a more pitiful sight. The hovels didn't look like they had been built by humans. They resembled giant mushrooms growing out of the mud. Traces of whitewash were barely visible here and there, but mostly they were covered in dirt from their bases to their rotting thatch roofs that could have only been improved by fire.

The whole place reeked of decay and dung and sour charcoal smoke. We saw no adults, just a group of filthy, half-naked children who chased two hostile goats around a trough. The moment we appeared, they glued their hungry eyes on us, but showed no intention of greeting us properly. I looked away to avoid their ugly faces and their pervasive odour.

As it was clear now that the path did lead somewhere, we spurred our horses, trying to outrun the falling darkness. Less than a mile from the village, the path came abruptly to an end at the entrance to a castle as decrepit and sunk into mud as the village had been. Its walls were perhaps twenty feet high, and its foundations were soaking in the green waters of a useless, narrow moat. The stones, covered in moss and eaten away by time, were held together by little more than sticky sludge, resembling a decomposing body.

This forgotten forest fort had neither gates nor drawbridge. A muddy causeway led to a gaping stone arch. Save for the painted shield that hung above it, bleached by the sun and half-eaten by the worms, I would have been sure we had accidentally come across some forest bandits' lair.

Even Father drew back a little. He sat on his horse, watching the whole scene in disbelief. "The old man is a drunkard," he commented, "but I had no idea they had sunk so low."

I didn't want to ask who, I just wrapped myself more firmly in my cloak to avoid any contact with the disgusting surroundings. There were no guards on the walls, nor did anyone come to greet us.

"Hey!" Father shouted. "Is there anyone here?"

Somewhere behind the walls, a dog started barking. Soon a whole pack joined it, loud enough to wake the dead. A tiny speck of light appeared in the depths of the castle yard and slowly grew bigger as someone approached us. It was a solitary old man, limping painfully with a lamp in his hand. He appeared to be some kind of guard, wearing a dented chest plate and a short sword on a piece of string. In the rapidly falling dark, he lifted the lamp towards my father's face.

"What do you want?" he asked, with no welcome in his voice.

"We want to see Gospodar Cervin," Father retorted. "He invited us here. I am the Vlastelin of Gozdny Dol."

"Perhaps he did invite you, but you won't see him, because he's drunk as a sow," the old man said. "I will ask the young master if he'll receive you." Without any further explanation, he turned and limped away as slowly as he came.

We were left standing alone.

"We could simply go in," one of our guards suggested.

"I'd rather wait," Father said warily.

So we waited, while darkness fell around us. I wondered what would happen if they did not receive us. Nothing could make me ride back through that forest in the dark, but the dogs started barking once more and the familiar spot of light appeared. The same old guard limped towards us.

"Gospodar Selern bids you welcome."

So, he styled himself *gospodar*, even though his father was alive. An upstart lordling.

Carefully following our ancient guide, we entered the courtyard. I couldn't see much in the dark, but it looked just as dilapidated as the walls, unpaved and dirty. Mossy stones, wooden stairs leading to the upper floor, stable leaning on the outer wall, a heap of dung in one corner, its smell permeating the whole yard, a broken cart left to rot.

I hoped this unplanned visit was just another one of Father's whims that would evaporate like dew in the morning, as soon as the sun rose and the horses were saddled. I saw no reason to linger. What could Father have to do with such people? He always strove towards better, nobler, richer company and tried very hard to avoid those below him.

"I apologize for such a welcome; we did not expect you," a voice said, and a tall, burly man with a lamp in his hand materialized before us. "I am Volk, His Lordship's steward."

"There's not much to steward, is there?" Father said coldly, but still, he dismounted and nodded to the man.

"Times are difficult, and my lord's health has been failing these last few months."

"Really? So, Gospodar Cervin is ill?" Father asked. "I haven't received any letters from him since last spring."

"Yes, I am aware of that, I write all his letters," Volk said. "His condition worsened."

"Condition? The guard said he was drunk as a sow," Father snorted.

"Karn blabbered it all out, I see," said Volk, equally cold. "Lucky for you that the young master can receive you. Let's go inside." He turned to the old servant, "Karn, take the lord's escort down to the kitchen and make sure they get something hot to eat. Afterwards, you can show them their lodgings." He turned back to Father, "And you, my lord, please follow me. This young lady is your daughter?"

"Yes."

"My lady." He looked me up and down in a manner I didn't like.

We climbed rickety wooden stairs leading to the first-floor open corridor that ran around the length of the building.

"Watch out, there's a stair missing here," he warned us, and I trod carefully, gripping the fragile banister.

The corridor, full of drafts and cobwebs, was lit by the pale moonlight and Volk's lamp, which bobbed before me as he talked with Father about the affairs of the old lord and the intentions of his heir. They mentioned some land on the border of their properties they had disputed for a long time, some letters and old agreements, but I soon stopped listening.

"Please," I whispered to all the gods who could hear me, "let all this be just a dream. The whole journey to Myrit, the tournament, Vairn, everything that happened, let it be just a messy dream that turned into a nightmare. Please, let me wake up at home, in my bed, with spring sunshine on my pillow and Silya's voice in my ears."

But there was no sunshine and the shadows suddenly lengthened, rushing through the corridor and swallowing the feeble light that led us. Although I walked as fast as I dared in the dark, I couldn't keep up with Father and the steward. Behind me, the cold draft stroked the hairs on my neck, the stench of something dead following me.

At one point it looked like Father and Volk turned the corner, but when I reached that spot, there was no corner to turn, just a straight wall. The dot of light disappeared, and darkness surrounded me. Something brushed against my skirts, a rat or a mouse, and I screamed and clung to the wall, too afraid to call for help.

The whole place felt wrong. I do not mean the poverty and neglect. It was not an accidental fall into ruin, time slowly grinding everything to dust. It felt intentional, something alive … or not alive, but conscious. It was behind everything: the woods, the village, the castle. Everything bore the mark of deliberate decay.

I have never been particularly pious, but at that moment, I found myself praying for help. Or at least trying to pray, for the words could not find their way out of my mouth. My palms were pressed against the stone wall behind me, and something rushed through it, entering me, taking my measure. I tried to pull away, but my body did not obey me. The wall was holding me, sucking me in. I squealed in panic, thinking I would be stuck there forever.

Someone said, "There you are, my lady. It is dangerous to fall behind in the dark." Volk appeared before me with a lamp. In a shockingly insolent gesture, he ran his hand down my back, removing me from the wall. "We don't want to lose you."

I wished I could slap and chastise him, but I was afraid he would walk away and leave me in the dark. Shivering with fear and anger, I followed him down the corridor that seemed longer than it should have been in such a small, decrepit castle. He opened a door and led me into a well-lit room whose walls were bare, except for several pairs of deer antlers and boar tusks that served as coarse ornaments. One side of the room was taken up by a big fireplace with a fire burning in it, for the night was cold and the castle even colder. In the middle of the room, there was a roughly hewn table with twelve chairs, only two of which were occupied. Father sat on one, and on the other was—I assumed—the young master of this rotting pile of stones.

"Elisya likes to wander off when no-one is watching," Father said instead of introduction.

"Elisya," his companion repeated my name and stood up, very slowly, as though he were trying to hoist rusty armour.

"This is Gospodar Selern," Father said.

Selern tried to smile, but his crooked teeth ruined the attempt. He was young, twenty or twenty-one perhaps, but at the same time, he looked as tired as an old man. He wasn't overly tall, but he stooped slightly, scrawny as a scarecrow. Sandy brown hair hung around his pale face in tangled wisps, and purple shadows underlined his blue eyes.

He looked neither attractive nor repulsive. Just another average boy. Not that it mattered to me. The only man I wanted was the one who had abandoned me.

"Welcome to my humble home. It has been quite a while since I wrote to Gospodar Tolmir, expressing my wish to meet you."

Still angry and afraid, I wanted to reply that he should have prepared a better welcome then, but my brain finally overtook my tongue, and I had a good look at the room and the people in it.

It all became clear.

"Oh, Father," I said sadly, "are we going to part like this?"

He was watching me with the same expression as ever, a combination of indifference and irritation, and said nothing. And then I realized another thing, much worse than the stupid, obvious ploy with *Gospodar Selern*. I realized my father did not love me. All my life, I had thought his austerity and impatience, his unreasonable demands and rigidity really meant that he cared for me. That he was measuring me, correcting me, directing me because he wished me well. That his manner towards me was really a sign of the love he didn't know how to express.

At that moment, I understood I had been mistaken. He did not care for me; he had never cared for me. All he cared about was using me as his tool. He wanted a lucrative marriage for me in Myrit not because he thought I would be happy there, but to gain access to the city and to his friend's wealth. When I ruined that opportunity, he decided to get whatever he could out of me. Father and the steward: a conversation in the corridor. Some land, some dispute. Even a neighbour as poor as this one could prove to be useful. He would think Father did him a great honour, and Father would get rid of an unwanted burden.

The last flicker of hope died in my chest. Father did not love me, Silya did not love me, my stepmother never pretended she cared for me, and Keldik I did not want to mention. And Vairn … truly … I wished he could see my situation. My rich lordling, my tournament hero. He could have been a man, not a coward. He knew which road we would take; he could have waited there for us, not to abduct me or do something foolishly romantic, but to talk to Father, who was so greedy and pretentious he wouldn't dare refuse such a meeting. He could have promised something, saved my honour, tried to repair the damage. After all, he could have married me against everyone's wishes. It only took a priest and two witnesses. Everyone would be angry with him, he would fall out of favour for some time, perhaps he would be less rich, perhaps some younger brother—if he existed—would inherit. But he would not end up in a dark hole like the one I was in, and he would not become a beggar or an outcast. And he would have me.

If he had wanted me, if I meant something to him, he could have done it. But he retreated with his tail between his legs, he attributed his cowardice to a higher authority and vanished. He would remember me with nostalgia and tell stories of how he once met a beautiful girl at a tournament, but it was not meant to be. It was possible that he would wonder where I was and what happened to me, but he would never do anything to find me. Because he preferred the life he had to me.

*Dear Elisya*, I said to myself, *you realized too late that nobody loves you. Silya has known it all along, you should have learned from her.*

I sat at the table feeling like an empty vessel, lighter than air. I let them pour me wine, drank, asked for more. While Father and the steward talked, Selern reached across the table and took my hand. His fingers were cold.

"My father and Volk wrote to your father. They were looking for a bride for me. I thought nothing would come of it," he admitted.

"My father wanted to marry me off in Myrit," I replied with an equal dose of honesty, "but I ruined the deal. I tried to elope with someone else, but we were caught. Now I am damaged goods."

I thought it would touch his nobleman's honour, and he would refuse me, but I was wrong. He just cleared his throat and shrugged.

"Do you like hounds?" he asked. "That's about the only thing I have here. Hounds."

"So you like to go hunting?" I hoped for at least some amusement.

"Oh, yes," he said, and I heard something like ardour in his voice for the first time. "Although lately ..." He didn't have time to finish, because at that point Father and Volk reached some kind of a deal.

"Everything is settled, then," Father said. "We can do it tomorrow."

"We have the bride, the groom and the priest, but that is all we have. Are you sure you don't want guests?" Volk asked.

"As far as I'm concerned, a contract will be enough," Father said coldly. "You can do the binding tomorrow if it means something to you. Or you can wait for the guests to come if there is someone you want to invite," he added, remaining true to himself.

It was pointless to argue. Had Selern thrown ten silver crowns on the table and said he wanted to buy me to wash his clothes and cook, Father would have agreed to it. He had decided he wouldn't take me back home; everything else was just tiresome fussing.

Selern turned to me. "Tomorrow, then?"

I nodded. That was his suit, I supposed.

We were shown to mildewy chambers that must have been empty for years, with dusty furniture and sheets untouched by sunshine or fresh air. There was no girl to help me undress, but I didn't want to lie down anyway, too afraid to extinguish the candle and close my eyes.

I wanted to try one final thing before I surrendered. I walked in circles on the bare stone floor, arranging the words in my head. My last defence.

I gathered the little courage I had left and knocked on Father's door, right next to mine. He wasn't sleeping. When he opened the door, he was still fully dressed.

"I want to talk. Please," I said.

He let me in, waved me toward a dusty chair and sat down, waiting for me to begin.

"Father," I uttered the words I had prepared in advance, struggling to keep my voice firm, "I have been ungrateful and disobedient. I was a bad daughter, dishonouring myself and disgracing you, who have always been lenient towards me. What I did is unforgivable."

"Yes." His voice was harsh.

"I know I do not deserve your fatherly love and you can disinherit me and leave me on the road if you wish. I am not asking you for forgiveness, I am not asking you to take me back in. But I do beseech one thing of you." I slipped out of the chair and kneeled before him, "I beg you, do not leave me here. Anywhere but here."

I pushed all my anxiety, fear and daughterly love towards him, hoping to make him feel at least a fragment of what I felt. He shuffled in his seat impatiently.

"Elisya," he sighed, "you are always the same, always stubborn. You don't like this; you don't like that. You refused Gospodar Bremir, now you won't accept Gospodar Selern."

"Please, Father, please, that is not the same. I made a terrible mistake with Gospodar Bremir, I was stupid and rash. It was a great opportunity for me. But this is no opportunity at all."

"This is the only opportunity you have now. It's not Myrit, I know; it is very remote. And I admit I was surprised to see how they have deteriorated since I last saw them. But they are an old noble family with an unblemished reputation. With your dowry, this place could be improved."

"Father, please, listen to me!" Tears welled in my eyes. "There is something wrong with this place, don't you feel that? Our guards noticed it as soon as we entered the forest. This place is cursed!"

"The guards are superstitious fools, and you, Elisya, you've read too many legends. Do you really think I would believe such a foolish story?"

I looked into his eyes; they were hard and cold.

I said, "Feel free to call me mad, unreasonable, stubborn, sly. Tell me I am imagining things, that I am superstitious, that I am telling you fables. Do not believe me, let everything bad about this place be a fabrication of mine. Let there be no good reason for me to run away. But take me with you anyway. For my late mother's sake."

He winced and I saw a tiny crack in his armour. He allowed himself to think about it.

"But what am I to do with you then?" he asked. "There will be no other suitors when the word gets around. No, Elisya, this is your best chance."

"Father—"

"No." He silenced me with a turn of his palm. "I've made my decision."

Thus, I returned to my room and waited for the dawn with my eyes wide open.

In the morning, a maid came to help me dress. She was a scruffy, thin, barefooted little thing. Her brown hair was a matted nest, and her arms were covered in scabs and old scars. She kept wiping her snotty nose on her ragged sleeve. I have seen beggars on the side of the road who looked better than that child.

I barely managed to show her how to lace me up. I felt it was appropriate to end everything in the same manner it started. Every stitch and every embroidered detail on my blue gown spoke of hope, friendship and grand plans. A token of the shiny future that waited for me. I brushed my hair, letting it fall in a golden mass of waves. I washed my face, pinched my cheeks, bit my lips, fixed my smile.

When I entered the room, they all gasped when they saw me, including Father. On the dirty grey background of the castle, my hair shone like the sun.

That was the first time I saw my future father-in-law, Gospodar Cervin. He had the same brown hair and blue eyes like his son, but all resemblance stopped there. The old lord's face was swollen, with a red, bulbous growth where his nose should have been. His body was skinny, but his belly was bloated and precariously balanced on two spindly legs. He was sober that morning, but according to his pained look, he wasn't taking it too well.

First, we signed the documents: my engagement, wedding and dowry contracts, everything was dealt with at once. Selern introduced the servants to me; I had already seen them all except the boy who took care of hounds and horses and who was so slow he barely spoke. The limping old man was Karn, and his wife was the half-blind cook, Freda. Tinka, the scrawny little maid, was an orphan they had taken in.

The mood was gloomy. My bridegroom must have seen disappointment in my face because he whispered in my ear, "I suggested we should do the binding outside, in the garden. It is much nicer there."

I was still little when my sisters married, but I could clearly remember the feeling when the pair's hands were tied together, and the priest called for a blessing. Something that surpassed a mere contract between two people happened at that moment. I remembered the priestess who performed the ceremony: she had a dress the colour of the leaves, greying hair in long plaits and a crown of flowers on her head. She looked fragile and small before the lords and ladies who gathered there, but she had the gift. People didn't become priests because they chose the calling, but because the calling chose them.

The ceremony itself was always simple, regardless of who the bride and the groom were. Signing the marriage contract might have been an extravagant occasion, the celebrations might have lasted for three days, but the binding was performed by the local priest, out in the open. The bride and groom would hold hands, the priest would bind them with a piece of string and call for blessing, first from their own divine patron, then from all the others. The bride and groom would promise to love, honour and respect one an-other.

I had always imagined I would stand like that one day with a man I was in love with, looking into his eyes while I said my vows. I glanced at the young man my father chose for me and tasted bitter disappointment when I compared him to the image in my head. With a leaden heart, I followed him out of the room.

We passed through the empty corridors and came to a low, arched door. Someone had hung an ivy wreath on it: the only decoration I saw that day. Selern took my hand and we stepped from the darkness into the bright sunshine outside.

He didn't lie, the garden was prettier than the rest of the castle. It wasn't big, but it had tall, graceful birch trees, quite different from the old, gnarled giants that grew in the forest. The ground was covered with a soft carpet of new grass. And the roses—someone had planted a few bushes and they grew, wild and unpruned, full of fragrant flowers, white, yellow, red.

When he noticed I was staring at them, Selern said, "They were a part of my mother's dowry, she planted them here. No-one has tended them since she died. But I hope you will still be able to find beauty in them."

I nodded slowly, remembering with longing the bloom-ing rose bushes in my father's garden, where I spent many lazy afternoons with Silya, dreaming about adventures.

"Let's go to the water," he said and led me down the gravelled path, turned by years of neglect into a dirty, over-grown track. It ended at a shadowy little pond covered with water lilies. Although it was a warm day, the spot in the shadow was chilly, and the water looked deeper than it should have been.

"Who will perform the binding?" I asked. "You haven't introduced me to a priest so far."

"Haven't I?" he replied. "Well, here he comes."

I should have known, I realized, as a cold breeze blew through the summer air and chilled my bones. He was dressed in his goddess' colours: dark green, grey and black, and his eyes were hard like two jet beads. Volk was more than just a steward, he was also the servant of Morana, the goddess of water and death. Never have I heard of Morana's priest being called to perform the binding.

"You can't expect him to—" I began, but Selern interrupted me.

"There is no-one else. Does it matter?"

I wanted to oppose him, to say that it mattered a great deal, that, although it was true all priests could perform the wedding ceremony, there was a good reason why some of them never did, but I bit my tongue. It was just another ugly duty my father forced on me. I wanted none of it, and I would not have changed my mind even if the Goddess of Love's high priestesses came to bind our hands.

Volk caught my eye and I felt he read my last thought. I blinked quickly and focused on a chalice he held, adorned with a garland of golden leaves and blood-red rubies.

When he commenced, calling the gods' blessing upon us, cold shivers ran down my spine. *Perun, father of gods, the wisest of all!* His voice was deep, coming from a great distance. *Dazbog, driving the sun chariot across the sky!* And yet, it was curiously flat, without resonance. *Vlasta of the hearth and family!* As if he were speaking in a small chamber, not a garden. *Stribor of the wind, protector of travellers!* Like he spoke into a box that didn't permit the sound to escape.

I looked up into the summer sky and it seemed fake, like a canopy stretched over our heads. The names of gods fell from his mouth heavily, like stones falling on the sand. I waited for the last one. *Morana, mistress of death and deep waters, bless this couple!* A sliver of ice pierced my heart and I shuddered. Cold water spread through my veins, dark and noiseless and deadly, dousing my fierce fire.

Volk took a piece of red ribbon and wrapped it around our wrists. *I join you before the eyes of gods and people, from now until death.*

"I take you to be my wife, from now until death," Selern said and took a sip from the chalice the priest gave him.

"I take you to be my husband, from now until death," I said and sipped the sweet red wine.

And then we kissed.

We were married.

# CHAPTER THIRTEEN

# IDA

## AUTUMN 361 A.C.

*Ida*, I told myself, hiding in an alcove, fearing for my life, *if you survive this, you will go back to Abia and be the sweetest, most obedient tavern wench the world has ever seen.*

You guess that things didn't go smoothly in that damned castle, and you guess right. We had a worse time than a beardless boy on a ship whose crew had not seen a woman for half a year. We had such a bad time that there is no-one but me left to tell the story.

Our arrival had been so promising. Once we stopped staring at the strong, smooth walls glowing in the moon-light, we rode in as a group of weary travellers who had heard of the lord's hospitality. I admit I had little experience with castles. Gair had never included them in Doctor

165

Bellemus's tours since there was always a possibility we could meet a real physician. And I had never tried to enter a castle on my own. I didn't want to be molested by the guards at the gates—which was probably as far as I would get. Besides, I hated the nobles. All they ever did was fight, drink and chase girls.

I had to remember I was pretending to be a lady, too. And trust me, that was bloody hard, much harder than on stage. I was trembling with fear and anxiety at the thought that I would find myself among lords, or even worse, ladies. What did they talk about when they were alone? How long would it take them to discover I was an impostor?

Such thoughts rushed through my head as we crossed the drawbridge and entered the courtyard through a dark passage. Did I notice anything strange? No, not at once. And neither did Criscer and his friends, who were far more familiar with noblemen's dens.

Before we managed to dismount, a large man appeared from a dark corner of the yard, carrying a lamp. The closer he came, the larger he seemed, until he finally grew as huge as a werewolf, dressed in leather and greasy wool, covered in grey hair from head to—I guessed—toes.

"We are travellers," said Criscer, introducing us. "The mistress at the inn in Haragov Dol said the master of this place gladly welcomes everyone who happens to stop by."

The wolf-man lifted his lamp to see our faces. His eyes met mine for a moment and I thought I saw a flicker of recognition in them, although I had never seen him in my life.

He spoke in a growl, deep and resonant.

"Welcome. My name is Volk, and I am Gospodar Selern's steward," he said. "It is true that his lordship welcomes guests. I hope you have travelled well and you're not too tired, because he will want to meet you tonight."

He whistled to the stable boy, who promptly appeared and took our horses. An old servant limped out to take our bags.

"You arrived just in time for dinner," he said, leading us upstairs. "I will let you rest for a bit, and then I'll send someone for you."

I didn't want to part with my companions, but Volk took us to a door where a scruffy little maid stood waiting for me.

"This is your room," he said. "Where's your luggage?"

I had no luggage. Criscer had burned my old dress and boots. "Why would a young lady carry rags and cheap trinkets in her bags?" he had asked reasonably. And so I carried nothing but the things I had in my pockets.

"My bags were stolen on the road," I lied.

Volk nodded, without questioning my words. "Tinka," he called the little maid, "ask her ladyship if she wants to help."

When they left me alone, I panicked, not knowing what to do next. But then I took a deep breath and looked around the magnificent room. It was a huge step up from my usual kitchen floors and haystacks, hard ground and fishing nets.

I couldn't resist running towards the featherbed and throwing myself on the fat cloud of feathers, excited like a child. I rolled around in it, spreading my arms, staring in wonder at the beautiful canopy above me, stunned by the grandeur of the moment: that enormous bed, that mountain of feathers fit for a lady, was all mine. I was tempted to crawl underneath the covers and sail away to the land of dreams.

But there was no time for dreaming. I had to prepare for my role. I fetched a jug of warm water and washed my hands and face. There were traces of dried blood under my fingernails. I scrubbed them vigorously. I warmed myself beside the fire. Everything in that room seemed prepared in advance for my arrival.

There was a knock on the door, and the rush of panic came back.

"Come in," I said, trying to control my voice. The little maid entered with a heap of colourful silk in her hands.

"Gospa Elisya bids you welcome," she said. "She will gladly lend you one of her gowns. Please take a look to see if any of these fit."

She spread the beautiful fabrics on the bed, and I had to bite my lip to prevent myself from gasping in wonder. Never in my life had I come near to owning a silk dress, and now there were three in front of me. Dark red with embroidered vines, green with sleeves trimmed with flowers and dark blue with tiny pearls.

"Her ladyship and you are of similar height," she said, eyeing me. "She's a bit rounder, but all three should fit. Which one do you like?"

I touched them: the fabrics were heavy, smooth and cold. They were not new, they showed signs of wear: a hem that was torn and stitched up, embroidery that was mended in a few places—but they were, without a doubt, the real thing. Nothing like those cheap, garish rags we wore on stage.

"I think the red one will do," I said in the most restrained tone I could muster.

"Come, I'll help you dress," the girl said.

And so I had to let her take my black wool off and dress me in red silk. My undergarments were, luckily, clean and of decent quality. I tried to convince myself a poor noble-woman from the South would probably wear a linen shift just like mine.

"I will comb your hair," the girl said and started to undo my braids and untangle my curls. She had deft little hands, but her skin was red and flaky from laundering. She plaited my hair again, this time more firmly, wound the braids around my head and tied them with a ribbon. The skin on her knuckles was worn so thin it bled, and I remembered how that hurt. I knew what it was like to be the youngest girl in the house, with too many hard tasks. When she finished doing my hair, I gently caught her hand. She shivered and tried to pull away, but I held her.

"I have something that will help you," I said, trying to be as kind as I could.

"I'm fine."

"Wait," I ordered and reached into the pocket of my black dress. I retrieved a little pot of unguent for wounds, blisters and frostbites.

"Give me your hands." She was still eyeing me suspiciously, but she obeyed. "This will tingle," I warned her, "but it will reduce the pain." I spread a thin layer of salve on her skin and she winced, but didn't move. When I was done, she sniffed it.

"Smells nice," she said.

I slipped the pot in her pocket. "Take it, you need it more than I do. Your hands are better now, aren't they?"

She nodded and whispered, "Thank you."

I thought it was a good moment to ask her a few questions.

"Tinka," I said, "that's your name, isn't it?" She nodded. "How long have you been here?"

"I'm not sure," she shrugged. "Quite long."

I took a good look at her, lit by the warm glow of the fireplace. She was small and probably looked younger than her age, but she couldn't have been older than twelve.

"When you say quite long, you mean a year or two …?"

"I mean very long," she repeated stubbornly. "Many years."

I thought she was a bit simple, then. She probably meant months, not years.

"Tell me something about your mistress," I said. "What is she like?"

"Good." Another shrug. "You'll see for yourself."

"Is there anything I should know about her?"

Ever since I had given her the salve, Tinka showed signs of embarrassment. She fidgeted and retreated towards the door. At first, I thought she was ungrateful. Then I thought she was probably not used to ladies being kind to her. But then it occurred to me her stance had nothing to do with my gift.

She looked around, although we were alone in the room, and came closer.

"You are no noble lady," she whispered in my ear.

"How dare you …" I wanted to act insulted, but then I saw the worry and fear in her face. "How do you know?" I hissed.

"I can always recognize another girl like me."

"What now?" I asked. "Will you tell someone?"

She shook her head quickly. "No, I'm not trying to blackmail you. I don't care what you and your companions do here. It's just …"

"What?"

"You were kind to me, so I'll be kind to you. Listen carefully …" She came so close that her cheek touched mine. "Gospa Elisya. Make her like you."

"What?"

"Make her like you." She grabbed my arm and squeezed so hard it hurt. "She is lonely, she needs company. Let her think you could be her companion. Do whatever you need to do, entertain her, flatter her, comb her hair and rub her shoulders, but stay with her all night, in her chambers. Do you understand me?"

"But why?"

"Do you understand me?" she repeated, squeezing even harder.

"I do," I cried. "But tell me …"

She took a step back and released my hand. "Thank you for the ointment. I must go now."

# CHAPTER FOURTEEN

## ELISYA

### SUMMER 320 A.C.

I didn't say a single word to Father that day. In the afternoon, when he and his guards mounted their horses, I came halfway down the wooden stairs and raised my hand. But when Father said, "Goodbye, Elisya," I looked away and went back inside. Volk leered from the shadows. He caught up with me before I reached my room.

"Gospa Elisya," he said. His voice was perfectly polite, but when I tried to go around him, he blocked my way. "A word, please."

He had filled me with terror even before I found out he was a priest. I wanted to turn and run away, crawl under my bed and remain hidden.

"You are not a little girl anymore, my lady," he said, reading my thoughts. "There is no nurse to save you from the monsters in the dark."

"Leave me alone," I said.

"I will, my lady, but before that ..." His enormous hand caught my arm. He didn't squeeze tight enough to hurt me, only to warn me that he could. I tried to pull away, but he held me anchored in the corner.

"No-one got what they wanted with this wedding. You wanted another groom. We wanted ... well, let's just say that the letter to your father was among the last we sent."

A wave of heat climbed up my neck.

"But things are as they are, and the sooner you adapt, the easier it will be," he continued. "Your only task is to keep the young master happy. Take care of that and I will take care of the rest. You are young and beautiful, and I understand you have experience with men. Use it."

My cheeks were burning, but we were in the shadow, and I hoped he couldn't see it. "Is that all?" I snarled.

Volk smiled. "There are worse things than spreading your legs." He bent to my ear and whispered in his deep, harsh voice, "There's darkness so thick it consumes you. There's deep, cold water and things that live in it, things that pull you under and devour your flesh while you're still screaming. There are corridors that do not lead where you want them to, there's a key that opens every door in this castle and there's me."

He squeezed hard before he let me go. My whole body shivered uncontrollably and I opened my mouth, but no sound came out. Volk gave a short, sneering bow and disappeared around a corner before I had time to think of a reply.

I stood there a long time, my heart filled with terror, but the corridor showed no intention of playing tricks on me. Reluctantly, I started an aimless tour, encouraged by the clear daylight. The castle was simple: stable and kennel in the yard; kitchen, armoury and storerooms on the ground floor. Upstairs, there was the big hall and five or six small chambers. Four empty towers with leaking roofs protected the corners. On the other side of the wall, there was a dirty moat. The castle sat in it like a tiny island in the middle of nowhere.

The maid found me when the sky changed from blue to purple.

"The young master would like you to join him," she said with a clumsy curtsy.

When my sisters got married, there were feasts in the evening with enough food for everybody, from the highest guests to the boy who cleaned the stables. Glasses and cups were never empty and everybody teased the bride and groom. I didn't understand the jokes, but I clearly remembered the laughter, the cheerfulness, the antics when it was time to go to bed. My elder sister drank too much wine and her husband had to carry her upstairs, to everybody's amusement. My younger sister was led to her bedchamber by her friends, singing songs I didn't understand at the time.

I was followed by a quiet, grubby little girl.

"My lady," she said, opening the door for me.

My husband's chambers were somewhat more comfortable than the ones Father and I had stayed in, but only because someone lived in them. There were some faded tapestries and threadbare carpets that had lost their ornamental function, but still kept the drafts and cold at bay. Several odd pieces of furniture had found their place there, including a monstrous bed which had probably been used by generations of lords and ladies. Selern was sprawled across its plush feather pillows.

"Elisya," he said and smiled.

I noticed a little table heaped high with food right next to the bed. I realized I had spent the whole day so anxious I had forgotten to eat and drink. I poured some wine, watered it down and drank it. Then I poured some more. I took a piece of bread and stuffed it in my mouth unceremoniously.

"You haven't eaten today?" he asked, sitting up.

I shook my head with my mouth full, too hungry to be ashamed. The food was simple: cold meat, cheese, bread. The old Elisya would ask for something better, but the new one didn't care for such things. I motioned him to sit beside me.

"I have already eaten, thank you," he said, but he accepted a cup of wine.

I watched that complete stranger who was now my husband, and it became clear to me why there were always so many people and so much wine at weddings.

We had no people but there was plenty of wine, so I poured myself a third cup and didn't bother with adding water. He was watching me in silence, his eyes gliding over my face, my hair, my hands.

"What are we going to do now?" I asked when the wine started working at last. "My friends and your friends should be here, getting us ready for the bedding."

"It's your father's fault there are no guests. Had he shared his plans with us in time, without rushing it, we would have been able to have a real wedding." He paused. "Why was he in such a hurry?" he mused. "Are you with child?"

175

"Oh, no," I blurted out, blushing. "No, I assure you."

"So … he did not lie. Damaged but not beyond repair."

I shrugged. I had nothing to add to that description.

"You don't like me," he said. It was a statement, not a question.

"I love somebody else," I said. If Selern were bigger or more dangerous, I would have kept quiet. Someone like Father was capable of breaking his bride's neck for that. But my new husband just raised his eyebrows.

"It's fine, it doesn't say anywhere that you must love me," he said with a sly smile. "You must give me an heir, and that's quite a different matter."

When his inept hands touched me, I started to cry.

I woke up at dawn, thirsty and cold, and looked at my sleeping husband, gently snoring with his mouth open beside me. I felt the weight of the canopy above my head, I smelled the oppressive, mouldy odour of the tapestries, I heard the cold water lapping in the corridors. Suddenly, I could not breathe. I ran to the window, clawing at my throat, choking. There was no life for me in that castle, no life at all.

My blue dress was on a chair where Selern had thrown it the previous night and I left it there. Wearing just my undergarments, I ran to my room, found my riding suit and boots and dressed hastily.

I rushed to the stable and was surprised to find it in better shape than the rest of the castle. The half-witted boy groomed the horses and cleaned up after them. I brought them apples and let them sniff me. There were ten stalls, but only four were occupied: an old workhorse long past its prime, a long-legged black courser Selern used for hunting, a lively black mare that probably belonged to Volk, and my gelding, who had carried me since I left home. I greeted it and stroked its neck. It replied with happy neighing.

"Saddle my horse," I ordered the boy.

He nodded and did as he was told. He guided the horse out into the yard and brought me a small mounting block. I took the reins and looked around. The castle had no gates; the path that crossed the moat and led towards the woods was clear. Was it really so simple?

"Are you going somewhere, my lady?" A voice startled me. Volk stood on the stairs, watching me. It was not so simple, after all.

"I need some exercise, and I want to see the surroundings," I said.

He nodded. "Return before dark. The woods become dangerous after nightfall."

"I will," I said, thinking, *if we ever see each other again, it will be too soon.*

I crossed the moat and rode down the path that led to the village. Although I was tempted to spur the horse and run to freedom, I forced myself to ride slowly and carefully. They knew where I was, and no-one tried to stop me. A loss of a shoe or, worse, a broken leg, would ruin my chances of escape forever.

It was a bright summer morning, but the mood in the forest was gloomy. The village was empty again, except for a few animals and children. One filthy little creature of ambiguous sex stood in my way, with outstretched arms. I had apples for the horse in my saddlebag, so I gave it one. The child devoured it in two bites, before the others arrived. In a couple of heartbeats, I was surrounded by a dozen little creatures. They grabbed at my boots, my dress, my reins with their dirty little paws. They grinned with their tongues lolling, like a pack of dirty mongrels, their teeth sharp and carnivorous.

I whipped them and spurred my horse, my heart beating madly in my chest. When we got out of their reach, I let the horse slow down again, too afraid of injuries.

I had taken nothing but water and apples in my bag, expecting to reach the road soon, planning to find a village or a farm and buy some food and perhaps ask for shelter. I progressed rather slowly, but I assured myself there was only one path leading from the castle to the road. Even someone as inexperienced as me couldn't take a wrong turn. To make sure of it, I tore my red scarf into thin strips, which I tied to the branches beside the path, to mark my way and make sure I wasn't riding in circles.

I rode for a long time, too long: the sun rose to its zenith and started descending and still there was no road in sight. I stopped for a moment, confused, to drink a sip of water and eat an apple. My stomach signalled it was long past lunchtime.

"I thought we were riding straight for the road," I mused. "Have we taken a wrong turn somewhere? Can there be more than one path?"

For the first time that day, fear replaced anticipation. Gnarled branches and ancient trees loomed behind me. The thought that the night would find me in the woods made me tremble. All day I ignored fear and disgust because I thought my adventure would be over soon. But the feeling that something was terribly wrong crept over me. The trees seemed to close in, reaching across the path with their skeletal hands.

There was no time to go back, the day was almost done.

"What are we going to do now?" I asked my horse. Tears of fear and disappointment blurred my vision.

The shadows lengthened, branches over my head turned into a thick canopy, oppressing me with their dark silence. We didn't find water on our way and the horse was thirsty and tired. Instead of rushing, we slowed down. When the sky turned from blue to purple, with no road before me, I started to tremble.

"Oh, gods," I whispered, "can you hear me? Lela, protector of the forests, if your grace shines on any of these wretched trees, please, help me."

My ragged breathing seemed to echo in the complete silence and even the horse froze, unwilling to go on. A breath of cold air touched my neck, a faint breeze smelling of graves and decay. Darkness fell around me and I knew, *I knew* there was something on the path behind me.

A whisper. *Elisya.*

I screamed.

My horse broke into a wild gallop, and I clung to the reins for dear life, as branches swished beside me, trying to grab my hair. We fled towards an opening in the trees, a faint smudge of light, but when we reached it, instead of the road, I saw a castle, surrounded by a dirty moat without a bridge, with a painted shield above the entrance.

"No," I whispered. "No, this can't be."

Like a dead thing preying on the living, the castle stood in menacing silence under the pale moonlight. I cried in desperation as we crossed the moat and entered the courtyard. The half-witted stable boy came to take my horse, with a blank, foolish smile stuck to his face. As he took the reins, his eyes widened and he pointed at something behind me, but when I turned around, there was only darkness.

"Are you afraid of the forest?" I asked him, but he disappeared in the stable without looking at me.

Staggering with exhaustion, I wanted to huddle in some well-lit corner, surrounded by people. The only place I could think of was the kitchen, so I went to see if there was anything warm for supper. Freda and Karn sat beside the fire. When I called her, she brought me a bowl of thick venison stew and a piece of dark bread. I had barely swallowed a mouthful when Volk walked in. In one hand he held half a dozen dead rabbits, which he threw on the table, barely missing my bowl. In the other hand, he held a larger animal, with russet fur.

"Look what I found in the forest," he said.

It was a dead fox, without traces of blood. Strangled, with a red ribbon wrapped around its neck. A ribbon from my scarf.

I sprang to my feet. "Did you follow me?"

Volk was a sturdy man, with thick grey hair and a beard. His eyes were two tiny dots of light burning deep inside their sockets. They pinned me down with interest and derision. He reminded me of a hungry wolf, a hairy mountain of malevolence.

"I don't need to follow you to know where you're heading," he said with a sneer. "My lady."

I fled from the kitchen, stirring the fury in my chest and smothering the fear, and burst into my husband's chamber. Selern was lying on the bed, in the same pose as when I had left him that morning.

"Elisya! I'm glad you're back. I was worried when Volk told me you went riding."

"Why?" I asked bitterly. "Did you think I would run away?"

He looked at me as if I were mad. "No, of course not. You wanted to explore," he said. "That was brave, but not very wise."

"Why not?"

"Because …" He sighed. "This forest is old, and it has its own rules. It is best to do what Volk says, he knows what he's talking about."

"Who is the master of this castle?" I asked him. "Is it you, is it your drunken father, or is it really Volk?"

I thought he would get angry, but he just sighed.

"Please don't quarrel with him. You will do yourself a lot of damage and lose in the end."

I couldn't sit down, so I paced around the room. "What do you mean?"

"You were out today, alone," he said. "I wish you wouldn't do that."

"Why?" I cried. "What is wrong with the woods? Tell me, please, I don't understand." Tears welled up in my eyes. "I'm not crazy, and yet …"

"Promise me you won't go there alone again."

"Why?"

"I'm afraid something might happen to you." He took my hand and his eyes met mine. "My mother went riding alone one day. She never came back."

# CHAPTER FIFTEEN

## IDA

### AUTUMN 361 A.C.

I remained in that lavish room, in a beautiful dress that rustled whenever I moved, beside the fire that kept me warm, but the joy had gone out of it. The little maid's words disturbed me more than my own doubts. But there was little time for thinking, for somebody was already knocking on my door.

"His Lordship invites you to join him for dinner." Volk filled the doorway, still dressed in the same hunting garb, worn leather and dirty wool. His eyes widened when he saw me. "You glow, my lady."

I reminded myself to lower my eyes shyly while I followed him out. *You are a lady,* I told myself, *a lady.*

"We rarely have the opportunity to entertain such beautiful women here," he said as soon as we left the room.

The corridor was well-lit, but still it had too many shadows. It was longer than I thought, and colder. I suddenly wished I was in a warm little room at some inn where I could hear people talking, singing and fighting through the floorboards. This castle filled with drafts and darkness frightened me.

"Thank you," I said.

"Are you engaged to any of the gentlemen you travel with?"

"What? No ..." Such a direct question confused me. "Criscer is my cousin, I'm not engaged."

His hand materialized on my shoulder. "Then you must be lonely." It moved down my back. If he had known I was just a common girl, he would not have wasted any time talking, he would have raped me against the nearest wall. Pretending to be a lady got me a somewhat gentler treatment, his hand on my bottom.

"Please," I begged.

He laughed and made me face him. His smell hit me like a fist: sweat, grease and dirty clothes. He pressed his bushy beard against my face, scratching my chin and cheeks, forcing his tongue into my mouth and his hand between my legs.

Disgust made me choke. There was no self-control that could have stopped me. I slapped him as hard as I could and screamed, "No!" He let go of me for a moment, but only to catch a breath for another attack.

"Ida?" a voice called from the dark corridor. I span and saw Criscer holding a lamp. "Is everything all right?"

"Yes," I lied, an angry flush spreading over my cheeks. "I just tripped in the dark."

"I deliver you the lady alive and well," Volk said behind my back.

Criscer glared at him. He was not stupid. But all he said was, "Thank you."

"Come, his lordship is waiting for you." Volk walked by me, throwing me a sneering look, and continued down the corridor. Compared with him, Criscer was the epitome of politeness. We followed him, Edon and Krasil joining us.

"You look wonderful," Edon whispered in my ear.

Volk led us into a bright, opulent room. Deer antlers and boar tusks decorated the walls, together with tapestries depicting hunting scenes. There was a table in the middle, laden with food, surrounded by carved, high-backed chairs. Light, warmth and the smell of food made me dizzy. It felt like I had stepped into another time and place.

"Welcome," someone said.

Gospodar Selern and his lady stood to greet us. Criscer took the lead immediately, introducing his companions, and exchanging a few words about our journey and the weather. All the while, I stood in the back and watched the noble couple. I had never entered such a grand house, not even as a servant, let alone a guest, and I had never seen a lord up close, without his horse, armour and entourage.

Despite his nice clothes and a heavy gold chain on his chest, Gospodar Selern looked disappointingly ordinary. Younger than I expected, just over twenty. Not particularly tall, very thin, with unruly brown hair and an unappealing face. If it were not for the brocade he wore, I wouldn't have guessed he was somebody important. He looked like a scribe or a small merchant and barely deserved a second look.

Gospa Elisya, on the other hand, in a shimmering green dress, with shiny golden hair, looked like a princess. Younger than her husband, strikingly pretty and pale as the moon. She behaved just as I imagined a noble lady should behave: she watched us with a mixture of indifference and contempt, a cold smile twisting the corners of her mouth. She greeted Criscer with a barely noticeable nod, and his companions with a long look of her piercing blue eyes. I bowed my head and gave her a deep curtsy.

I'd always had troubled experiences with mistresses, in every place I'd worked. They always doubted me, they were envious of my looks, uncertain because of my impertinence and intelligence. They saw me as a rival in their husbands' hearts, a temptation for their sons, a firebrand among the servants and a girl who was generally more trouble than she was worth.

"My lady, this is Ida, my cousin," Criscer introduced me.

I wondered what the lady would see in me. I wasn't coming to her as a servant. And I was certainly not prettier than her.

"Welcome, Ida." She gave me her delicate white hand with one slim gold ring on her little finger. "The dress becomes you, I see."

I looked at her coyly and smiled. "Thank you, you are very kind."

She was so enchanting my companions couldn't take their eyes off her. But I sensed something false in her beauty, as if we were both actresses, meeting on stage.

"Sit beside me," she said, her eyes flying towards her husband, who was already chatting with the men.

I listened carefully while Criscer talked about himself and his companions. He mentioned his father's name and lands, far in the southwest of Larion—they might have actually been real. He was indeed a lord's son. He presented a lively picture of young men eager for adventure, travelling from one inn, town or castle to the next, wasting time and money as if they had them in unlimited supply.

"Our generation missed all the great events," he said. "Conquests, wars … even the tournaments are not as they used to be. So we need to find excitement on the road."

"And? Do you find any?" Gospodar Selern asked.

Criscer shot a long look towards the lady, and Krasil replied, "Oh, yes, sometimes we meet outlaws, or somebody tries to rob us in a tavern."

"And if we don't find the excitement, we create it," Criscer smiled at the lady.

"We have quite enough excitement here, trust me," she replied coolly, untouched by his broad smile.

"I like hunting," her husband said. "You never know what you might find in this forest."

I looked at the trophies decorating the walls. The last remains of at least a hundred animals hung over our heads. A shiver went through me, but then we started eating and I was so hungry I forgot everything else.

Never in my life had I seen so much food for so few people and I didn't understand how they managed to prepare such a feast so quickly. White bread, broth with meat and vegetables, eels in jelly, fish pies, meat pies, venison stew, almond and honey cakes. And wine, sweet and strong, that went straight to my head.

"Tell me, my lady," Gospodar Selern spoke to me directly, "what do you think of travelling with young men looking for adventure? Is it tiring?"

"Oh, I've been with them for a very short time. Criscer was so kind as to offer to escort me on my journey."

I was afraid our story would look fake, but as Criscer and I told it, our audience listened without a blink. The tale of an orphaned girl travelling with her cousin proved to be plausible enough.

"I hope my journey will end soon; the road is no place for young ladies," I added in the end, so earnestly that Gospa Elisya squeezed my hand under the table.

We sat there for a long time. The servants took the remains of the meal away, leaving only the wine and the sweets. It seemed to me the laughter became shrill as the candlelight turned into little golden balls surrounded by the growing darkness. The place became less real. As if the world around me was both flatter and deeper than it should have been. Flatter because it felt like a backdrop, painted on the pupils of my eyes. Deeper because there was another world behind it, taunting me that if only I could turn my head at the right angle, and look from the corner of my eye, I might see what was hidden in the shadows.

I didn't know how late it was when the final act played out: the laughter was still ringing in my ears when the first blade appeared. Criscer held it under the lady's throat. I wanted to call out, but my tongue was heavy in my mouth. His friends got up, carefully watching the lord.

"Thank you for your hospitality," Criscer said brightly. "I apologize for being rough, but as you have no guards up here, I think it's best to end this quickly."

He ripped the lady's necklace off her neck and the golden net off her hair. She gave a muffled scream, but the blade pressing harder against her skin cut it off. I looked at Gospodar Selern, expecting him to do something, but he just sat there, pale and limp like a dead fish.

The lady's hand found mine under the table, and this time it was me who offered an encouraging squeeze, although I had no courage. Nobody had told me of this plan. I knew Criscer and his men were swindlers and thieves, but I thought their methods were more elegant: persuading the lord to gamble with them or emptying his coffers at night and disappearing. Anything but this violence.

"Do not bother calling for help," Krasil said, while his tiny eyes flickered. "The servants are far away and your steward … if you try to call him, you will lose your pretty wife, which would be a real shame."

Gospodar Selern nodded carefully. "Take what you want."

I watched the scene quiet as a mouse, trying to remain invisible.

Criscer gave a sign to his friends. "Escort the lord to his chambers and take whatever is valuable. Be quick. If I hear you shout or if you take too long, there will be blood."

When they left, Criscer, still holding the blade to Gospa Elisya's throat, winked at me. "Give me some wine, lass."

Silently, I gave him a full glass.

"What are you going to do with us?" Gospa Elisya asked.

"Nothing, if you do as we say. We will take your gold and ride away into the night. You and your husband will be tied and gagged so that you can't raise an alarm too soon, but we won't hurt you."

I had no need to look into his eyes to know he was lying. The plan was too neat; it implied they would meet no-one on their way out, that they would saddle their horses by themselves, open the gate, ride into the night and find the right way in the dark.

"The servants are still awake downstairs," the lady said. "The guards won't let you out."

"Then we will have to take a hostage."

That was a lie, too. What would they do with a hostage on the road? They planned to kill them and disappear before the bodies were found. It was the middle of the night; the servants and Volk were away. Criscer and his friends were armed and used to fighting, unlike our hosts. Who could stop them?

I felt sick. Stealing from the rich was all right, as was tricking the fools and cheating the gullible. Killing someone in self-defence or in the war … I understood that, too. But to rob and kill the people who received us so generously? That I could not accept. I didn't have much to do with the gods, but I was certain an act like this was sure to make them very angry. And, with my bad luck, the last thing I needed was the wrath of the gods.

Gospa Elisya threw me a quick glance. Was she trying to say something? Ask for help?

I made my decision in a heartbeat. I opened my eyes wide, jumped to my feet.

"Criscer, look out, they're behind you!" I cried.

He turned, quick as a cat, removing the dagger from the lady's neck. I grabbed a heavy wine jug from the table. He was already turning back when I hit him as hard as I could on the side of his head. The jug broke and the wine spilled over the table and into the lady's lap. Criscer stumbled and fell on his back. I wasted no time. I took her hand and dragged her up.

"Let's go. Is there another way out?"

"There's a hidden door on the other side of the room."

Behind our backs, Criscer got up, swearing and calling for Krasil and Edon. We dashed into a low passage and into a labyrinth of corridors and stairs. Shouts echoed in the dark, but no running feet followed us.

"We must tell the guards," I said, catching my breath.

The lady shook her head in silence and continued to run through the darkness. I lost my sense of direction; left, right, up, down. I had no idea where we were. At last, she pulled me through a pitch-black doorway, hidden behind a heavy curtain. She slammed the door behind us and latched it. We were in a spacious chamber lit only by moonlight. A large, canopied bed heaped with velvet pillows took up most of the room. Carved chests and a mirror in a silver frame stood in the corners.

"Are we safe here?" I whispered.

To my surprise, she started to laugh softly. "As safe as we can be in this castle, yes."

I was expecting tears, I admit it. Panic, fear, worry for her husband. Definitely not this quiet, scornful laughter.

"My lady," I whispered, "are you all right?"

The laughter stopped. "No," she said gravely, "I'm not. I haven't been all right for quite some time."

"We must call for help; your husband is in danger," I tried to reason with her. "Criscer and his companions ..." I hesitated, but I decided to say the truth. "They will kill him and run away with the gold."

"If only," I thought I heard, but it was just a gust of wind in the dark.

"If you tell me how to reach the guards, I can go alone," I tried once more.

"If you leave this room tonight, you will die," she said, and her voice was suddenly completely clear, completely cold.

I shut up immediately. I could tell the difference between a threat and a fact. I approached the bed and sat cautiously on the lush cover. She stood by the door for a bit longer, listening, and then she joined me.

"It's cold," she said, "it will snow soon. It's still early in the year, the winter will be long."

"Yes, my lady. The earth was frozen this morning, and the fields covered in frost."

"The fields …" she repeated dreamily. "You have been travelling, lucky you. What's new in the world?"

This change of subject surprised me, but I played along. As long as I was safe in a locked room, I was ready to humour her.

"We have peace," I said, "most of the time. Autumn fairs are over, the roads are empty. There was a great tournament in Myrit, the king and the queen had another child, a girl."

"A little princess," she said. "I remember a tournament in Myrit when a princess was born." She chuckled. "Oh, gods, that must have been a long time ago, who knows what happened to all those champions and their beautiful ladies? Dead, probably … Tell me, Ida, are the Leven nobles still so conceited? *We are the heart of the kingdom; without us the sun would not rise in the morning?*"

"I know nothing about the Leven nobles, my lady," I admitted. "I've never left my home before."

"Ah …" she said, "your first flight. When I first left my father's house, I thought a grand adventure awaited me. Do you feel you're in a grand adventure?" She gave up sitting and stretched herself on the covers.

"Adventure, my lady?"

"Well, you've joined a band of thieves and murderers, you must have expected an adventure." She snorted. "Or did you not know what they were? Lie beside me, it's cold." She moved a little to make room on the feathery cloud. "I used to have a friend who slept with me, a long time ago. It was nice, I liked to have someone I could whisper with in the darkness. I thought it would be the same after I got married, but men are different." She waited for my comment, but I had nothing to add. "Tell me all about yourself, please do. I don't care if you are a thief and murderer, I promise I won't tell anyone. Tell me your story. The night is long, and I am not sleepy."

*Which story do you want to hear?* I thought.

"I was born on the border between Larion and Elmar," I said, "my father had a small estate and an even smaller castle, little more than a border fort in the White Mountains. I grew up among the shepherds: they hid my mother and me when the Seragian troops came. My father remained at the fort with his men, and fought, and died."

"I'm sorry."

"It was a long time ago. When the war ended, my mother took over, but there was no money for repairs and barely any food. We scraped by somehow until she got ill and died. Then I decided I would not waste my life in such a bleak place. My mother had a sister in Leven, I wrote to her."

"So Criscer …"

"… is my cousin. When he appeared with his friends and said they would escort me … I realized soon enough they were swindlers, but I had no idea … I'm sorry …"

"Oh, you don't have to apologize," she said. "Your visit is the most exciting thing that has happened here in the last ten years. A dagger under my throat, I wondered for a moment what would happen if he cut … but no, impossible. Tell me, those boys, do they have any special skills, besides cheating and stealing?"

"Skills, my lady?"

"You must know some legends," she turned, and I felt her breath on my cheek. "The legend of Lela's bow, that young hunter, brave as a lion, fast as lightning, beautiful as a summer dawn? That's what I'm thinking of, something exceptional, something invincible."

"But, my lady," I said, confused, "that's just a story. And this is reality."

"Reality, reality, I've heard that somewhere already," she sighed. "But it's not true. There's nothing real here but you and me and these dresses we're wearing. This is a story and I walked into it, and you walked into it, and your friends as well … and if one of them is not a hero …"

"What then, my lady?" I asked.

"Then they'll be dead by morning. It always ends like that. And therefore, don't worry about the guards, alarm, robbery and escape. It only made the evening a bit more interesting. I am sure Selern and Volk are mightily amused," she added, and her voice was weird, flat. "They are hunters, and no prey has ever escaped them."

I thought she was mad. Or that she was shocked by the events. But she sounded so cool and composed. *Think, Ida!* There was something wrong with that castle, I had known it the moment I entered it, but I ignored the signs because I believed Criscer and because I was too busy pretending to be a lady to pay attention to what my road instinct was telling me.

"This is a cursed place, Ida. Nobody leaves it, neither the living nor the dead."

She did not deign to explain further.

*Ida,* I thought then, *you are a practical girl. You do not suffer from hallucinations or hear voices in your head. You must believe something strange is happening around you.*

193

And that scared me. I had no experience with such things. That world belonged to the gods and nobles; it was divided between the heavens and legends.

Gods had never been my friends. When I was little and my life was bad, I must have prayed to someone, believing a higher power might right the wrongs. But I soon learned prayers didn't work. Above me were only the masters and mistresses, knights, nobles, lords, and their task was creating injustice, not mending it. Gods had nothing to do with that.

Afterwards, on the road, I adopted some habits of the people I travelled with without much questioning. Actors would always pour a cup of wine for Dazbog before the show. Girls would make crowns of flowers and hang them on the branches so that Lada, the Goddess of Love, would grant them wishes. When the road was dangerous, when they lost their way in the dark or when they were threatened by avalanches or floods, travellers would ask Stribor, the god of winds and journeys, for protection. Those were the little rituals that, even if they didn't help, at least could not harm anyone.

Legends were an entirely different thing. I loved listening to them, I memorized them and performed them whenever I got the chance. Beautiful stories of the ancient heroes and princesses, stories about the gods who played with human destinies, about wars and great loves. Bigger than life and as far from me as the moon in the sky. Things like that did not happen to girls like me.

What did happen to girls like me was that they sometimes disappeared without a trace on the road. Not because they found a fantastic feast in a castle in the middle of the woods and joined it never to return, but mostly because someone killed them and hid the body well.

"My lady, what will happen to me?" I asked.

She was quiet for a long time. And then she said wistfully, "Selern and I have been alone up here for years. I have begged him for company, many times. Sometimes a woman or a girl would arrive here. *Let me have a companion*, I would say. And sometimes he did. But it always ended badly. Nobody lasts here but the two of us."

Winter on the road suddenly didn't seem so terrible in comparison with this place. "What happens to them?" I asked.

"I don't know," she said softly. "Sometimes there is a big feast, sometimes just a dinner or a gathering … but when Selern and Volk begin their nightly errand, I shut myself in here. In the morning, I'm too much of a coward to ask what happened. I'm sorry."

Insincerity infused her voice. She was not lying to me, not quite, but she was certainly omitting something. She knew what happened to the guests, she just chose not to tell me.

"My lady, if you help me get out of here, perhaps I can help you. I will find someone who—"

"You cannot help me," she cut me off, "and I cannot help you, do you understand? It's every man for himself here. Or woman," she added.

I clambered out of the featherbed and put my feet on the cold floor.

"Then pardon me, my lady, if I don't stay with you and whisper in the dark, waiting for someone to find us here. I'd rather try my luck alone. As far as I know, castles are difficult to enter, not so difficult to exit." I turned around, cursing the damned dress, heavy and long, not at all practical for running. "You told me I would die if I went out, but now it seems I will die anyway. I have no idea how. Your husband must be some kind of spider, killing every guest that wanders into his web."

"It's not his fault, it's the curse—"

"I don't care, my lady. I tried to save you when I thought you were in danger. And you know well what threatens me and you won't help me."

I thought she would say something to that, offer a way out. But she only said, "I'm sorry."

"Being sorry never helped anyone." Seething with anger, I pulled the latch, opened the door and stepped into the pitch-dark corridor.

# CHAPTER SIXTEEN

# ELISYA

## SUMMER 320 A.C.

Next morning, two saddled horses waited for us in the stable. The sky was clear; the sun had just come out, promising a warm day.

"You wanted to go riding, so let's go riding," my husband said. "Will that make you happy?"

"You want to go riding with me?" I gaped at him, not entirely sure why I was so surprised. After all, he had tried to be kind to me from the beginning, in his own strange way.

"Of course. I want you to be happy here. Let's go deeper in the forest," he suggested. "There's a river there, flowing over a bed of black stone …"

"I'd rather go in the opposite direction," I cut in impatiently.

He scrutinized me, narrowing his eyes. He could have refused me. But he did not.

"All right," he said, "I can show you the way to the road, if you promise me you won't go there alone."

"I promise," I said.

He didn't trust me completely. But the previous night, it had occurred to me I could make him love me, if only I was ready to forgo my own wishes and fulfil his. My stepmother and Silya had been acting like that their whole lives and it served them well.

We took the same path I had taken the previous two days, through the filthy village and onwards. While we were passing the dilapidated huts, the children watching us in silence, he said, almost as if he was apologizing, "My father neglects his possessions. But I have other plans, and a deal with your father. Soon we will start clearing the forest and harvesting timber. The king is building ships in Abia, and your father promised we can get an order from the royal shipyard. That would make us rich," he looked at me and smiled, showing his crooked teeth. "Have you ever seen the sea?"

"No," I said. I wondered if Father really had enough influence to secure a deal like that, but I said nothing. "What does Volk think of your plans?"

"Volk?"

"He is your father's steward, isn't he?"

"Volk is …" he paused. "Volk takes care of many things."

"Has he always been that weird?"

"Weird?" He was surprised. "I thought all priests were like that. I've known him all my life. He came here long before I was born. He's always had his way of doing things.

When my mother disappeared, and my father started drinking, he raised me as a son. He's always been good to me."

"But as your father's steward, he allowed it all to go to ruin," I insisted. "He keeps you in isolation."

He gave me a sharp look that made me question how much he really knew about the castle, the woods and all the strange things that happened there. Perhaps it was all normal to him, perhaps he didn't realize it was odd.

"Volk did the best he could, when there was no-one else to do it."

There was a long pause while I weighed my words, trying to decide whether I should keep silent. But no, he was my husband, for better or worse, and he should know.

"Volk threatened me," I said. "He grabbed me, he hurt me, he followed me in the forest and killed an animal as a warning to me."

My voice came out shrill and childish, and I could hardly believe myself. Selern shook his head. His hard expression reminded me of my father, although there was no physical likeness.

"I wish you'd stop being so stubborn and fanciful and obey me. I cannot protect you if you don't."

I bit my lip and said no more.

We rode in silence for a long time, and I carefully watched where he was leading me, looking for unexpected turns or secret trails. But there was just the one path I had already seen twice. I expected to spot the castle through the branches anytime soon. But instead …

"There, we've reached the road," Selern said. "It's time to go back, if we want to get to the castle before dark."

I didn't trust my eyes, but no matter how many times I blinked, the road was still there, visible through the trees: a wide trail of beaten earth and gravel. I let my horse go a little way towards it.

"Elisya," Selern said behind me, "come back, we must return."

I could have turned my horse and returned to the castle, I could have lived with the man I was forced to marry and waited for him to make his dreams of wealth come true. Or I could have escaped while the road was still in front of my eyes. I didn't dare look away; I was too afraid it would disappear.

I would never be able to find it alone, of that I was sure.

"Elisya," he repeated.

Instead of replying, I dug the spurs into my horse's side and let him fly so fast I almost fell.

"Elisya!" He rushed after me, and I spurred my horse even harder. The opening between the trees was getting closer, the road was right before me. A hundred steps or less.

Behind me, his horse screamed with a terrible, almost human sound. A moment later, Selern's shout was cut short by a crash that shook the forest. I had no time to make a conscious decision; I turned my head automatically, reining my horse. They lay on the path behind me, the horse on the rider. The animal's legs jerked in the air as it tried to get up. Selern was crushed under it, screaming in pain.

I didn't hesitate, I swear, although the road was a stone's throw away. I turned my horse and rushed back. In the meantime, Selern's horse managed to get up and hobble towards me. Selern fared much worse. He was sprawled on the ground, and his left leg was twisted as no leg should ever be.

"I'm here." I fell to my knees beside him, lifting his head and shoulders off the ground. His breathing was shallow and irregular, and his face was a grimace of pain. "We must get you back to the castle."

I realized how futile my words were. I wasn't able to bring him back. He had a broken leg; he couldn't ride. His horse was hurt and probably unfit to carry him. And I couldn't even lift him off the ground.

"If I leave you here and ride as fast as possible ..." I was thinking aloud. By the time I reached the castle, it would be dark, by the time we got back, midnight. Who knew what might happen to him?

"Don't ride back, ride forward," he managed to say.

I thought he was hallucinating; I paid no attention to his words. I folded my cloak and put it under his head. And then I went to catch my horse, who was grazing on the sparse grass beside the path.

"Haragov Dol might be nearer," I mused, thinking about riding there, searching for help. I looked towards the road.

But the road was not there.

Through the opening in the trees, just like the previous days, I could see the castle sitting in its green moat.

"How?" I turned to Selern, but he was unconscious.

I blinked, shut my eyes and tried again. But nothing changed. The castle was in front of me, as if there had never been a road there, as if I had not been riding towards it.

I could forget my plans of escape. I mounted my horse and hurried to get help.

# CHAPTER SEVENTEEN

## IDA

### AUTUMN 361 A.C.

I wandered through a net of narrow passages, each leading to a locked door. There was no light, so I felt my way around, tiptoeing carefully along the flagstones, mindful that my footsteps produced no echo. I explored one passage after another, to no avail. After the tenth or eleventh dead end, I realized I was moving through a labyrinth that stretched for miles through the depths of the castle.

*I've been walking for too long; perhaps I'm walking in circles.* It was easier to think the fault was mine, despite my senses telling me the opposite. I was tired, sleepy and thirsty. And more frightened with each step I took. The long hours passed with no exit in sight and no light. It began to dawn on me that I could be walking until I fainted from exhaustion, and then cold or thirst would kill me.

I turned into an alcove, leaned on the wall and closed my eyes. There was no point in walking blindly. I wasn't moving through a real space. Something was playing with me.

"Look, I stopped," I whispered. "What now?"

Silence. *If I ever manage to get out of here ...*

And then I heard a sound, distant and rhythmical. Someone was running towards me. I froze, thinking of the wolf-man and his grasping paws, of Gospodar Selern's cold, expressionless eyes. Stories about monsters I had heard in the long winter evenings flitted through my mind. I flattened myself against the cold stones, hoping the darkness would hide me.

And then a familiar voice called my name. "Ida, where are you?"

"Criscer?" I could hardly believe it. "Is that you?"

I stepped out of the alcove. He was carrying a lamp, and I saw it was really him, irritable and winded.

"Ida, you stupid girl," he snarled, "what came over you back there, attacking me and running away like that?"

"I'm sorry, I thought you were going to hurt the lady. You're not angry with me?"

"We'll deal with that later." He waved it off. "Come, we must run."

Gospa Elisya's words about her husband's lethal game still rang in my head. I was confused. "You are unharmed?"

"Unharmed? Of course I am. Everybody is alive and whole. What did you think, that we were killers?" he said, pulling my arm. "Come on, our saddlebags are full, horses are ready. Servants are asleep or tied and crammed into a locked room. The boys wanted to leave without you, but I disagreed."

"But the lady said—" I started as we ran down the corridor, but didn't continue. The lady herself admitted she was not well. Why did I trust her words? She had taken me to a room tucked away in the middle of the labyrinth and told me strange stories.

We ran straight ahead. "You know the way out of here?"

He turned his head, but didn't slow down. "The way out? This is just a corridor."

He was right. It was a corridor, straight and wide, with no branches. The labyrinth I had been wandering through for hours suddenly seemed like a waking nightmare.

"Hurry up, we must get out before the dawn. I don't want to be found here!", Criscer said.

And so we ran even faster. I glanced at the courtyard through the arches. The stars were still in the sky, but somewhere far towards the east, I could see the first pale light of dawn.

"Faster!"

We flew down the stairs, into the yard. I looked for Edon and Krasil and saddled horses, but I couldn't see them.

"Where …?" I asked.

"Behind you," he said.

I spun around. There was just one man standing in the shadow of the stairs. I recognized his enormous frame right away. Before him, on the stone flags, lay three bodies in a pool of blood. They were thrown one over the other like rag dolls, broken and limp. I recognized Criscer's handsome face, deathly pale and frozen.

"But—" Alarmed, I turned back to my companion. Instead of Criscer's warm brown eyes, I met the cold blue stare of Gospodar Selern. It pinned me down like a fox pins down a rabbit, and when I saw a movement, it was too late.

Without a sound, a thin dagger pierced the pretty dress Gospa Elisya gave me and sank into my belly.

"Lady of the Depths, I dedicate this death to you," he said.

I bent over with a sigh, wondering where the pain was. I tried to reach for the dagger, but he pulled it out just as fast and warm blood spilled over my fingers. My knees buckled and he took me in his arms. As if he were dancing the last dance with me, he led me to my companions and then pushed me over. I fell on the heap, staring at the sky above me.

"And that's four," said the lord. "Just in time."

"It's dawning," Volk said.

"Yes, I must go. You take care of this."

I heard Selern's footsteps leaving over the stones and climbing the wooden stairs. Volk coughed and spat. His huge figure loomed above us. Neither a blink nor a breath revealed I was still alive. He looked at us calmly and then spat once again.

"There's no hurry," he said, replying to the lord who couldn't hear him. "The day is long, and the job is better done when you're not tired."

And then he left as well.

I lay in the cold wind, looking at the sky changing colours from black to blue to the grey-white of snow clouds. I was waiting for death: I had a bleeding wound in my belly, I was out in the cold, and I did not have a single friend in that cursed castle.

I tried to call my companions, hoping they were still alive too. I whispered their names and shook them, but they made no sound. They were silent and still.

*Little Ida,* I thought, *you have always known you were one wrong step away from death. It was bound to happen sooner or later.*

I was waiting for the end, but the end was not coming. It was so cold that the blood on my dress froze. My hands were two slabs of ice. The cold threatened to kill me before the wound.

Also, I was bored.

The first snowflake fluttered from the sky and landed on my cheek whole, without melting. I moved my head, forced my frozen hands to push, and dug my heels into the ground. I didn't dare try to sit, too afraid it would make the wound bleed heavily. Instead, I wanted to turn over, get on my knees and try to get up. But my heel slipped, the bodies beneath me shifted and I rolled to the ground with a silent moan. I lay there shivering, trying to press the wound with my fists to stop the bleeding.

The silence was broken by the sound of quick footsteps. I had revealed I was alive, they were coming to finish me off, and I was too stiff and weak to get up.

"Oh, gods!" said a quiet female voice. "You're alive! It has never happened before." Little head with mousy hair tied back in a braid. Tiny hand moving my fist covering the wound.

"Tinka," I said. "Help me, please."

She looked at my belly and my face. Then she looked around the yard.

"They will kill me for this," she said. "Still, that's a better fate than living here. Come."

She helped me get on my feet and let me lean on her skinny shoulder. Slowly, step by step, we stumbled over a thin crust of ice. Through a fluttering curtain of snowflakes, a completely different scene emerged before my eyes: a decayed, shoddy forest fort, overgrown by moss and ivy, but I had no breath to waste on questions. I focused on the walking, one step after another.

"Here," she said, opening a door. "Nobody comes here but me."

It was a dark, damp larder full of broken things, cobwebs and mice. Tinka threw a few old sacks in a corner and laid me there.

"Water," I implored. I yearned for a fire to keep me warm, but I knew I couldn't get close to any fireplace and remain hidden from Volk.

"I'll bring you some food and water," she said. "And something to dress that wound. Wait for me."

I do not know if I fell asleep or unconscious, but her voice woke me sometime later.

"Let me see the wound. Help me lift that gown."

I let her undo the laces and lift my skirt and underskirts over my hips, revealing my belly. She washed the wound and dried it gently.

"It's not bleeding much," she said. "If it were anywhere but on your belly, I would say it was fine."

"Lift me so I can see it."

She helped me up. I have seen a few stab wounds in my life, but never on myself. *Do not faint.* Tinka was right: the blade was thin, and it didn't go in too deep. I had no way of knowing how much damage was done inside, but if it had cut something important, I would have been dead already. I was lucky.

"You will have to sew it," I said. "Can you do it?"

She cocked an eyebrow, tilting her gaze my way. Her eyes were much older than the rest of her face. "And why do you think I brought needle and thread?"

She pushed a piece of wood between my teeth and got to work. I bit the plank hard as the needle pierced my skin. Even worse than the jab was the feeling of the rough thread passing through the hole. I gave a muffled moan as tears streamed down my cheeks.

"Done," she said. "I'll cover it now."

"Thank you."

She shrugged. "I brought you some soup. It's still warm."

It was thick and hearty, and it helped me warm up, as did a shabby woollen cloak she wrapped me in.

"They do this to all travellers who come to the castle?" I asked.

"Yes."

"But … but … I saw Criscer alive. He was as real as you and me, his voice, his clothes, everything. How did they do that?"

Tinka gave me a wry smile. "Do you think they share it with me?" She wiped her nose with her grubby little hand. "If they can transform this cold, dirty place into a beautiful castle, I guess they can transform other things too."

"Has no-one resisted them yet? Given them a dose of their own medicine?"

"Big merchant caravans do not come here, and neither do the armed troops. Just some random travellers, lost in the woods, or naive fools sent by that bitch, the innkeeper in Haragov Dol. Volk pays her to keep her mouth shut when somebody asks about the people who vanished."

The innkeeper had appraised Criscer and his companions well, I thought. She knew no-one would come asking questions about them. I was just an accidental addition. My luck.

"What will happen to me?" I asked, although I could guess the answer.

"If you stay here till nightfall, they will kill you," she said. "His lordship usually does not appear during the day, and after a night like this, Volk likes to sleep till the late afternoon. Which means you still have a bit of time. But if you want to survive …"

"… I have to run away," I finished the thought. "But …" Something occurred to me as I was looking at her pale face. "If it were easy to run away, you would have done it a long time ago, wouldn't you?"

She nodded.

"Can I negotiate?" I asked. "The lady mentioned she wanted a companion. Or perhaps they need a servant; you probably have too much to do, and that ancient cook can't see what she's doing."

She shook her head. "All the servants have been here from the beginning. There's been nobody new since things changed. And that story about a companion—if you think the lady will protect you, you'd better think again."

"I must escape, then," I said. "At night. While it's snowing. With a wound in my belly. That's what I call laughing in the face of death. What else is against me? Come on, let's see what else I'm fighting against, while I'm in a good mood."

A faint smile appeared on her lips. "You're brave," she said. "That's good. I haven't seen many brave people here. Mostly they beg or bargain or think they can hide in the corridors of the castle. But the corridors have only one master when the night falls."

"You scare me," I said. "Don't do it. Tell me this: if I sneak out of the castle in the evening and go through the forest towards the road, what will happen to me?"

"If you take the path, it will bring you back to the castle. You'll think you're walking in the right direction; you'll turn back in fear, convinced you left the evil behind you. You'll walk for hours. And then, you'll see an opening through the trees and believe it leads to the road. You'll run, thinking you are free. And then you'll find yourself in front of this cursed castle."

She had tried that, I realized. She was telling me her story.

"And then?"

Instead of answering, she turned her back to me, took off the kerchief covering her neck and pulled her dress down, revealing the skin on her nape. Thick silver lines covered it, like a cobweb. I winced.

"They whipped you."

"Volk," she said, tying the kerchief back. "I was not able to put a shirt on for two weeks, or lie on my back for two months."

"Have you tried to run again?"

"Oh, yes. I decided I wouldn't take the path but cut across the forest."

"And? What happened?"

She withheld her answer for a while, weighing her words. And then she just said, "I wasn't brave enough. I went back."

It was the shortest and least helpful explanation I had ever heard. But something in her eyes told me pressure wouldn't help. I tried to go in another direction.

"Gospa Elisya mentioned some legends to me; she said this place was like walking into a story."

Tinka laughed, but her laughter was deep and mocking. "Oh, Gospa Elisya, with her head in the clouds, perhaps this is a story to her. She thinks she is a princess in a haunted castle and believes one day some prince will walk in and save her. Everything revolves around her; she is the only one important."

"I thought she was a prisoner here," I said, confused. "Like the rest of us."

"Oh yes, she is. But she is also the lord's wife. And if she wanted, she could make so many things better. Instead, she lies in her huge, rotting bed in her freezing room, waiting for someone to save her. She pretends she has nothing to do with us, or the guests, and tries her best to ignore her husband as well. A princess in a tower, that's her." Contempt seeped from her words like poison from a broken stem of deadly nightshade. "When she arrived here, she was so sad we all felt sorry for her. It was a mistake, though, for she has no pity in her heart for anyone but herself."

I took her small hand, trying to wrap my mind around the fact that Tinka wasn't a child. How long had she been trapped in that castle, and in the body of a little girl? I was too afraid to ask. Already overwhelmed by the ordinary things that were against me, I couldn't wonder about the extraordinary. So I squeezed her hand.

"Thank you," I said. "If I ever get the chance to return the favour—"

"Leave it," she smiled. "We girls have to stick together."

It was the first time I heard something like that. In the company I had kept, and in the houses I had worked in, no girl had ever thought we had to "stick together". They believed I was a dirty intruder, stealing food and men, and they wanted me gone.

"I have to get back to work, or they'll notice I'm not there," Tinka said. "Rest now. I'll come to get you before the dark and show you the way out."

I dreamt of a place I had never been to. A spacious corridor, wide as the largest hall, high as a three-floor building. Huge pillars that three men could barely encircle with their arms carried a ceiling as vast as the sky, in muffled tones of green and blue, and a rare glint of silver and gold. The marble floor gleamed like the surface of water; waves trapped in stone. The mosaics above my head glimmered in a diffuse light whose source I could not see. Even the air itself was thick and cold like water, and when I breathed out, I expected to see bubbles coming out of my mouth.

I was barefoot, and as I stepped on the icy marble, it felt like walking on water. My dress, a garment made of blue gauze I had never seen before, stuck to my body. I turned my head in awe; the place was magnificent, incomparably beautiful. Somewhere in the depths of my memory I thought I had heard of it, there had been a name, but I couldn't remember it.

It was empty and still, except for the rays of light playing on the ceiling. I wanted to call out, but when I cleared my throat, it echoed like an explosion. I turned around, the vast hall place around me stretching into eternity, with no beginning and no end, just the blue fog dissolving the shapes. I chose a random direction and started walking as softly as I could.

The noise of water lapping in the distance, rhythmical and muffled, rose somewhere behind my back. I turned around, but there was nothing to see in the foggy darkness. I continued walking, a little bit faster now. The noise grew louder, like the breaking of the waves. I risked another look over my shoulder: nothing. My legs were wiser than my head, and I started running, lifting my skirts. In that instant, I slipped on the marble floor, lost my balance and fell hard.

The noise behind me became louder, its rhythm faster. It wasn't the sound of waves anymore, but of wet and heavy footsteps. A gust of air reached me, bringing the smell of stagnant water, of wet plants and rot. My whole body ached from the fall, but I somehow got to my knees and turned around once again. Far away in the shadows, a dark shape shambled forward. It resembled a human being as much as a decomposed corpse in a lake resembles a person. I knew I was dreaming, but somehow I also knew I would die if it caught me.

A small white hand suddenly shot out of the shadow and pulled me up. It belonged to a woman, neither young nor old, with very fair hair and a dress of silver scales. A sweet scent of jasmine filled my nostrils, obliterating the rotten stench. Her face was rigid with fear, perfectly reflecting my feelings, but her eyes, grey and clear, were calm. She lifted her other hand, revealing a small scallop shell. She pressed it into my palm and closed my fingers around it.

"Tell him to call his father and he will come," she said. "And now, run like the wind, you foolish girl! This is my dream!"

# CHAPTER EIGHTEEN

## ELISYA

### SUMMER 320 A.C.

Volk and Karn brought Selern into the room while the old Gospodar Cervin stood in the corner and muttered to himself. Volk cut Selern's hose and revealed his leg. A wave of nausea washed over me, and I had to turn away from the sight of a white bone protruding from the torn flesh.

The little maid brought bandages, and Volk pushed a piece of wood between Selern's teeth.

"In case he wakes up," he said.

He tied his hands and his good leg to bedposts and showed me how to hold his head.

"Be ready now," he said. And went on to set the bone.

Never in my life had I heard such a horrid scream. Selern opened his eyes and started jerking violently. There was a sound of bone grinding on bone, and the reek of urine filled the air when his bladder gave out. Every muscle in his body trembled, but the ropes held fast. It lasted a few moments, but it felt like a lifetime.

"There," Volk said, as Selern lost consciousness again.

We washed him with a rag, bandaged the leg and changed the soiled sheets.

"Tell Freda to brew some willow bark tea, he'll need it when he wakes up," Volk ordered the maid.

"Why did he fall off his horse?" Gospodar Cervin suddenly asked from the corner. We had forgotten he was there, but he had been watching us in silence all the while. "Selern is a good rider. Why did he fall?"

"Because the forest path is full of potholes," I retorted. Volk put his heavy hand on my shoulder and gave me a little squeeze of warning.

"I will escort you to your room, my lord," he said. "You must be tired."

And so I was left alone with the man I had tried to run away from. Later that evening, the maid brought the tea and a bowl of broth for me, but nobody else came to see us. In the long, dark hours, I was unsure who to pity more: him or myself.

I must have fallen asleep because his voice woke me up before dawn.

"Water," he begged. I gave him some willow bark tea. "It hurts," he said.

"I know. The tea will help. I'm sorry," I added.

"You were running away from me," he said.

"No. I was running away from this place." He nodded, but he was too oblivious to understand the difference, so I added, "I will stay with you until you get well. I promise."

But my promise was empty, and we both knew it. When the morning sun appeared at the window, I took a look at his leg. The wound had stopped bleeding. What worried me was the skin around the wound, red and hot to the touch. He cried in pain as soon as I brushed it with my fingers.

Volk appeared around noon and joined me at his bedside. He took one look at the wound, and I saw he thought the same as I. We changed the bandages in silence. I had the servants bring me a pallet bed, changed my clothes, ate some food and prepared myself for a long wait.

By evening, the wound was inflamed, and Selern was burning up with fever. I was giving him willow bark tea, but I doubted it could blunt the pain that harried him. When the night came, Volk appeared again.

"He is worse," I said. "He is in constant pain. He slips in and out of consciousness. I'm afraid the wound will fester."

He nodded. When he removed the bandages, the smell was putrid.

"You must do something," I said. "I know nothing about healing."

He took a long, hard look at me, and I understood he knew all about my escape attempt.

"Do I look like a physician to you, my lady?"

"No, but perhaps you can send for someone. My father has a man …"

"Whoever we send for now, he will be too late."

I winced. He did not say it was all my fault, though he meant it.

"But you are a priest; you must help. I thought you cared about your young master," I added bitterly.

"I am Morana's priest, my lady. My goddess sees death as a gift."

A surge of anger flashed in my chest, but I recoiled at the thought of quarrelling by my husband's deathbed. I got up and went to the window, wishing I could release all the fury inside me, hit something, scream my lungs out.

"Stop pretending you are powerless, will you?" I said at last, not looking at him. "This whole castle and the forest around it, there's a divine hand at work here, only a fool could miss it. How is it possible that the forest *knows* who is passing through? How is it possible for the paths to turn according to your wishes?"

He watched me with a steady, dark gaze. "Every god wants something," he said slowly. "The question is whether we mortals are ready to give it."

"Do not speak to me in riddles!"

He remained silent until the last echo of my angry words vanished, until the only sound in the room was Selern's laboured breathing. And then he said, "The Goddess of Death will take a life as a sacrifice."

The picture appeared from nowhere, right in front of my eyes: Volk in the woods, his hands bloody. I didn't see what he had killed. *Whom* he had killed. But …

"Are you telling me someone has to die for Selern to live? Is that the meaning of your words?"

"I am telling you the Goddess of Death will sometimes receive a sacrifice and grant a wish. If you know how to ask," he added.

He smiled, and it was the ugliest sight in the world.

"Get away from me," I said. "You scare me."

He just shrugged. "As you wish, my lady. I'll come in the morning with clean bandages."

217

The agony lasted for three more days. The wound oozed blood and pus, and the whole leg up to the groin was hot and swollen. Red stripes spread like lash marks under the skin. Selern's fever was so strong that cold compresses couldn't bring it down, and he did not regain consciousness, for which I was grateful.

On the third night, his breathing became very fast and shallow. The previous day I had tried in vain to force him to swallow a few sips of tea; nothing passed his lips. He was completely lost to the world. I had no experience with dying men, but I was sure the end was near.

I called the little maid.

"Tell Gospodar Cervin his son is dying. Perhaps he wants to see him," I said, unable to hide the bitterness in my voice.

"Yes, my lady."

It took her a long time and when she returned, she was alone.

"His lordship doesn't want to come."

I could barely keep my eyes open; every bone in my body hurt from sleeping on the pallet. My stomach churned from the stench of pus and vinegar compresses. I had been left alone with Selern for three days and nights. Volk hadn't returned after our conversation, and Gospodar Cervin never once came to see his only son.

"Wait here," I told the girl.

I entered the lord's chambers without knocking. I found him sitting at his desk, drinking wine, with his eyes fixed on the flickering oil lamp.

"Your son is dying," I said without introduction. "Come and see him."

"My son is dying," he repeated slowly, still staring at the flame. "She says it just like that, like she had nothing to do with it. Tolmir's spoiled daughter. Oh, how he carried himself, like he was doing us a massive favour, when in fact he delivered damaged goods. A woman who does not know her place. A wife who runs away from her husband."

"You have no time for this," I said. "He's dying."

"Dying?" He lifted his eyes and looked at me. "No. Selern will get well. Volk promised me."

"Volk?" I didn't understand.

"It is fair that the one who caused the accident pays for it." He struggled to get up. "If you had any decency, you would do it yourself."

"What?"

He grabbed my wrist, and I suddenly understood what he was saying. His other hand reached for my throat. I pulled away with all my strength. He tripped and crashed to the floor, dragging me along. He was drunk, old and clumsy, but still stronger than me. We rolled on the floor, snarling like two curs. He grabbed a fistful of my hair and slammed my head against the floorboards. Black stars exploded in front of my eyes. I clawed at his face. My thumbs found his eyes and I dug in as hard as I could. He screamed and pulled out a handful of my hair. I jerked my knee into his crotch. He lost his grip, and I slid out from under him. I crawled to the desk and pulled myself up as his hand wrapped around my ankle. Wine spilled from the heavy silver chalice as I swung it at his head. He fell to the floor without a sound.

I collapsed beside him, struggling to catch my breath, when I felt someone's eyes on me. I grabbed the chalice, my only weapon, and sprang to my feet. Volk stepped silently from the shadows.

"He wanted to kill me," I said.

"Yes."

"Why didn't you help me?"

"Because you had to do it on your own."

I put the chalice back on the desk and motioned towards the unmoving body on the floor. "You told him the same thing you told me, didn't you? About the goddess, and one life sacrificed for another?"

"Yes."

"But I killed him by accident, it was no sacrifice," I said wearily. "I killed him in vain."

Volk made a deep, unfamiliar sound akin to a growl, and I realized he was laughing.

"He is not dead, my lady. But he will be, when we're done with him. If that's what you want."

His eyes met mine. An old drunk in exchange for a young man dying in agony? An old man who tried to kill me in exchange for a youth whose death I had caused?

I nodded in silence.

"No, my lady," he said. "You must say the words aloud."

"Do it, yes," I said. "Do what you must."

"Very well." He bent down and picked up the old lord's body. He threw it over one shoulder, as easily as if it were a rag doll. "Let's go."

I followed him through the dark corridors.

The moonlit garden smelled of roses. I could hear the wind whispering among the leaves and a rustle of wings of some solitary bird above us. Volk laid the old man on the wet ground at the edge of the pond. He dipped his hands in the black water and bowed down, his forehead almost touching the surface.

"O mistress of death and deep waters, the most just of all the gods, before whom we are all equal, you who accept us all in the end," he chanted. "O, Morana, you who give us our final rest, hear me now."

He paused, and I pricked up my ears. The water was completely calm, reflecting the moonlight like a mirror, and it seemed to me there was no answer. But Volk didn't wait for one.

"O goddess, your faithful servant begs for your gift, the gift of life and the gift of death. Receive the life of Gospodar Cervin as a sacrifice in exchange for the life of his son, Selern, who lies dying. Hear my prayer and take one life in return for the other."

And with those words, he grabbed the old man's body and submerged his head in the pond. The cold water awoke the lord, and he started to struggle. But Volk was much stronger. Involuntarily, I held my breath until I heard my heart beating in my ears. My whole body shook in horror and disgust as I clenched my fists so hard that my nails bit into my flesh. The old man twitched one last time. Volk waited until the old lord was motionless, and then he waited some more, just to be sure. Only then did he drag the body out.

I barely dared to look, for fear of seeing something terrible. But his face was just as swollen and pale as before. He didn't look dead, just drunk.

"Help me hang him," Volk said.

I didn't understand what he meant, but I followed him anyway to a silver birch tree. He took a length of rope from his pocket, slipped it under the old man's arms and tied it behind his back. I helped him hold the body upright. He threw the end of the rope over a sturdy bough, lifted him up, wrapped the remaining rope around the trunk and tied a knot.

"Is that all?" I asked suspiciously. "Nothing happ—"

The world flashed and then sank into darkness.

When I opened my eyes, I was lying on the ground. Beside me, Volk was kneeling, holding his head. My body was frozen and painful. I searched the sky above me for the moon and found it already sinking behind the roofs of the castle. I had been unconscious for quite some time.

"Selern," I said abruptly. "We must see what happened to him."

I got up and ran, too impatient to wait for Volk. I burst into the sick room like a whirlwind. The bed was empty.

"I am here." He stood by the open window, both his legs equally straight and strong. There was no trace of his injury.

"You are alive!"

"No," he said slowly. "Not entirely."

He reached towards me, and I took his hand. It was cold, colder than the night air, colder than the stones of the castle, as cold as the black water in the lake.

# CHAPTER NINETEEN

## IDA

### AUTUMN 361 A.C.

"I da, Ida, wake up!" Tinka gripped my shoulder, shaking me awake.

I opened my eyes.

"Call your father and he will come," I stammered.

"What? What are you talking about?"

"I was dreaming," I said, still out of breath, as if I had been running. Something hard and sharp nestled in my right hand. "But it was also real." I lifted my head slowly. A small white scallop lay in my palm. "A woman in a silver dress. She … do you know who she is? Pale, small, blonde? Sharp grey eyes?"

"I have no idea what you're talking about." She looked at me like I was mad. "Ida, it will be dark soon. You must go."

That brought me back. I slipped the scallop into my pocket. The castle, Criscer and his companions, my wound …

"My belly hurts," I said. "I don't know if I can walk."

"You must. They will find you here." She helped me get up. "Take the cloak. And this bundle; there's some food in it."

She opened the door and peeked into the corridor. I turned around quickly and grabbed a wooden stick for support. Feeling weak and dizzy, I followed her with a dull pain in my stomach, yearning for the warm glow of a fireplace.

"Let's go, now."

We stepped out into the deep shadows of the corridor. "But the exit is not in that direction," I whispered and stopped.

"You don't think you could just go through the main gates, do you?" she hissed. "Come on, if I wanted to betray you, I'd have done it already."

I followed her to a door she unlocked, down a flight of stairs, into a cellar: there were vegetables buried in sandboxes, game left to hang, cured meat, barrels of wine. I saw a small trapdoor in the corner. She lifted it and lowered the lamp just enough to show me a deep hole.

"It leads down to a tunnel under the moat."

The hole looked bottomless. There was a ladder on one side. I leaned on my stick, trying to breathe slowly and calmly.

"Come on," she said. "Start climbing down."

"I … I don't think I can. It's a grave." I looked into her eyes with dread, pleading silently. Any other way but this one.

But then we heard heavy footsteps outside. Without ceremony, Tinka pushed me into the hole. The stick fell out of my hand and into the pit. I barely managed to catch a rung when she slammed the trapdoor down. I was left in complete darkness.

And then I heard Volk's voice, the soft growl of a predator.

"What are you doing here, Tinka?" he asked.

"I came to get the carrots for supper, sir." Her voice was calm, barely audible.

My hands shook. Very, very quietly I started descending, away from that creature.

"That girl who came yesterday, she disappeared. Have you seen her?"

I didn't dare to breathe. My hands and feet searched for the rungs blindly.

"No, sir," Tinka said above my head.

"Then why are you standing on a trapdoor that leads out of the castle?"

I reached the bottom and felt around for my stick. No way out but through the tunnel.

"What trapdoor?"

There was a blow, a scream and another blow. Tinka wailed. I staggered forward as fast as I could. The tunnel was narrow and barely high enough for me to walk upright. It was supported by beams every five steps or so. Tinka's cries echoed behind me, but terrible as they were, they meant he was still too busy beating her to follow me. I was surrounded by the heavy, moist smell of earth, reminding me of fresh graves. Water dripped from the ceiling as I passed underneath the moat, but it became dry again as I continued farther on beneath the forest.

The tunnel looked nothing like the vast corridor I had seen in my dream, but the sound of the trapdoor opening warned me the monster was behind me once more. I tried to move faster, but I stumbled. I felt around me in the dark and found roots growing through the ceiling supported by rotten beams. The ground shook under Volk's heavy footsteps. I was too slow to run and too weak to fight. He would kill me with one blow, like an annoying mole, and drag my body back to that heap of dead men.

Overcome by panic, I dragged on the roots above my head and loose earth rained down. Was there a way to make the tunnel collapse? If I had to die, at least I could drag him down with me. With all the strength left in my shaking hands, I grabbed my stick and kicked at the crumbling supports. The rotten wood split and broke, and the earth poured down. But the steps were getting closer.

"Dig, girl!" he laughed. "There's no way out of here."

My courage betrayed me, and I fled like a rabbit just to get as far as I could from that voice. I hadn't damaged the tunnel enough; the beams were still standing. The heavy echo of his footsteps was again the only sound in the darkness. But then, suddenly, there was a loud crash and the whole ceiling behind me fell. I ran, ignoring the sharp pain in my belly. A cloud of dust caught up with me and pushed me down. I thought I was buried.

I didn't know how long it was, but when I lifted my head, everything was completely silent. The sickening sound of moving earth stopped, and the beams above me held. I crawled forward. I expected to hear him behind me or, even worse, feel his hand grabbing me. A muffled sob escaped my lips. Nothing happened.

I allowed myself a moment of rest. I turned over and touched my belly, praying the stitches were still in place. My fingers felt only the dry, crusted blood, nothing fresh and wet. Tinka had done a good job.

"I'm sorry, Tinka," I whispered, thinking of her cries. Then I moved on.

I spent an eternity dragging myself through the darkness, stumbling and pushing through, hoping the tunnel wasn't blocked. The roots grabbed my hair like dead men's fingers; the earth whispered I should lie down and close my eyes, that death would be painless like sleep. Cold made my movements slow and clumsy, until I barely moved at all.

My outstretched fingers hit something. Earth. The tunnel was blocked. But then I touched a wooden rung, and then another one: a ladder. I started to climb up. Rotten wood broke under my foot, and I slipped and remained hanging, my belly stretching painfully. I searched for support in panic and found the next rung. Up towards the light and the fresh air.

There was a wooden trapdoor above my head. I pushed it. Nothing happened. It was locked from outside. No, it couldn't be locked, this was an exit from the castle. It must be blocked because no one had used it for a long time. Leaves or snow, or worst of all, a fallen tree. Cold sweat broke on my forehead. There was no way back, no staying there. I had to find a way out.

My fingers searched for the edge of the door and the wooden frame around it. Barely keeping my balance, I pushed the end of my stick between them to make a lever. On the first attempt, it only slipped and almost sent me flying down into the pit. I tried again, and again, until it lodged itself in a tiny hole.

"Don't break," I whispered. "Please don't."

I nudged lightly and felt resistance, but then the door moved a fraction of an inch, just enough to push the whole tip through, and let in a gust of freezing air and a sliver of bright light. Snow. I rammed the stick harder, trying to make the door jolt and shake the snow off. Propping the door with my shoulders, I climbed, digging the tips of my boots into the earth, and pushed with all my strength, lifting it high enough for my head to come out.

The white brilliance of snow blinded me.. I grabbed the hard, frozen bushes and started dragging my body out of the hole, scrambling with my feet until I found some support. The trapdoor was heavy, and it mashed every part of my body as I pulled myself out, but I persisted, refusing to remain trapped under it. Then I yanked my stick and it fell down with a thump. The snow beneath me was bloody. My wound had opened.

Something warm and wet touched my hand—a tongue? I opened my eyes. A fox was sniffing the hand that rested on my belly, digging the snow with its nose and licking the blood.

"Get lost!" I growled and tried to slap its muzzle, but my hand refused to move. I was paralyzed. Or dead, and this was just my ghost watching. I blinked. No, I was not dead. The urgent need of the living pressed my bladder. How long had I been lying there?

"I'm frozen," I told the fox, who took a few cautionary steps back and watched me from a safe distance. "And I'm covered in snow, but I'm not dead. Sorry, no lunch today."

I focused on moving my feet, just a little at first, forcing my blood to flow and bring some warmth. I started to shiver, which was good. I was lucky. Were it not for the fox waking me up, I would have remained there forever.

"Thank you, fox," I said, clumsily getting up.

Snow was falling heavily from the grey sky. It was late afternoon or early evening. I looked around and saw nothing but trees: no castle, no path. There was no moon, no stars in the sky, nothing to help me find my way.

I hitched my skirts up and relieved myself in the snow, then checked my wound. The stitches were still there. Dragging myself out of the hole had not torn them, just made the wound bleed some more and then stop, frozen. There was no way for me to do anything about it: it would either hold or it would not; it was in the hands of gods. I picked up my stick and wrapped myself tightly in the cloak Tinka had given me.

"Take me to the road," I told the fox. "Show me the right direction."

The fox answered with a short bark and ran ahead of me.

The snow shimmered on the ground, perfectly new and white, settling on the branches and sticking to the rough trunks. It drove out the threatening darkness from the woods, the night pursuing the traveller. It fell thickly and covered my traces, reminding me I had to keep walking.

The fox was a red dot between the trees, a flame burning in the white bleakness. Much faster and nimbler than me, it could have disappeared at any moment. But it did not. It would run forward and stop, waiting for me to catch up, stumbling through the drifts. I followed it without a second thought. I didn't need Tinka's stories of her failed escape to know the forest was not a good place: it was alive and conscious, and it was watching me. It radiated with the malevolence only intelligent creatures could have. It scared me out of my wits. But the fox was not a part of it; it was just an animal. An animal who understood my words.

"Are we moving in the right direction, fox?" I asked. "Are you leading me towards the road or deeper into the forest?"

The fox barked again and lolled its tongue, grinning, reminding me of a skinny dog with a pointy muzzle. I could see a new fair attraction in my head: a girl and her clever fox, performing tricks together. I smiled for the first time that day.

It was impossible to measure time, but I progressed slowly and painfully. A hood covered my head, long sleeves hid my hands, but there was nothing I could do about my legs. I lost all feeling in my toes, then in my feet. Moving them inside the boots, which were large enough to cram two pairs of thick socks inside, didn't help me feel them again. I knew well what frostbite did; I had seen it on other travellers.

"Your paws are bare, fox," I whispered. "Don't you feel the cold?"

I was exhausted and hungry, and I had the means to solve just one of those problems. Tinka had given me a little bundle of walnuts and dried fruit which relieved the cramps in my stomach. Exhaustion and cold were more cunning enemies: they crept behind me, made me slip and stagger, and whispered reasonable advice in my ear. *You must rest for a bit or you will collapse,* they said. *Just for a little while, a moment or two, sit here and close your eyes.*

I shook my head and pinched my forearms under the cloak. It was too cold for sleeping. If the way to the road was really that long, the wretched forest needed no evil spell. Everyday, natural things were enough to kill me: the cold, the exhaustion, the snow.

"Is the road far away?" I asked the fox, almost expecting it to answer me. The wise animal paused, looked at me and barked.

"What are you trying to tell me?" I asked. But then I realized the fox wasn't looking at me. It was looking at something behind me.

Someone behind me.

"Idaaaa …" A croaking, distorted voice in the silent forest.

He surprised me for the second time in two days. Gair, damn his bones. I turned around quickly, my fatigue erased by fear. He stood behind me, leaning on a tree. There were no footsteps in the snow around him, like he had walked right out of the trunk. And his face was …

When I had left him in the forest, I had not bothered to look at him, unwilling to let his crushed snout haunt me in my dreams. But at that moment, in the darkness lit only by the snow's reflection, every line of his ugly face was perfectly sharp, from the crooked teeth and bristly cheeks to the eyes filled with malice. His temple was smashed, his shoulders and chest soaked in blood from his broken skull. When he opened his mouth, I saw what the stone had done to his teeth. I thought he was growling, cursing me, but then I realized he was laughing. He poked at his belly with the tip of his finger; my wound amused him.

I had nothing to say. There was no apology or regret inside me, just burning rage. I made two steps towards that bastard and swung my stick as hard as I could. It connected with his skull with a blow that shook my bones. And still, the whoreson laughed.

One step back, and then another. His laughter turned into snarling and our eyes met.

We moved at the same time. I lifted my skirts and ran as fast as my legs could carry me. But he was unencumbered by skirts or cloak. When his icy hand grabbed me, I screamed at the top of my lungs.

And Gair was laughing and cawing like a crow.

"Let me go, damn you!" I shouted, fighting with all my strength. He wrapped his cold fingers around my neck, blocking my windpipe.

*Think, Ida. The dead that walk.*

I had heard the stories, yes, mostly around the kitchen fires, with winter winds howling outside. There was always someone with a scary story. About a soldier who rode all night to warn his companions that Seragian troops were arriving, and his companions discovering in the morning he had been killed in an ambush the previous day. About a pregnant girl killed by her lover who wanted to marry another, appearing on his wedding day with a baby in her arms. And there were also the gods playing with the mortals, raising them from the dead when it suited them, for justice or vengeance or a cruel joke.

But this was not a question of justice, for which god could have been on Gair's side? The bastard had tried to kill me, and failed only because I was faster. No fair judge could say his fate was undeserved. No, it was some kind of dark divination, the same one I felt at the castle.

*Perun, by your godly blood, what is this abomination, festering under your sky?*

I thrashed desperately, but his cold, dead weight held me down like a millstone, and the fingers around my neck kept squeezing. There was no air in my lungs to scream. The world before my eyes sank into darkness.

And then I heard a voice. A live, human voice, the neighing of a horse, the sound of hooves in the snow. The weight was lifted off me and the sweet, freezing air filled my lungs.

"Get away from her," someone shouted. And then a short, sharp gasp of terror when he saw Gair's face. "Oh, gods, what …?"

Gair threw himself at the man. I could only see he was young and frightened. He had a sword, but he had no time to pull it out of the scabbard before Gair dragged him to the ground, where they fought like wild animals in the snow. I tried to get up, but my legs failed me. I touched my belly: instead of cold, crusted blood, I felt sticky warmth. I sobbed in anguish.

My saviour managed to get his dagger out and stab Gair in the shoulder, but Gair caught the hilt, pulled it out and threw the bloody blade into the snow. I crawled towards it as Gair scrambled on top of the man and started choking him. He opened his broken jaw and moved towards the man's face, snarling like a rabid dog.

My fingers found the hilt in the snow. Gair stuck the remains of his teeth into the man's cheek, bending his skinny back in a sharp arch. I grabbed his matted hair and pulled his head back. The dagger in my hand was sharp; it cut through skin, muscle, tendons and vessels spurting blood, grating only when it met the bone.

"Stop it, stop it," the young man shouted. "He's dead, you don't need to cut his head off."

A pair of arms hugged me, warm and alive. I let the blade fall out of my hands.

"It's all right," he whispered. "I'll take you back to the castle, to safety."

"No," I moaned. "Please, no."

"It's over." He held me close. "Let me help you."

I wanted to push him away and flee but the last remains of strength left my body and I fainted.

# CHAPTER TWENTY

## ELISYA

### AUTUMN 361 A.C.

"The girl has escaped," Selern told me in the evening. I stood in front of the fireplace, knowing that it was his least favourite spot in the room, but he joined me there, nevertheless.

"Oh?" I said. Escape was a word he liked to use, although no-one had ever escaped the castle, not really. I saw in his face that he had a story to share, so I asked, "How?"

"Through the old tunnel under the moat. Volk followed her, but she managed to make it collapse on his head." He chuckled. "It took Karn the better half of the afternoon to dig him out."

I found nothing funny in that image. I wished they were all dead: dead and buried and gone forever from my life.

"Will you go hunting?" I asked.

"I thought we'd have to, but it seems there's no need. She'll come back to us soon enough. With some very interesting guests." He touched my wrist with his icy fingers, and I shivered. "Wear your blue dress tonight. The one I like the most."

When he left, I thought about the girl with a sharp pang of regret. Ida—that was her name. Black hair and dark eyes, thin lips curved in a lopsided smile. Not beautiful, but fetching in some sharp, scrawny way. I committed her face to memory; it was all I could do.

Tinka came in to help me dress, scowling, a livid bruise covering her cheek making her look even more pathetic than usual.

"The blue one," I said.

As she laced me up, I heard shouts coming from the yard, the sound of hoofbeats, someone calling for help.

"We have guests," I said. Her eyes met mine in the mirror. "Selern said Ida would return. Go out and check what's happening."

For the briefest of moments, there was an expression of such violent hatred on her scruffy little face that I thought she would sink her teeth into my neck, but then she nodded and turned away. I pinched my cheeks and bit my lips, but I still looked like a frozen corpse, lifeless and pale.

"My lady!" Volk called from the corridor. "Ida is hurt."

Another show for guests, then. I opened the door and there he was, none the worse for having been buried, carrying Ida's limp, bloody body in his arms. I could not understand why he bothered to bring her to me, but I had learnt not to ask questions.

"Put her on my bed," I said.

"A brave young man saved your companion in the forest. Alas, I don't think she will pull through."

Behind him stood my husband and another man, tall, blond and frightened. A lost lamb rather than a hero. I sighed.

"You'll be needed later, my lady," Volk said.

"I wish to stay—"

"Later." He walked out, his footsteps disappearing down the corridor.

I turned to look at the girl on my bed. If it were not for the slight movement of her chest, I would have thought her dead. She was still wearing my lovely red gown, all bloody and torn now.

"I told you I couldn't help you," I whispered. "It would be best for you if you just died."

She did not hear me, prostrate on my bed, oozing melted snow and blood, barely breathing. All that courage and resolve, and for what? To end up in the garden with the others, a sacrifice to a voracious monster.

It occurred to me that there might be a way to help her. I took a pillow.

"If I don't say the words, I think you will be free," I whispered. "You won't belong to her." My hands shook as I gently pressed the pillow to her face.

"What are you doing?"

Tinka's voice startled me, and I quickly pushed the pillow under Ida's head.

"I'm just trying to make the poor girl more comfortable," I snapped.

"Leave that to me, my lady. I'll get her out of these dirty clothes and wash her."

I was a useless coward, nothing more.

# CHAPTER TWENTY-ONE

## TELANI

### AUTUMN 361 A.C.

An old hound emerged from the shadow, looked at us with his rheumy eyes, sat on his skinny rump and greeted us with a long howl.

"Don't move," said a voice from the darkness. "I have crossbows aimed at you."

The dog stopped howling, and we lifted our heads, looking for the speaker.

"What kind of welcome is this?" I said. "Aren't you familiar with the rules of hospitality? We come in peace."

"No," the voice interrupted me, "you don't."

I saw a flash of light on the metal and a dark silhouette under an arch. A tall, bearded man stepped out from the shadows on the first floor. He was indeed holding a crossbow, aimed at my chest.

"There's another one, on the other side of the yard," he said. "So don't try anything if you don't want to be shot without warning. And you will be shot, trust me."

I did trust him. He was holding the weapon like a man who knew how to use it.

"But why?" I asked. "We are just travellers."

"Dismount, please," he continued, paying no attention to my words. "The stable boy will take care of your horses. And then lay your weapons on the ground, slowly and without sudden moves, and take two steps back."

"Do as he says," said my lord.

We obeyed him. I surrendered all my visible blades.

"You have a knife in your right boot; take it out, please. And the dagger from the pocket on the back of your jerkin."

I stared at him, trying to recognize his face under the beard. Had we met before? I took out the hidden weapons and threw them on the heap. I felt naked.

"I hope that's all," the man said. "If I see you with so much as a penknife, I'll shoot you immediately."

"That's all," I said. My lord shrugged in silence.

"Right," said the man. "Tinka, take these weapons to my chambers, I'll have a look at them later. There are too many fine pieces here for two brigands like yourselves."

A little girl in a shabby dress stepped out from behind the stairs and gathered our blades without a word.

I thought then it was all a simple misunderstanding.

"We're no brigands," I said. "I don't know where you got the idea."

"I'll also ask you to shut up," the man said, descending into the yard. Gods, he was huge, as tall as my lord and twice as wide, like a brown bear from the woods of Virion.

And just as hairy. "There's no point in barking now, there's a trial awaiting you."

"Whose castle is this?" my lord addressed him for the first time.

"It belongs to Gospodar Selern, the Vlastelin of Tamny Dol." I had never heard of him. "Come on, start climbing."

We went up to the first floor with the crossbow aimed at our backs. When we reached the top of the stairs, a hunched old guard appeared, holding another weapon. I quickly calculated the possible moves and the probability of staying alive. The odds were not too low. My lord touched my arm in the dark. A tiny motion of his head towards the guard. I nodded.

"Now," he said, and threw himself backwards at the bear man, elbow smashing into his face.

The giant's crossbow bolt whizzed past my ear as I jumped at the old guard and threw him to the floor. He was little more than a bag of stinking bones. I wrenched the crossbow out of his hands and shot the bolt at point-blank into his head.

I threw the now useless weapon aside and yanked a short sword from his belt. I rolled to the writhing knot of bodies a few paces away. My lord had pinned his opponent down, but the monster thrashed beneath him, growling like a rabid dog. I could not see well enough to strike, so I stabbed him under the ribs. It should have been enough to kill him, but it wasn't. He jerked violently, pushing my lord off him. I clung to the hilt desperately. Had I pushed deeper, I would have lost the sword. Instead, I pulled the blade out and staggered backwards.

My lord jumped to his feet, and before the man could rise, kicked him viciously in the face with his boot. When he fell, my lord stamped on his neck, crushing his windpipe. He crouched, pulled the giant's dagger out of its scabbard and slit his throat.

We both looked around, breathing heavily, the blood black on our faces and hands. The corridor was silent and dark.

"We need to get our horses," I whispered, trying to see the staircase that led into the yard. The corridor somehow seemed longer than before.

"Not without Raden." My lord rose with the dagger in his hand. "Come."

There was a soft scratching noise behind him. I peered through the darkness. The man I had shot in the head lifted his hand and clawed at the bow sticking out of his eye. Terror gripped my chest, and a gasp escaped my lips as my lord grabbed my shoulder and shook me.

"Move!"

But I couldn't. I stood frozen, watching the two people we'd just killed come back to life. "What's this cursed place?" I whispered.

"Haven't you seen that giant's garb?" my lord spat. "He's a priest. *Her* priest."

He didn't say the name; he didn't have to. Everything clicked into place, crystal clear: the dark forest, the weird castle, the murderous welcome. Morana.

This was not a random trap; this was a ruse to catch my lord. This was a decades old divine grudge.

"You have to *run*," I hissed. "You *have* to run."

"Too late," he said. "Let's find the boy."

We rushed through the corridors. But they were all wrong: long and winding and leading nowhere. The doors were all locked, the arrow slits so narrow they let in slivers of pale moonlight that bathed the floor in a ghostly light. When I peered out, all I could see was the forest. The castle was a labyrinth.

"It can't be this big," I whispered.

"It's not." My lord stopped and shook his head. "It's not. All this is wrong, this castle is a collapsed heap of stones and a very strong illusion. I can just about discern it, if I don't focus too hard."

I had learned to trust such talk from him. His blood, his mother's gift for divination, his brush with death—gods knew where it came from, but it was always true. I squinted. "I can't see anything."

"Come." There was another locked door in the wall behind him. "Close your eyes and touch it."

I did as he said, expecting to feel the smooth, warm wood. Instead, my fingers found wet, rough-hewn stone. I gasped and opened my eyes. The door was still there. I forced my trembling hand to brush its surface once more: it was wood.

"Your fingers reveal the truth when your eyes don't tell you what to expect."

"But we can't walk around with our eyes closed."

"No. I'll keep mine open; I see some of it. And you'll close yours and guide me. Take my hand."

And so we proceeded, shuffling in the dark like two blind beggars. My skin prickled, every hair on my neck rose when the cold draft touched it. I tried to ignore the soft sound behind us: something wet and heavy following us, still far away but coming closer. A sickly sweet scent of decay filled my nostrils. My instincts screamed at me to run like a wild beast, and it took every morsel of self-discipline to steady my terrified heart and keep on walking.

We found one real door and opened it. I saw a magnificent chamber, but my lord said, "It's just an empty bedroom filled with cobwebs."

We carried on, ignoring the steady sound of pursuit behind us. Another door materialized under my hand.

"There's light inside," my lord whispered. Gentler than a summer breeze, he pushed the door open and peered inside. "Let's go."

We walked into a large room filled with hunting trophies, lit by the fire from the fireplace and several candles placed on the long table. A hunched figure sat at the table nursing a cup.

"Raden," my lord said.

The boy looked up. He was still dressed in his travel clothes, the worse for wear. Covered in blood, but with no injuries save a bite mark on his cheek. Recognition sparked in his eyes, and he cried out and jumped to his feet so quickly he overturned his chair.

"Get away from me!"

My lord paused. "Raden," he repeated, "we must leave."

"No," the pup said. "Stay away. I know you're here to kill me."

"What?" I cut in. "All we're trying to do is save you, you fool."

Raden lifted his head, looking rather sick, and shot my lord a raw look. "You know it's true," he said softly. "The king wants me dead."

His words were followed by a deafening silence. Mounted deer gazed down on us through empty sockets. The castle held its breath.

"Yes," my lord said at last. "He does. But I swear I will not harm you. Come, this is a foul place."

But the boy shook his head. His hands trembled, and he hid them behind his back. "You barge in covered in blood like a butcher and expect me to trust you? I know who you are. I know *what* you are. You're a murderer and I don't believe you'd spare me." He looked behind us, towards the door. "Gospodar Selern gave me sanctuary." And then he took a deep breath and screamed, "Help! They're here!"

Footsteps drummed in the corridor and the door burst open. I threw myself to the floor before I heard the click of the crossbow. The bolt flew over my head and lodged between a pair of antlers on the wall.

My lord grabbed the boy by the scruff of his neck, I seized his arm, and we ran, dragging him towards the other side of the room—suddenly as long as the longest hall in the royal palace in Myrit. I risked a glance over my shoulder. The huge priest stood at the door, whole and unscathed, and inserted another bolt in the crossbow.

"Let me go," Raden cried.

"The door," said my lord.

There was indeed a hidden door, a faint line in the dark panelling. Just as we ran towards it, it opened, and a man stepped in. He was slim, unremarkable, finely dressed, and he held a sword. "Stop," he said.

We stopped short before his blade. I looked around for an exit, but the castle was playing its tricks on me again. The room was so vast now that the walls disappeared in the darkness. The glass eyes of the stuffed animals glittered like cold, dead stars.

"It's them," the boy said, tearing himself out of our grasp. "They've come to kill me."

The old servant appeared behind us, holding another crossbow. This time, he and the giant were clever enough to aim at us from a safe distance. We were outnumbered, and we had nowhere to run.

They tied our hands behind our backs and forced us to sit at the long table.

"Volk, Karn, thank you," the slim man said to the giant and the servant, who retreated behind us, their crossbows cocked. He sat down across from us and motioned to Raden to sit next to him.

I studied our host's face. It was so pale the blue veins showed through, and rather plain, framed by light brown hair that fell in straight, untidy strands. His red and brown brocade was expensive, but this close up, I noticed threadbare elbows and cuffs and the strange, old-fashioned cut.

He greeted us with a slight nod, without blinking.

"I am Gospodar Selern, the lord of this castle." He shot an intense look at my lord, expecting him to introduce himself next. The silence dragged for a few long moments. "Perhaps you could be so kind to say who you are," he continued. His face showed no emotions, but there was an edge to his words.

"I don't see the point," my lord said, and turned to Raden. "I'd never harm you."

"Why should I believe you?" The boy's voice trembled. "You have never refused to carry out the king's orders, you have never endangered the welfare of the kingdom."

"Not this time, not with you." My lord's words came out uneasy, as if it took a great effort to say them. "I'd have hidden you in Abia."

Raden's face, marred by scabby toothmarks, remained confused and frightened.

Gospodar Selern cut in with a smirk. "This young man is a hero." He put his hand on Raden's shoulder, eliciting a shiver. "He saved my wife's companion, who was attacked in the forest. The girl is seriously hurt, but without his help, she would have been dead. Therefore, when he told me he was chased by two murderers, I offered him sanctuary."

I threw a quick glance at the boy, who stared at the floor, flustered.

Gospodar Selern continued, "This brave young man accuses you of following him through the woods and sneaking into my castle with the intention of killing him."

"This is ridiculous," I said. "We lost our way in the forest and stumbled upon your castle looking for shelter. As for Raden, all we've ever done on our journey was try to keep his miserable head on his shoulders. I have no idea what he bases his mad accusations on."

I looked at my lord, hoping for an explanation, but it was Raden who spoke next.

"I'm Amris's heir, too, and the king knows it." The boy's voice was barely audible.

The hall around me turned insubstantial all of a sudden, a flimsy stage set for the millstones of gods' schemes, grinding our lives once more. "Heir? Flesh and blood?" Confused thoughts rushed through my head. Gospa Lenka's tearful words, the morning in her stable when the boy joined us ... "My lord, surely he can't be—"

"Mine?" He shot me the palest of smiles. "Goodness, no. He's my father's. The last bastard he sired."

I looked into the cold, calculating eyes of Gospodar Selern as the whole image in my head suddenly became sharp. Amron V had several natural children with baseborn women who were no threat to the throne. But a tall, blond son of a rich Leven noblewoman, with the proper education and a talent for divination? It was a long shot, but there were always people mad enough and ambitious enough to use such a pawn. The king had every right to be worried.

However, our host did not look like someone who would be interested—or willing to participate—in dynastic struggles. This was not politics, this was malevolence. Both my lord and Raden sat there hurt and angry, paralyzed by the inability to understand each other's behaviour, while he gloated.

Gospodar Selern played us all for his amusement, feeding on our quarrels.

"This is not about the king and his orders," my lord said softly. "For someone gifted with second sight, you are surprisingly blind. Can't you see this place for what it really is?"

The boy lifted his head and looked around like he had just woken up from a dream.

"Enough," said Gospodar Selern. "I don't need to hear more lies. There was an order for assassination and the plan that Raden—a young man of royal blood—should be followed and killed on my land."

Despite the dread crawling up my spine, I struggled to understand that he was serious. He thought he had jurisdiction, the right to judge a prince of the blood, when in reality he didn't even have the right to address my lord without his permission ... and yet ...

We had no men, no weapons, no way of letting anyone know where we were.

"Considering all that," he continued, "along with the fact that the two of you are determined to cause as much harm as possible, even when unarmed, I have no other option but to take on the heavy burden and decree ..."

"I want a trial by combat," my lord said.

"What?" Our host's features twisted in surprise, showing emotion for the first time that night.

"I want a trial by combat," my lord repeated. "If someone must decide my fate, let it be the gods."

"I don't ..." Gospodar Selern stammered, but he was interrupted by a growl from the corner.

"It's done," the huge priest said behind our backs. "We can break all the laws of the kingdom and nothing will happen. But we cannot deny the gods their right to judge."

He moved towards the table, and his huge shadow swallowed the light in the room. Gospodar Selern's importance disappeared, his ridiculous interrogation and his puny authority vanished into thin air. There was a presence in the room at that moment, and it was as vast and undeniable as the night outside.

"The Goddess will decide. At dawn." The priest nodded towards my lord. "As the accused, you have the right to choose the weapon and name your champion."

"I will fight," he said. "And I choose the sword."

The big man nodded and turned. "Raden?"

Raden stared at Volk, helpless. "I don't have a champion."

"You will have to do it yourself, then." I thought I heard a trace of amusement in his voice.

"But he'll kill me in two strikes ..."

"Do you doubt the judgement of the Goddess?"

"The gods are not just," said Raden softly.

And my lord laughed so hard his laughter reverberated off the ceiling.

They shut us in a room in one of the towers and the little maid brought us rye bread, cold meat and strong wine. Laying them on the table, she turned to my lord and said very quietly, so that the old guard standing outside couldn't hear her, "Your Highness, I knew it was you right away. You resemble your royal father so much."

My lord was taken aback, but he had enough presence of mind to nod and smile. She looked no older than twelve. His father had been dead for almost twenty years.

"My lady will want to see you when I tell her who you are," she whispered. "And when she comes, request to speak to Ida."

"Ida?"

"The girl from the forest. She can help you."

When she left, we washed the blood off our hands and threw ourselves at the food like two starving strays. My belly filled, I examined the room. The floor was made of stone, the walls curved and bare, with no secret doors or passages. A good fire blazed in the fireplace, but the icy wind blew in through the arrow slit, making us shiver. I looked down on the endless treetops and the frozen sky above them.

"It dawns late at this time of year," I said. "There's plenty of time until the sunrise; you should rest."

"Later," he replied. There were no quills or ink in the room, but he produced a few sheets of paper and a stick of charcoal from some pocket and sat down to write.

I lay on the floor with my cloak under my head and closed my eyes, listening to the sound of the charcoal scratching the paper. But my exhausted mind refused to sleep, trying to arrange the events of the day into some rational order instead.

"The boy got us into deep trouble," I mused. "No wonder the king wants him dead."

"But I don't," he said. "I don't agree with the king's decision. I see why he thinks the boy is dangerous, but there is a big difference between a potential heir and the real pretender to the throne. No." He shook his head. "The king doesn't think the boy can do it, not really."

"But what does he think, then?"

"I can only guess," he shrugged, still writing furiously. He had a knack for talking and writing at the same time. "I'd say that he counted on me disobeying him. He knows me well enough."

"And what then?" I asked, disbelieving. "There's nothing he can do to force you …"

"It's not that simple," he waved my words off. "I'd keep the boy in Abia, but I would fall out of his favour, and he could accuse me of plotting against him. I'd be banned from Myrit for a time. Which means that he does not want me there anymore." He managed a brief, pained smile. "He only had to ask; I would have gladly removed myself."

"Rather ungrateful of him."

"Gratitude is not a virtue of kings." This was the third one he had served; he knew what he was talking about. "But none of that matters," he added tiredly, rubbing his hands to warm them. "We're in another kind of trouble now."

"Why? I don't see the duel going in any direction you don't want it to go. If you want him to surrender and withdraw his accusations, you'll make him surrender and withdraw his accusations. The boy can barely tell which side of the sword he has to hold in his hand."

"Oh, but do you think *she* will judge fairly?"

My heart sank. "No. Of course not. Damn the boy. It's all his fault." The words escaped my mouth, and I did nothing to stop them. It was easier to be angry than afraid. "How could he be so stupid, so blind?"

"Because he is terrified and inexperienced. Because he honestly believes we are out to get him, so every ally who can stop us is welcome. Don't hold it against him. He is her tool, nothing more."

"They all serve her," I said. Neither of us wanted to mention the Goddess' name.

"Yes. This is bigger than us, Telani. I would be tempted to use that unfortunate expression, *the divine plan*, if I weren't so confident the gods do not make plans. Instead, they conspire, waylay and plot revenge. They are particularly fond of revenge," he added thoughtfully. "It is not beneath them, not even when it's against mere mortals. And I, of all mortals, have insulted her the most. I pulled myself out of her claws once. I will not be given the opportunity to do it for the second time. Even the gods learn from their mistakes."

Cold comprehension trickled down my spine.

"Let me be your champion tomorrow," I said. "It will spoil their plans."

"No," he shook his head. "The cards have been dealt. Your role is to be the messenger."

I watched in dismay as he folded the two letters he was writing. The first one he tied with a piece of blue ribbon he pulled from his pocket.

"In the unlikely event that something goes terribly wrong," he said brightly, "this is for my wife." Then he gave me the other letter. "This one is for you. Instructions and such. You have to promise me something."

"Whatever you want, my lord."

"If something happens to me, Raden must come away unscathed. He is important. Protect him. Do whatever it takes to get him out of here."

"But, my lord—"

"Telani, I won't argue with you," he said mildly. "It's not yours to decide on his life and death."

"Yes, my lord." I bowed my head. "I promise."

"Thank you." He went to the table and poured two cups of wine. "To the king's health."

"To the king's health," I replied and took a sip. I should have choked, with so many black thoughts running through my mind. "What now?"

"What now?" My lord smiled and sat beside the fire. "Pull the other chair over here, please. We are expecting a visitor."

"A visitor?" I was surprised.

"Oh, Telani, you always underestimate women. It will be the death of you."

# CHAPTER TWENTY-TWO

## ELISYA

### AUTUMN 361 A.C.

Useless coward, nothing more.

Tinka walked into my room carrying a sword, and for an instant I thought she would unsheathe it and run it through my black heart. Instead, she offered it to me, belt, scabbard and all.

"What am I supposed to do with that?" I asked.

Tinka's eyes flashed with derision. She was half a head shorter than me, but her gaze slapped me as if I were a stupid, wicked child.

"We have two guests in the north tower," she said. "This sword belongs to one of them."

"So?" I took it from her. I didn't know much about swords, but this one looked as ordinary as they come, and well-used. The scabbard's leather was faded, the metalwork chipped and tarnished. Years of lying snugly in someone's hand had polished the grip to dark smoothness. No precious metals or jewels adorned the pommel or the guard. But when I unsheathed it slowly, the steel sang, perfectly sharp and deadly. Blue ripples ran across the blade as it caught the light.

"He is a prince of Amris's blood."

A cold shiver ran through my body, freezing me in place, rendering me unable to utter a single word. With the sword in my right hand and the scabbard in my left, I must have looked like some ancient statue of vengeance.

"Use it to do some good, for once," the insolent girl said and walked out even though I hadn't dismissed her.

Bitter tears welled in my eyes and ran down my frozen cheeks as I stood there, torn between despair and faith. All those terrible, lonely nights I'd shivered in my freezing room, praying for help, for the smallest sign that I hadn't been cursed for eternity. The thin gold ring glittered on my little finger, reminding me of the promise made so long ago. With trembling hands, I slid the sword back into the scabbard and ran out of my room.

The door to the north tower was unguarded and latched from the outside … I stood before it in the darkness, squeezing the scabbard so tightly my fingers turned white, heartbeat drumming in my ears. I heard the prince's voice, a clear baritone muffled by the thick oak door. Another man answered in a heavy southern drawl.

*I must do it. It's the only chance I'll get.*

I touched the queen's ring for courage. She had known, may gods have mercy on her; she had been right, all those years ago. Hope, long buried under the bleak layers of sorrow, blossomed in my heart. But I was guilty, and weak.

My fingers touched the rough wood, lifted the latch and rapped gently. Before I lost the little courage I had mustered, I slipped into the dimly lit chamber. He was sitting in a chair by the fire.

I expected someone glamorous, a fairy tale knight, young and vibrant. Someone dazzling, an obvious hero. Instead, the man who stood up to greet me looked closer to forty than thirty, his face grey with fatigue, his eyes framed by dark shadows.

"My lady."

He smiled and it lit up his features, dispelling the gloom. For a heartbeat, I was sure we had met before. Then I realized he looked familiar because he had his mother's clear, keen gaze, and his father's sharp nose and high cheekbones. Not stunning, but handsome enough, with an air of calm self-possession.

*You two will meet*, the queen had promised.

"Your Highness, you must come with me right away." My trembling legs refused to carry me, and I fell to my knees, offering him his sword. "My name is Elisya and I'm the lady of this unhappy place. Please take your weapon and come with me."

He lifted one eyebrow, but there was no surprise on his face, just a hint of reluctance. For the briefest of moments, as he helped me rise, I felt sixteen again, artless and innocent.

"Come where, my lady?"

His hand was warm and dry, and I hated to let it go.

"I can show you the way out of the castle, help you get your horses," I blurted out. "My husband and Volk are busy planning, they don't know I'm here, I never visit our guests. But we don't have much time."

There was a soft rustle in the shadows. I had almost forgotten there was another man in the room, the Southerner whose voice I'd heard through the door. He cleared his throat. "With all due respect, my lady, why should we trust you? This place is full of tricks and lies."

I paused. "Oh … Of course, you are right." I turned to the prince. "Your Highness, I must give you something." I removed the thin gold ring from my finger and placed it on his palm. "This," I said. "Do you know what this is?"

Instead of replying, he lifted the ring towards the light, studying it closely. In his long fingers, it looked like a toy, a trinket made for a child. No gems, no special decorations or inscriptions, just the simple gold thread, woven together in an endless knot, worn down by age.

"I know what that is," he said. "It's a promise."

"It was given to me by—"

"My mother, yes. She told me the story of the tournament in Myrit and the girl who tried to elope. She told me we would meet, you and I."

"Yes."

"But, my lady," he said slowly, turning the ring so that the light flickered on its surface, "it's been forty years since, and you don't look a day over twenty."

There was a high, mournful sound in my ears, like the wind whistling in the reeds. "Forty years?" I whispered. "I haven't counted, believe me, days go by in a fog here, and nights are filled with nightmares. Oh, so much time lost!"

He took my hand and gently slipped the ring back in place. "This belongs to you."

I tugged invisible wisps of hair behind my ears and touched the ring for reassurance. "We must hurry. You are in greater danger than you think. Selern and Volk, they like to play tricks on guests, they like to set them against each other, confuse them, make them angry and scared. And then at dawn, they kill them."

"I see." Still no surprise on his face, just serious attention, a slight furrow to his brow.

"No matter what game they're playing, you will be dead by sunrise." I pressed my eyes with the heels of my hands. "I know what you're thinking, I grew up among knights. You have your sword, and there's just the two of them plus that old guard. Yes, that's all, three men capable of carrying weapons in the whole castle. And you and your … companion," I looked at the black-haired, hard-featured man in the corner, "you are excellent fighters, I'm sure. But you don't stand a chance because the game is rigged. You cannot kill them. You must run away."

"But how, my lady?" he asked. "This castle has walls that are not there. It's a labyrinth. And the forest …"

"I know the way through the castle, I will lead you out. As for the forest … You know, don't you? You have your mother's gift. You know about Mor—"

"No!" he stopped me abruptly, and then added, "Please, don't mention that name. The name invokes them."

"Yes. You are right. So, you know?"

"I know."

"Then you must come with me, or my husband will sacrifice you to her. If anyone can find the way through the forest, it is you. You won't be fooled by her tricks, and you can fight her monsters."

His companion snorted in the corner, laughing softly, though I couldn't see what was so funny about my words. The prince just closed his eyes.

"And you would go with us?" he asked.

"I hoped … I hoped that you would take me."

"What about the other guests? What about Raden, and that girl he saved?"

"I'm afraid I can't—" The Southerner's snigger irritated me. "What's so funny?" I snapped.

"I apologize my lady; I'm laughing out of despair."

"Despair? But why—" Then it dawned on me. "You won't do it, will you?" I asked the prince.

"I can't do it." He shrugged.

"I don't understand. I thought you were here to save me." A monstrous weight crushed my chest: a dark violet tide of wretchedness extinguishing the flame of hope. "Your mother saved me once, despite my best efforts to turn my life upside down. She was kind to me when nobody else was, not even the people who were supposed to love me." I touched the ring again. "She gave me this ring and a promise that carried me through all these years." I bit my lip so hard my teeth drew blood. "I am an evil person and a coward. I have done a terrible thing, I invoked *her*, and I had no idea what it meant. No idea. I thought I was saving someone. But I did not know that when the gods give you a gift—"

"They take much more in return," he finished.

"You know?"

"I've experienced it myself."

"Then you understand me." I shook my head. "None of my prayers were answered the way I hoped. We became her creatures, and the guests started to arrive. That's why you are here, in grave danger, and I'm trying to help you, but if you won't go …"

"I can't go. I cannot run away and leave everybody else behind."

His eyes were a strange shade of blue-grey, dark like the winter sea, and there was no trace of derision or judgement in them. I felt weary and hopeless and old as the bleak, ragged mountains on the horizon. I had imagined a different hero just as I had imagined a different life, but gods had their own plans.

"I think I should leave now," I whispered.

"My lady." He took my hand. "Wait. Please. You can still help me. I need you to take me to a place you can find much quicker than I."

"What place?"

"I need to see the girl Raden saved. The one who was your companion."

"Ida?" I wanted to tell him she had never been my companion, that she was just a girl unfortunate enough to stumble upon this lair of monsters, but truth evaporated on my lips. "She hasn't woken up. I think she's dying, and I cannot … I cannot stand more death."

He buckled his sword belt. "Tonight you must," he said.

# CHAPTER TWENTY-THREE

## TELANI

### AUTUMN 361 A.C.

The corridors of the castle turned into a labyrinth as soon as we stepped out of the tower.

"Give me your hand," Gospa Elisya said to my lord and turned to me. "You too."

I took her small, soft hand; her palm was cold and wet. She set a brisk, resolute pace, with her eyes closed. "It's less confusing this way," she apologized. A couple of times I thought we would walk right into a wall, but then a new corridor opened before us.

At last we arrived at a small wooden door hidden under an arch. It was latched on our side but not locked.

"We're here," she said.

My lord breathed in sharply as he walked in. "But ... this is not a room."

"No. It's the heart of the castle."

It was a garden, moonlit and entirely drained of colour, black in the shadows and grey where there were none. A bone-coloured moon sailed above our heads: not the gods' sacred vessel, but a pale disc illuminating the wasteland that surrounded us.

The ground was covered in fine sand that stuck to our boots. In full light it might have been white, but we saw it in various shades of grey. The trees were just skeletons, smooth and cold, and I knew they had never produced a single leaf or flower. And on those trees …

"The sacrifices," my lord said. "Is the girl here? Is she dead already?"

"No, no—"

"Then why did you bring us here?"

Gospa Elisya buried her face in her hands, like a child who does not want to see the monsters in the dark. "I'm sorry."

People were hanging from the trees. Dead, or something like it, suspended from ropes that didn't go around their necks, but under their arms. Completely still, for there was no wind in the garden. I expected the stench of death and rot, but there was none. Only the scent of something old and dry, like a chest full of scrolls buried in the desert sand.

I had seen battlefields, long sieges, slaughtered villages, the worst carnage of war. There was no such gore, no blood and decay in the garden, but it was just as horrible. My stomach heaved and I ground my teeth, breathing through my nose to prevent myself from retching.

"Gospa Elisya." My lord gently pulled her hands away from her face. "Why am I here?"

"Because *she* is here," the lady whispered. "You were meant to come here. You're the hero, you're supposed to face her."

My lord took a step back, sand rippling beneath his feet. "I should face a goddess? On her own sacred ground?"

The idea was as naive as it was monstrous, hatched in some gilded book of legends, where glorious young knights fought demons and beasts, and won.

"I offered you escape, you refused it," she said in a small voice.

I wanted to grab her shoulders and shake her, but my lord turned on his heel and walked away. The lady remained there, arms wrapped around her chest, head bowed in a parody of remorse.

There was nowhere to go but forward, among the grisly trees. I followed him as he slowly approached the first figure. It was an old man, balding and bloated, with a swollen belly and thin legs. His clothes stuck to him as if they were wet. Surprised, I checked the ground under him. There was no trace of water.

"Let's go on," my lord said.

We watched them closely in that strange light, with the sharp shadows that made no distinction between the living and the dead. We saw the traces of their deaths on them: wounds, strangling. Their eyes were shut, as if they were sleeping.

There were young people and old people, men and women, nobles, merchants, soldiers. Some had old-fashioned clothes, armour and weapons that had not been used for forty years. We even found one Seragian messenger, with Prince Nykodios's coat of arms on his chest.

I looked for familiar faces but, luckily, found none.

"I wonder how they choose guests?" I mused. "How they avoid luring a group of ten well-armed hunters? Or soldiers? Or just someone very careful and very well equipped, searching for these people? Some of them must have been missed."

"I don't know," my lord replied. "The forest has its own paths and I think they are not the same for everyone. Some travellers never reach the castle, for sure. And some ... some were guided here for a purpose. Why did Raden ride into the forest? If he was so afraid of us, why didn't he try to slip away at night from some inn? Why did he risk getting lost in the snow?"

"I can't say," I admitted. "I thought the boy was rash and imprudent, but perhaps it was something else." I paused. "And that woman he found, the companion ..."

"I wish we could reach her," he said. "If she knows something that might help us." He shrugged. "At least she's still alive."

"If we turn back and try to navigate the corridors alone, we might find her." I looked back over my shoulder towards the small figure huddled by the door. The lady was no obstacle. But the corridors harboured worse creatures than her, and I had no wish to fight the huge priest in vain again.

"No," he said, walking to a tree with three gaudily dressed young men hanging from the branches. These were the last sacrifices; after them there was only a handful of bare trees, an expanse of smooth sand and a perfectly still pond in the distance. "Perhaps the lady's reasoning was not completely wrong, you know. Perhaps this thing should be dealt with at its heart."

We left the copse behind us, and I should have felt relief, but the dread that grasped my heart still held fast. The pond was narrow enough to throw a stone across. The water resembled ink, black and stagnant. A perfectly straight line divided it from the grey sand. I knelt down to study it and saw the tips of my lord's boots when he stopped beside me, a good two feet from the water. Its blackness was impenetrable; I could not discern the bottom, not even at the very edge. I had a terrible sense of foreboding that something would reach for us from the depths: something cold, toothy and dead. Something feeding on human flesh.

My lord fell to his knees beside me. His eyes were filled with fear.

"I don't know what to do," he whispered very softly. "I don't have a plan. I don't know if I can face her again."

His wife knew the truth of his death and return to life, but all the rest of us had was the legend. I never dared to ask him what happened when he voluntarily gave his life to Morana to save the kingdom. I did not know how he escaped, if escape was what he did. He was dead, and then he was alive. But not entirely. *Borrowed time*, he told me once. *When you have eternity at your fingertips, you can afford to lend a tiny piece*.

On those nights when nightmares haunted him, we would sit together under the wide canopy of stars, and he would tell me about the fear. Not of death, as such, but of death that gives no peace, no rest, no oblivion.

"The thing you fear the most," his breathing was laboured as he bowed down, "always catches up with you in the end. She promised me we would meet again."

His teeth bared in a grimace of pain, he touched the black water with his fingertips.

"I'm here, Morana," he said. "Show yourself."

Silence. And then a black tentacle shot out of the pond and wrapped around his wrist. His whole body jerked as it pulled him forward.

I jumped and grabbed him, digging my heels into the sand, pulling back. I would be damned if I let her have him. More tentacles appeared, cold and slimy and putrid, but so incredibly strong. I grabbed the dagger my lord took from the priest. I stabbed and slashed like a man possessed, but for each one I destroyed, two more appeared, until they were wrapped around my arms and legs and chest, squeezing the air out of my lungs, holding me above the ground, tied, suspended, helpless.

The black water in the centre of the pond swelled as a figure surfaced and began moving slowly, fitfully, towards the shore. My lord cut the last tentacle that held him and staggered backwards, his face a mask of absolute horror.

There was something eerily familiar about the creature moving towards him under the harsh light of the crooked moon. A corpse, dripping wet and entangled in black reeds. Fair hair, darkened by water, falling to its shoulders; rotten rags hanging from its tall frame; face destroyed beyond recognition, empty sockets and bared teeth.

A heap of decaying bones held together by dark magic.

Yet I *knew* those bones. I knew them better than I knew myself. I opened my mouth, a scream exploding in my lungs. But the night swallowed it as soon as it left my lips, and the only sound I heard was the water lapping and my lord's heavy breathing as he watched his own corpse approach him.

Neither said a word. My lord shivered, his arms limp, his sword hanging uselessly. The creature carried its perfect copy, undistinguishable from where I watched. Despite being little more than a few scraps of rotting flesh hanging from a skeleton, it swayed it smoothly, attacking as soon as it came within reach. My lord reacted slowly, like a person moving in a dream, but his fighting instincts kicked in, and he blocked the advance and retreated.

I struggled against my bonds, stone-hard and unyielding. I could neither move nor make a sound. All I was allowed to do was watch.

The creature attacked again, and I noticed it didn't just look like my lord, it moved like him too. It had the skill and grace of one of the greatest swordsmen in the kingdom; it fought like my lord did when he was rested and focused. It was the best version of my warrior prince, unlike the living man who retreated before it, exhausted and terrified and so excruciatingly slow.

When the first blow landed, I tried to close my eyes, only to discover I was unable to. My lord staggered, black blood flowing down his leg. The creature hacked at him, a grisly smile fixed on its ruined face, its hollow sockets gleaming with black malevolence. Another cut, above the left elbow, then a shallow graze across the ribs. My lord leaped back, the creature's blade swishing through empty air where his chest had been a fraction of a heartbeat before.

There was no fairness to that fight. It was a cruel setup, a monstrous divine joke. And my lord was losing.

# CHAPTER TWENTY-FOUR

## IDA

### AUTUMN 361 A.C.

I was on the snowy plain in the middle of the forest, running. My boots kicked the snow as fine as dust, raising a white cloud that whirled around me. Somewhere in the distance, I spotted a red dot and headed towards it.

It was a fox. No, not just any fox, it was my fox, the fox who had saved me. Only now it didn't really look like a fox. When I approached it through the blizzard, I saw it was a woman, red-headed, sharp-faced, with eyes as shiny and black as jet buttons. Her lips parted in a sharp-toothed smile, the tip of her pink tongue darting out to wet them.

"Little Ida," she said, "always running away."

Something was off. I peered through the snowflakes, searching for the dark shape chasing me.

The wind was sharp, the snow untouched, yet there was a whiff of something unpleasant in the air. A stench of wet, rotting places.

"Come closer," said the fox woman. "Let me see you."

"No." I took a step backwards.

"Don't be afraid." She reached towards me with her clawed paws. "I can lead you out of here."

I was wrong, it was not my fox. I knew those eyes; I'd seen them before.

"Once more, you took something that belongs to me," the Goddess said.

"I have nothing." I tried to retreat, but my feet were trapped in the deep snow.

"Almost nothing." She laughed: it came out as a bark. "That little shell in your hand. Give it to me, and I might let you go."

Only then did I become aware that I was indeed holding a small sharp object in my right hand.

"No. It doesn't belong to you."

"Oh, be reasonable." The wind was picking up and her hair flapped wildly, longer and darker than it had been a moment ago. Her smile was all teeth now. "A fair exchange: an empty, dead shell for your freedom."

"If I give it to you, will you let me leave the forest alive?"

Dark tendrils of her hair reached towards me although the wind was blowing in the opposite direction. "I will. You'll wake up in bed in Haragov Dol and all this will seem like a bad dream."

Was it a trick? I dared not look into her eyes.

"A long and happy life or eternity in the darkness, what will it be?"

I had nothing to lose but an empty shell I had no use for. I lifted my fist and slowly opened my frozen fingers. Light poured out of my hand.

Here, on this windswept plain that didn't belong to the mortal world, the shell was a jewel, a radiant star in my hand.

Black tendrils reached for it, but I closed my hand and shoved it in my pocket. "No. You can't have it."

With a shriek of rage, the Goddess launched herself at me, her hair turning into vipers that wrapped their sinuous bodies around my legs, my arms, my chest, tearing me apart. I screamed in terror.

"Ida! Ida!" Someone was calling my name, patting my cheeks.

I gasped and opened my eyes.

"You were crying in your sleep," he said. "Are you in pain?"

I was in pain.

Blinking, I forced my eyes to focus on the face above me. The light was weak, one fluttering candle on the nightstand, but I recognized his blond hair, fine features, blue eyes. The young man from the woods.

"Here, drink some water, you must be thirsty. Don't try to get up, you have a stab wound in your stomach. And frostbite, I think. And—"

I lay in a large, soft bed, under a brocade canopy of blue and gold, in a comfortable room with carpets on the floor and tapestries on the walls. Gospa Elisya's bedroom.

Darkness poured in through the glazed windows: another night had fallen.

"You brought me back to the castle?" A frustrated moan escaped my lips. "You fool, you idiot, we're all going to die."

"What?" He flinched. "No, we're safe here, Gospodar Selern promised me protection."

I stared at him. He did not look like there was something seriously wrong with his head, and yet …

"Did you not see that dead thing in the forest?"

"Yes, but we're safe from it—"

"They're murderers. Gospodar Selern, and Volk, and even Gospa Elisya, that lying bitch. They kill their guests. This is a cursed place, a deadly labyrinth, and you brought me back here." I was so furious I might have screamed, had I not been too afraid to draw attention to myself. "You brought me back."

The corners of his lips twisted downwards, spoiling his looks. He was my age, or a bit older, but he looked like a petulant child.

"I thought you were Gospa Elisya's companion."

I laughed despite the pain. "They lied to you. I was a prisoner here, like everybody else."

"I'm sorry," he said, shrugging like my destiny was a footnote in his own great book of adventures. "I was desperate to escape the prince and that vile secretary of his. They followed me here, trying to kill me."

"The prince?" I wasn't sure I'd heard him correctly. "There's a *prince* here?" My thoughts flared up, overturning the dusty drawers of my memory. There were just four princes in the kingdom, to my knowledge. Three of them were toddlers. The fourth one though … "Just to be absolutely clear, you're not talking about some drinking mate of yours you nicknamed *Prince* because he is the ruler of every tavern he walks in? You're talking about His Royal Highness, Prince Amron?"

"Of course," he said with a grimace of distaste. *Mind your tongue, Ida.* The boy looked highborn, but I hadn't realized he was quite that highborn.

"The prince has his soldiers here, right? His armed escort?"

"Well, no, actually," he explained calmly, like it wasn't the worst possible news, "they rode for Haragov Dol. The prince is alone with his secretary, and I'm supposed to fight him at dawn, and I have no idea—"

He prattled on, but I ignored him. Useless, useless.

"Help me get up," I said, pushing the covers aside.

Someone had cut me out of that damned red dress, leaving me nothing but a thin linen shift. The boy flushed when he saw the outline of my breasts through it, his hands retreating as if I were some delicate, shy lady.

"Help me!" I propped myself on my elbows, grunting in pain. He hugged my shoulders, supporting me.

"I'm not sure you should—"

"Shut up. Ah!" I tried to get up, but a sharp pain ripped through my belly. I would have crashed to the floor had he not caught me.

"You're bleeding!"

"What?" I checked my shift, it was unmarred by bloodstains, my new bandages firmly in place. It was something else. Blood was dripping from my right hand, curled up tightly in a fist.

"Sit down, please, you're hurt."

"No, it's not that." I opened my hand. It was still there, the sharp little shell, plain and dead.

But the boy exclaimed, "What *is* this?"

"A shell," I retorted. "Isn't it obvious?"

"No. Don't lie to me, girl." His hand materialized on my shoulder, his fingers digging into my flesh. "I have second sight; I can see it. What is this thing, where did you get it?"

I looked at him again and this time he didn't look like a newly weaned pup. Sharpness infused his features, along with noble arrogance.

I sighed. "You won't believe me."

"Try me."

"I got it in a dream. I was in a huge hall covered in marble and mosaics. It looked like some exquisite underwater kingdom. One of the Goddess' creatures chased me, and I knew I would die if it caught me. Then a woman appeared before me, gave me this shell and said, *Tell him to call his father and he will come*. And then she said it was her dream and kicked me out."

He frowned, though he didn't accuse me of lying. "What did she look like?"

"The woman?" I closed my eyes, trying to remember the details. "Slight, pale, with silvery-blonde hair. Heart-shaped face. Grey eyes so sharp you could cut yourself on her gaze."

"Oh, gods," he muttered, wide-eyed, shocked. "She can't be still around … or can she?" He looked up, as if he could see the sky through the ceiling and cleared his throat. "And she said, *Tell him to call his father and he will come* in those exact words?"

"Yes, yes, she did." I nodded. "So, do you know who she was?"

"Of course I do." He looked at me as if I was the slow one. "Queen Orsiana," he added.

Queen Orsiana. She was dead, I knew as much. There were also legends and wild stories …

"But why would she tell me to call my father?" he asked, reaching for the shell that still laid in my hand. I let him take it. "I never met my father."

"Wait." I bit my lip, thinking. "What if the message is not for you?"

"What do you mean?"

"Queen Orsiana, she was Prince Amron's mother, wasn't she?"

"Oh." He stared at me and something raw and injured glinted in his eyes. "Of course. It's about him. It's always about him."

I couldn't have cared less about his whining. My wound hurt. I was too scared to look at my toes, fearing that some of them were missing. There was a fair chance I wouldn't survive the night. I was in no mood to stroke his pride.

"You must find him and give him the message and the shell."

"But … the duel," he stammered. "He'll kill me if I appear before him."

"Every creature in this castle will try to kill you tonight. You'll be dead before the dawn if we don't figure a way out. I'd go myself, but I cannot walk. Please." I grabbed his shirt. "Do it for me."

And then I pulled him close and kissed him.

# CHAPTER TWENTY-FIVE

## TELANI

### AUTUMN 361 A.C.

My lord fought on stubbornly, with the grim determination that had seen him through so many battles. He parried and blocked and retreated, gliding over the grey sand, under the bone-coloured moon. The creature pressed on, showing no signs of fatigue, no impatience. Cuts and blows could not injure it; no blood flowed from the rotting flesh. There was no stopping it.

I could not watch him die. I could not.

*Damn you!* My furious thoughts flew towards the black sky. *You scheming, greedy, useless monsters! Do something!*

The gods remained mute, and the two figures kept hacking at each other while the moon shone its ghostly light, indifferent and distant. Time stretched, immeasurable, irrelevant in this place where there was no life, no change. No hope.

And then a sound reached my ears: low, rhythmical. I averted my eyes from the fight and spotted a dark figure running among the trees. Blond hair, long limbs. Raden.

He stopped short when he saw the duel and unsheathed his sword. But he dared not approach the fighters.

"Over here!" My voice came out as a rasping whisper. He heard me, though, and turned his head. "Cut me loose."

He ran to me, his eyes wide with shock. He cut through the tentacles that held my body in their iron grasp. I fell to the ground, bruised but whole, and tried to massage some life back into my stiff limbs. Raden stood with his sword in the air, waiting for an attack that didn't come. Whatever that monstrous creature was, it did not move again.

I stood up and lurched towards the dagger on the ground.

"What is going on?" the boy asked.

"Later."

My lord and his counterpart circled, mirroring each other's poses perfectly. As I approached, the sickening stench of the corpse hit my nostrils. I moved slowly, carefully: one wrong step could have shattered my lord's crumbling focus.

There was no point in throwing the dagger, no point in stabbing the creature.

"Cut its head off," whispered Raden behind my back. "That's how Ida vanquished the thing in the woods."

I tried to catch my lord's eyes, but blood and sweat dripped down his forehead and I doubted he could see anything but his enemy before him. My strength and speed were paltry, wiped out by the stiffness and exhaustion. While the creature's back was turned to me, I took a chance and attacked. My rigid muscles betrayed me, though, and I staggered, crashing into its back. The horrible stench engulfed me and something cold and slimy covered my face. I thrashed, unable to breathe, biting the cold, rotten flesh that blocked my mouth.

A crunch exploded in my ears as something hard connected with the decaying bones. My lord's boot smashed through the corpse's ribcage and the hand that covered my face fell away. I grabbed the creature's hair and pulled its head back, cutting through the decomposing flesh until it grated on the bone. I slid the tip of my dagger between the vertebrae and felt them split with a sickening pop.

The creature stopped moving.

My lord pushed its remains off me and grabbed the severed head. He swung it as if it were a sack of grain and threw it into the pond.

At that moment, the dead trees behind us let out a sigh. No, not the trees, the people. All the dead heads turned towards us, all the dead eyes looked at us. *She* looked at us. And laughed from a hundred dead throats.

I screamed in terror and pain.

My lord fell to the ground. Raden rushed to him.

"I'm sorry," he said. "I'm so, so sorry."

My lord rolled to his side and spat black blood on the grey sand. "No time for apologies now." He was bleeding from half a dozen injuries, his left leg was drenched in blood, and there was a nasty gash on his forehead that needed urgent stitches.

"Oh no!" Gospa Elisya cried, emerging out of the copse. I'd forgotten all about her, and had there been any strength left in my limbs, I would have grabbed her by the neck and thrown her into the pond, to join the monsters who dwelt there.

She fell to her knees beside my lord and, demonstrating considerable dexterity, bandaged the wound on his thigh with her scarf, then offered him her handkerchief to wipe the blood off his brow.

"I saw you beat that thing," she said. "I thought it would end the curse."

I looked around. The bone moon remained motionless in the sky, the dead bodies hung from the branches like macabre fruit. Nothing had changed; we were still trapped inside the nightmare.

"Well, you were wrong, my lady," said my lord. "And now I still have a duel to fight at dawn." His gaze pierced Raden. "Why are you here?"

The boy swallowed hard, tucking a loose strand of hair behind his ear. "I have a message for you," he said.

"From whom?"

"From … your lady mother," he stammered, and Gospa Elisya gasped. "The girl I saved in the forest—Ida—she had a vision; she saw the queen in the submerged halls of Amraith—"

"Stop it," my lord growled. "Telani, help me up."

I rushed to him and offered him support to rise without leaning on his wounded leg. The boy stared at him, mouth half-open.

"You know your history well, Raden. But using my late mother …" He turned to Gospa Elisya. "What did you tell him?"

"Your Highness?" She feigned perfect innocence. "I've never even talked to him. He doesn't know I met her."

277

My lord was as upset as I'd ever seen him, standing there, struggling to keep his balance. His eyes narrowed and he gripped my shoulder harder than it was necessary. His rage was cold, contained.

"This place is a tapestry of lies," he said. "You can spin any stories you like, but I'm leaving."

"Please, wait." The boy jumped to his feet and reached into his pocket. "Ida saw her in a dream, a blonde woman with grey eyes, and she gave her this." He opened his hand, revealing a small, scallop-shaped object that shone like a precious stone. "The queen told her, *Tell him to call his father and he will come*."

"Call my father?" My lord turned to the boy, anger dripping from his words like deadly nightshade. "My father, your father, our father. He is dead, boy. Not spirited away by magic, not stolen by gods, not hidden in other people's dreams. Dead. I saw his body, I kept vigil over his remains, I buried him." He took a long, ragged breath in the stunned silence. "And when he was alive," he continued, "he thought of no one but himself. Even if I could call him, he would not help me. He never did."

He turned on his heel and we staggered together towards the trees. No one tried to stop us. When we had moved out of their sight, my lord said, "Let's sit here. I need rest."

We found a comfortable spot between the roots of an unoccupied tree. I didn't have to ask him anything to know how badly he was hurt. There was no point in mentioning it: neither one of us could have helped it. There was something else as well, a mood radiating from him that I hadn't felt in a very long time. A sort of brittleness of a blade under so much pressure it could not bend further. A breaking point.

"This place grinds me down and I'm too tired to think straight," he said. "Do you think the boy is lying?"

My first impulse was to say *Yes*, for I hated and mistrusted everything about Raden. This was not about my feelings, though. "Well …" I said, weighing my words, "if he is, then it's easy to ignore him. But if he isn't, perhaps there is something we missed."

"Like what?" He pressed the lady's handkerchief to his forehead, but the blood still seeped through. Needle and thread were in my saddlebag, buried somewhere in the bowels of the castle.

"I have never spoken to your lady mother, so this may be a presumptuous idea." I hesitated. Every family had a history of betrayal and heartbreak, and the royal one was no exception. "She was surely familiar with the relationship between you and your father. So if she had one crucial, life-or-death message for you, would she tell you to call him?"

"No."

"But if Raden is telling the truth—"

"Then the message does not mean what I thought it meant." He sighed. "It's a riddle. That's more like her, I think."

I waited for him to explain, but he looked up with an uncannily wistful expression. For a brief moment, we were in a different time and place. The great burden that lay on my chest lifted, allowing me to breathe freely.

Then I noticed the great starless dome above our heads was fading to grey towards the east, and dismay whispered its corrupt song in my ear once more. "It will be dawn soon," I said.

He touched the bandage on his leg and shuddered. In that odd, colourless world, it was hard to say how much blood he'd lost.

"I wish you'd let me be your champion," I said.

"No need," he replied. "I can beat the boy with my eyes closed. It will be all right, Telani. Trust me."

# CHAPTER TWENTY-SIX

## ELISYA

### AUTUMN 361 A.C.

I remained sitting on the cold sand beside a decomposing corpse and a visibly upset young man. Tears of agitation—or dread—ran down his cheeks. He wiped them off angrily and ran his fingers through his golden locks as if he wanted to pull them out.

"Raden?" I laid my hand on his shoulder. "May I see that shell?"

He opened his hand. The little scallop had its own light, pearly-white and alive in this dead world.

"I met the queen, you know." I showed him my ring. "She gave me this."

But he wasn't listening to me.

"He's my brother, and he despises me now," he said. "My task was to deliver the message, and I failed because I was afraid of him." His eyes were rimmed with red, as he rubbed them raw. "No, that's not true. I'd been jealous of him long before I was afraid. All my life, I listened to stories about him, wishing that I could be a hero like him. And then, when I met him, I realized he was sent to kill me."

I squeezed his arm to break his reverie. "Don't do this to yourself," I said. "The mistress of this place reaches into your heart, takes your dreams and twists them into something poisonous and rotten. There are no heroes in this place, only villains."

He shot me a bitter smile. I remembered the tournament in Myrit, the king who liked girls and the girls who—apparently—liked him back. The consequences of our actions, reverberating through the years.

"He will kill me in the end," Raden said, "whether he had planned it or not. He'll duel me at dawn, and he'll kill me."

I didn't understand why he was mentioning a duel, but then a sickly blue torchlight approached us through the trees and Volk said, "This way."

It was just another one of my husband's schemes.

The four of them walked out of the copse, Volk and Selern leading, the prince and his man following them.

"Do you have your weapons?" Volk asked.

The prince nodded, wrapping his hand around the grip of his sword. He was leaning on his companion, grey-faced, like it was an immense effort just to stand upright.

"I don't want to fight," Raden said, and turned to my husband. "I withdraw my accusations, I was wrong. I apologize for it." His eyes were wide, filled with ill-considered hope, as if Selern would ever be satisfied with anything but blood.

"The time for talk has passed," said Volk. "Now it's time for the duel." Not waiting for an answer, he stepped forward and opened his arms, looking up. "O gods! Turn your eyes to these mortals now, fighting in your honour, searching your judgement. Morana, mistress of death, we call for your blessing and your gifts."

The sound of her name reminded me of the stench of pus in my husband's sickroom, of Volk's false promises whispered in the dark. Of the blood on my hands, invisible but always present.

"Unsheathe your swords," Selern said, his eyes hungry.

Steel rang as Prince Amron lifted his sword and kissed the hilt. Torchlight danced on the blue blade. He whispered something in his man's ear, who retreated, leaving the prince to face Raden alone.

The young man reluctantly drew his blade.

"Stand here," Volk pointed. "And wait for my—"

"I don't want to fight," Raden repeated. "Your Highness—"

"The signal, please," the prince said to Volk.

"No ..."

"Now," Volk said.

The boy shut up for a heartbeat, deathly pale, while the prince swung the blade lithely, slashing through the air. He was so fast I only saw a flicker of light where his sword was.

"So, Raden," he said slowly, "are you a coward?" Even in that weak light, I could see the boy blushed to the roots of his hair. The prince limped towards him. "Or are you ready to defend your words?"

"I told the truth about the king," Raden replied, lifting his sword. "You know I did."

"You should have trusted me." The prince attacked. Raden blocked the blow and retreated. Prince Amron continued to circle, blood trickling down his face.

"I was wrong," Raden said. "Gospodar Selern—"

But the prince didn't allow him to finish. He attacked again and Raden stumbled, barely avoiding the blade.

"I don't want to die," said Raden.

"Too late." The prince fell on him, but the blows came in a controlled rhythm, reminding me of the long afternoons when Silya and I had watched my brother sweating in the practice yard. He was saving his strength, or he didn't have any left.

I lifted my gaze and saw the first light of dawn above the roofs of the castle, the stone shimmering where the sun touched it. The boy defended himself as best he could.

Selern and Volk stood together, watching the duel like hounds watch a slice of ham. I rubbed my little ring desperately. What was the point of promises and signs if they meant nothing? The ring, the scallop, the prince walking into this nightmare and doing nothing to save me?

I glanced towards the dark Southerner: his eyes followed the prince's every move. His face was harried, tarnished with fear.

Raden cried out when the blade nicked his right arm. He tried to stop the bleeding with his fingers.

Sunlight lit the roofs, melting them into clouds of light and fog.

"Oh, gods!" the young man wailed.

"Fight!" the prince roared. The towers of the castle evaporated in the air like images from a dream. "The heir of Amris's house? My father's son? Where is your courage?" He lunged at Raden who clumsily blocked the blow, but the prince rammed his forearm in Raden's face, throwing him to the ground. The boy retreated on all fours, the prince coming at him, staggering as blood soaked the bandages. "What are you? A coward hiding behind his mother's skirts, whining and snivelling?" He lifted his sword. "You'll never be worthy of Amris's name."

"No," Raden screamed and jumped to his feet. "Shut up!" He gripped his sword hard.

The last traces of night were gone, and the sun rose in the sky, illuminating the fallen towers, walls overgrown with moss, broken windows, rot and decay. In its golden light, the castle was no more than a ruin.

Snow shone like polished steel. Two figures, two dark silhouettes, fought one another. I was blinded for a heart-beat. I heard the steel ring and hit something hard. Raden was shrieking. One dark figure fell on the white sand.

*It is done*, he got him.

I blinked, moved my head. The glare was gone. Raden stood there, swordless, stupefied.

Raden *stood* there.

# CHAPTER TWENTY-SEVEN

## TELANI

### AUTUMN 361 A.C.

I did not remember how I got to my lord, but I knelt beside him, dry sobs rasping my throat. The blade had gone through his chest and remained stuck between his ribs. He lay on his back, his eyes looking at the sky, blood frothing in the corner of his mouth.

There was nothing I could do. No one could survive such a wound.

He whispered, "Perun, father of the gods, I dedicate this death to you."

I saw movement with the corner of my eye and turned my head. Volk approached Raden from the back. The boy was staring at us, motionless, unaware right up to the moment when Volk pulled his dagger and cut his throat. Blood spurted out in a long arc, the boy lifted his hands in vain and fell to his knees without a word.

Volk said, "Lady of the depths …"

My hand reached for my dagger, but it wasn't there. I turned, slow, stupid, shocked. Gospodar Selern stood behind me. I managed to raise my hand, he cut my fingers to the bone. And then he grabbed my hair and ran the blade across my throat. I didn't feel the cut, just the hot blood pouring out over my frozen skin. I fell beside my lord.

"They all belong to the Goddess now," Gospodar Selern said.

I watched my blood spread across the sand and merge with my lord's. I wondered how he had made such a terrible mistake.

The world lost its colours; they faded like banners in the sun. Red blood, blue sky, and green moss became grey. The garden was still there: Gospodar Selern was leaving, Volk stood with his hands on his hips, frowning at the bloodshed. He looked even bigger, more real, as if he were more present in this world I was seeing now than in the other, belonging to the living.

My thoughts flew to the dead, hanging like fruit in the branches. We were guests now as well; we had a bough waiting for us. It wasn't the death I knew, and it terrified me. Would I be conscious as they hung me there, seeing, hearing, feeling forever?

I saw my lord's wide-open eyes, the dark dots of his pupils, and the deep grey-blue of his irises. He was looking at me. He took a breath; his chest rose and fell. And then nothing. I waited, counting the heartbeats that were no longer there. The colour drained out of him; his eyes turned a dull grey. He was gone.

In that moment, the world changed. A golden ray of sun pierced the mist and illuminated first him and then the whole garden, painting it in vivid colours.

And then the gods came.

They were nothing like the legends or the pictures in books. They didn't bother to take a shape mortals could see, but I felt their enormous presence like a clam feels the ocean surrounding it. They came through the light and chased away the shadows haunting us. A terrible tempest raged around me, although not a single hair on my head moved. The last traces of illusion were swept from the castle; the spell was broken as time started to move forward. Its current captured Volk, who was still standing there, his hands raised in a confused prayer. The years flew across his face, ravaging it, decades passing in a blink: a middle-aged man became old, then dead, then just dust, carried away by the wind.

A muffled thunder rumbled in my ears. I thought the walls were coming down, but then I realized it was just my heart beating again.

My lord blinked.

Suddenly it was all over. The gods climbed up through the light, ignoring us.

All but one.

He materialized out of thin air, a tall man with a copper beard. He was clad in black wool, and a hooded grey cloak covered his shoulders. Perun, the father of gods, the sire of Amris the Golden-Haired. He approached my lord and gave him his hand.

"Get up, my boy, you did well," he said in a voice I heard with my mind rather than with my ears. "My sister got carried away and we could not get in."

"I was not sure," my lord said in a stunned, faraway voice. "I had to summon you. There was no other way …"

"No. And it's your time, too. I've left you for too long."

The god and the prince held hands.

"There's so much I wanted to do," my lord said wistfully.

"That's the fate of mortals," the god replied.

The rays of sun illuminated them, passed through them—and then I realized I was looking at nothing.

# CHAPTER TWENTY-EIGHT

## IDA

### AUTUMN 361 A.C.

I opened my eyes in the dim light of the winter dawn. I was alone in a large, warm bed, under a heavy brocade canopy. Gospa Elisya's bed. I sat up, my heart beating like a wild thing in my chest. Stitches on my stomach tugged painfully. There was an odd shell-shaped scar on my palm.

I remembered a golden-haired young man, stubborn and frightened, and a strange conversation about princes and queens. Did he deliver the message in time?

Angry voices made me stagger to the open window. A garden, curiously devoid of snow, covered in white sand. A black pond that looked like a slice of night lying on the ground. And bare, unfamiliar trees adorned with ... dolls?

*They're not dolls, Ida. You know what they are.*

Beside the pond, two men hacked at each other with swords, and the sound of steel ringing brought back memories that made me shiver. I closed my eyes and opened them again when sunlight kissed my eyelids. The first bright rays pierced the mist and touched the roofs of the castle. Someone screamed.

In an instant, the whole world changed.

Air was sucked out of my chest, and I fell to my knees, gasping. Hot pain slashed across my belly as all my stitches tore. A harsh, searing wind rushed through the window, burning my skin. My mother's face flashed before me, her soft features and dark, worried eyes. *Little Ida.* I was dying.

*Gods, have mercy! Gods* ...

It ended as abruptly as it had begun.

I rose slowly, my hand on my belly. The stitches were gone, but so was my wound, leaving only the warm, smooth skin. I took a deep breath and realized the heavy, oppressive grasp of fear was gone.

A glance through the window revealed that the castle was now little more than a heap of mossy stones. A pool of blood, ruby-red in the sunlight, slowly soaked into the sand. The trees shook, murmuring in human tongues.

A familiar voice said, "We are alive."

Tinka was somewhere down there.

I wanted to rush out immediately, but I had only a fine linen shift on. I opened the lady's chest and grabbed the first dress I found, a heavy, dark, woollen thing, and pulled it over my head. My boots were hidden under the bed, together with my old, blood-stained clothes. Too impatient to search for a cloak, I opened the door and ran down the corridor to the stairs that led to the garden. The castle was so small now that there was no chance of getting lost.

An old woman, dishevelled and wailing, covering her face with her hands, ran up. I moved out of her way as she rushed past without sparing me a glance. The blue gown she wore—I'd seen Gospa Elisya wearing it.

A small voice in my head said, *It might be another trick.*

Upset and confused, I passed under the low arch and stepped into the garden. "Tinka?" I called.

"Ida?"

On the edge of the copse stood a short, grey-haired woman, hardly bigger than a child. She wore a dress too short and too tight for her. I knew that dress.

"Tinka." I gawked, approaching her. "How old are you?"

She was bare-footed, but that didn't stop her from walking across the frozen sand.

"Fifty-two," she said, "or fifty-three. I'm not sure anymore." She caught the tip of her grey plait. "I have no mirror. How do I look?"

*Old*, I thought, but a voice behind her said, "Does it matter? It's over."

"It's over," she echoed in wonder, turning around, examining the ruined castle. "They're gone. Gospodar Selern and Volk. I lost all hope we would ever be rid of them. Thank you."

She moved to reveal a black-haired man kneeling in a pool of blood. His clothes were drenched from neck to boots, his rough, dark face unshaven and muddy. Tinka helped him get up.

"Don't thank me, thank His Highness. When he appears." His brown eyes found me, and a glint of recognition appeared in them. "You must be Ida. I'm glad you're well."

"I … thank you. But I don't know who you are."

"My name is Telani." He motioned towards a young man lurching towards us. Tall, thin, with a mass of blond hair matted with blood. "And that sad excuse for a man is Raden. But you've met already, haven't you?"

That face, that hair: I knew him. The young man who had saved me from Gair, who took the scallop from me and went in search of the prince. "Did you deliver the message?" I asked him. "Who broke the curse?"

"I don't—" Raden started, but the dark-haired man cut him off.

"Prince Amron broke the curse," Telani said, his face entirely devoid of triumph or joy. I've never seen anyone claim victory with such anguish. I looked behind him, curious to see the hero in the flesh, but there was no one else beside the pond.

"We're alive," Raden said slowly, amazed. "We can leave this place."

"No, we can't leave until—" Telani started and then inhaled sharply. "The guests! The trees!"

He rushed towards the copse, and I saw that the garden had changed as well. It was not the barren, sandy desert I'd seen from the window. It was an overgrown, snowy thicket glimmering in the winter sunlight. Like refugees from some war-stricken city, a group of at least two dozen ragged people stood among the trees. They looked around in wonder; one woman was crying. I noticed Criscer's handsome face in the crowd; he blinked, too shocked to recognize me.

*The guests, of course.* That is what Gospa Elisya had tried to tell me, in her sly, furtive way. *Nobody leaves this place, neither the living nor the dead.*

"What is this?" asked Raden, who had caught up with us.

"A mess we need to take care of," Telani replied. "Tinka, Ida, I need your help."

Telani took over smoothly, for everyone else was just standing around uselessly, waiting for someone to tell them what to do. He found a room whose ceiling had fewest leaks, made us drag in a solid desk, lit a fire and started to examine people, give out orders, make lists and write letters filled with incredible statements.

I helped him, coaxing and comforting the guests, leading them in and then out, taking them to the kitchen, where Tinka was struggling to feed them all and find them a place to lie down. Some of the guests wanted to leave immediately, and we needed to reason with them. There were no horses, no entourage and no supplies for the journey.

Sometime around noon, a group of soldiers appeared in the castle.

"We've been waiting for you the whole night at Haragov Dol," they told Telani. "When you failed to appear by sunrise, we turned back."

"But how did you pass through the forest?"

"There's a path leading straight to the castle. It's snowed in, that's why it took us so long to reach you."

"You didn't notice anything … strange?" I cut in.

Six hard, rugged men looked at me as if I were mad.

I left Telani to explain the recent events and went down to the kitchen.

"I'll stay here for a few days," Tinka said, wiping the sweat off her brow, handing out bowls of thin broth, "just because he asked me. There are no servants left in this place."

"Where's the mistress? I think I've seen her briefly this morning. She didn't look well."

"She'll be fine," Tinka said with sour contempt. "She's locked in her room, wailing."

Her pretty face was gone forever, then. I had no reason to feel sorry for her.

Out of the corner of my eye, I saw Criscer and his companions sitting beside the fire. There was a situation I had to deal with soon.

"And where is that young man … Raden?" I asked.

"Sulking upstairs because I made him draw and warm his own water. He demanded a bath, can you imagine that? In the midst of all this?"

I chuckled. "I'll take care of him."

She took her eyes off the broth for a moment to give me a sharp look.

"I owe you my life," I whispered. "Keep my secret and I promise I will pay you back."

"How?"

"I have a plan. Now, let me help you with feeding all these people."

# CHAPTER TWENTY-NINE

## TELANI

### AUTUMN 361 A.C.

Getting used to breathing again was harder than dying. Every muscle in my body hurt, every bone creaked when I tried to move. And my head—my head felt like it would explode even before the suddenly revived guests and their demands gave me a blinding headache.

Every time I laid my eyes on Raden, my hands shook with an almost irresistible urge to stab him and watch him bleed to death. But I had made a promise to my lord. The damned pup was safe from me.

"We need to talk to the lady of the castle," he said, "but she has locked herself in her room and refuses to come down."

"She's safer that way. She has many enemies among the guests."

"Perhaps she should be tried—"

My hand shot out and grabbed his shirt.

"Haven't you had enough of that folly?" I growled. "I don't know if she willingly participated in her husband's doings or not, but I don't want to be responsible for her death when some rash fool breaks her neck. We've had enough death here as it is."

I let go of him, and he stumbled backwards, pale and furious. I took a deep breath and thought of the sea, calm in the moonlight, cold and bottomless.

"Let's visit her together," I said, "and see what she wants."

We knocked on her door.

"Go away," said a voice, "leave me alone."

Raden shrugged but I knocked again.

"It's Telani, my lady. I've come to arrange your departure, if you want to leave the castle."

Silence, and then a soft creak as the door opened a fraction.

"I have nowhere to go," she said.

A narrow strip of light fell on her face, and I saw what time had done to her. Gospa Elisya no longer had her golden hair, her lovely figure and her creamy skin.

Behind me, the idiot boy gasped.

"No, don't look at me," she cried and would have slammed the door in my face if I hadn't blocked it. When I pushed forward, she escaped to the opposite corner of the room and huddled there.

"My lady, please," I said. "I'm here to help you."

There was a broken mirror beneath her feet.

"You can't help me. You might as well let them kill me. There's nothing left for me in the world now, I've been here too long."

"Surely you must have some family left," Raden said behind my back.

She drew her hand over her eyes.

"I've heard that Keldik, my brother, was killed in the war, and I've never met his heirs. My sisters are dead as well, Volk brought me the news long ago." She sat down on the edge of her bed with a sigh. "The only person I know nothing about is Silya, my cousin. But she would never …" Her voice trailed off, heavy with grief.

"Where did she live when you last saw her?" I asked.

"In Myrit. I think she stayed there. She was to marry my father's friend. Gospodar Bremir."

"Gospodar Bremir?" Raden asked.

"Gospodar Bremir and Gospa Silya, yes."

"But," he gaped, "those are my mother's parents."

"Oh," she said and fell silent, trying to come to terms with that. At last, she said, "I owe her an apology. Is she still alive?"

"Oh yes, very much so. She is the richest widow in Myrit."

For the first time that day, a faint smile appeared on her lips.

"We parted on bad terms, and I regret it very much. Do you think she would want to see me?"

"I'm not su—" the fool started, but when I gave him a sharp nudge, he continued, "Of course she would."

I added, "One group will leave for Myrit soon. You can go with them, my lady."

"Myrit." There were tears in her eyes. "I'd love to see it again. Come closer, child."

He had no choice but to approach her, kneel down and let her stroke his blond hair and blushing cheeks.

"You don't look like them," she decided, with a hint of disappointment.

"No, my lady," he said seriously. "I was told I take after my father's side."

I winced, but stayed silent.

"Well, you are a handsome young man," she said. "I'm glad all turned out well in the end."

Anger flared in my chest. "As well as can be. For some."

All those bewildered people who had lost their places in the world. I thought of the grey-eyed woman who cried when she realized her husband was long dead. I thought of the senile nobleman whose sons had played with wooden swords when last he saw them. We had to tell him that they had grown up and died in a war he had never heard of. I thought of the merchant whose heirs squandered his money while he was away. And I thought of all those who didn't come back because their time ran out.

Even the happiest of endings are unhappy for someone.

I ran around all day, ordering, begging and comforting. I was surprised when I saw the sun setting and I found myself tired, hungry and lacking a whole night of sleep. Tinka brought me a bowl of soup and a fresh loaf. I had no idea where I could lie down—every bed, pallet, bench and heap of hay was already taken.

I was waiting for my lord to return. I expected to hear his voice at any moment, saying *Telani, what is going on?* I expected him to walk in and take over this whole mess, as he had always done. He was somewhere near, I could feel him, and a couple of times I thought he was standing behind me, looking over my shoulder, reading the letters I was writing. I started sentences thinking he was listening and wondered why there was no answer.

When I went to change my clothes, I found his things as he had left them. I put away the letters for his wife, but only to give them back when he returned. I went down to the garden, among the leafless winter trees and snowy bushes, to get away from people. There were no traces of any divine presence, no sense that I walked into another world.

I approached the pond that was no more than a frozen puddle now. I knelt down and touched the ice: cold and wet and devoid of magic. Behind my back, the moon rose in the sky and spilled its silver light, restoring some of the castle's decaying beauty. I heard raised voices in the distance; something fell, someone was shouting, but the garden around me was silent.

I was alone.

I was completely alone. In the garden, in the kingdom, in the whole world.

"You are not coming back, are you?" I spoke to the wind and the clouds. "Just like that, for no reason. Neither a battle nor a conspiracy nor a court assassination, but this miserable little place, a nameless dot on the map. A mistake of the gods they corrected between two heartbeats. What am I going to tell your lady? What am I going to tell myself?"

But the clouds remained silent, and the wind continued whistling its song through the branches.

"I know you think differently, but they did not deserve it, none of them did, damn them. The spoiled bastard, the lying lady and all the other ungrateful, insignificant people."

Up in the sky, the stars shone their cold light. Gods were frolicking, fighting or plotting against each other, deaf to the grief of mortals.

I opened the letter he had left me and read it under the light of the moon. *Thank you for your loyalty*, it said. *Do whatever you deem fit.*

"I am going to finish this job," I said, "but you shouldn't have left me like this."

# CHAPTER THIRTY

## IDA

### AUTUMN 361 A.C.

It was already dark when I knocked on the door of the room that had previously belonged to Gospodar Selern but was now occupied by Raden.

"Come in," he said.

I slipped through the door, my eyes downcast.

"What does he want now?" he snapped.

"My lord?"

"Telani. What does he want? He sent you, didn't he? He's been pestering me all day, telling me what to do, sending me this way and that. And why should he be the one to command us all? He's a mere secretary, a scribbler, a servant to a dead prince. I want to be rid of him as soon as possible."

I sighed and reminded myself there were no easy tasks in this world. Not for me.

"Yes, my lord."

"So?" He tapped his foot. "Out with it."

I looked at him, standing in the middle of that decaying room with his hands on his hips. He was no longer a frightened boy from the woods, but a young noble claiming his birthright. Firelight turned his hair into a golden flame: a thing of wonder, wasted on a man. The rest of his face was drab in comparison: hard, angry eyes, and a mouth twisted in a dour curve that ruined his fine features.

"I'm here because I want to thank you," I said softly. "For saving my life."

"Oh."

There was a slight change in his demeanour. Someone had taught him to be polite to ladies, and I was wearing Gospa Elisya's dress and a sweet, modest expression on my face.

"You fought a monster who attacked me and then rode through a blizzard to get me to safety. That's the bravest thing I've ever heard of."

That threw him off balance.

"Thank you. I wasn't … In the forest, I just heard …" He cleared his throat.

"And thank you for delivering the message to the prince. Without it, he wouldn't have been able to break the curse."

"Did Telani tell you that?"

"No. I guessed it myself."

He looked up, his fingers creasing his tunic while he struggled with himself in silence. "Well, the prince did the right thing in the end, whatever his initial intentions were." His lips twisted. "Speak well of the dead, and all that."

Gratitude was not among his virtues, obviously.

His eyes returned to my face. "Your wound? Has it healed?"

"Yes." I slid my hand down my belly drawing his attention to my waist and hips, but the fool was already turning away. Had he forgotten my kiss so soon?

"I'm glad to hear it. You must excuse me, my lady, I have so much to do."

"Oh, I don't want to trouble you," I whispered. "But it's been so hard ever since I came here. I had no-one to protect me."

"You almost escaped. You finished off that monster in the forest. You are a brave, strong young woman." He shuffled through a heap of papers on the desk.

"I was afraid and trapped, just like anyone else," I said. "I didn't choose to come here. I was travelling with my cousin, when we chanced upon this cursed place. Gospodar Selern, he killed him, he stabbed him with a dagger and there was so much blood."

Fat tears started rolling down my face. I let out a sob to make him look up.

"I'm sorry. But your cousin, he's all right now?"

"I tried to run away," I said, ignoring his question. "The forest terrified me. And the thing that attacked me, I still see him when I close my eyes. His eye fell out of its socket and his mouth was a bloody hole full of broken teeth. If it weren't for you, it would … it would …"

I was weeping now, and it wasn't all acting. It struck me that I'd survived unspeakable horrors. I had every right to cry.

"Don't cry, please. Please." There was a hint of panic in his voice. "You are safe now."

I covered my face and stood in the middle of the room crying my heart out, oblivious to his words.

He came closer.

"There, there," he said, patting my shoulder as if I were a skittish mare.

My whole body shook. His hand hovered in the air like a clumsy, reluctant bird. I leaned towards him a little. Had he stepped back, I would have fallen flat on my face. But he remained where he was and let me fall into his arms, closing them awkwardly around me. I pressed my face against his chest, breathing in the scent of clean clothes and lavender soap. He stiffened when my arms slid around his waist, resisting for a moment and then relaxing, burying his face in my hair. I drew him close and let his body do the rest.

Now he trembled as much as I did. His fingers touched my face, caressed it.

"It will be all right …"

I licked my lips, lifted my head, and widened my teary eyes, willing them to shine. my eyes wide and brilliant like two moonlit pools.

"Ida."

His mouth found mine, our teeth crashing in a hurry, his tongue hot and intrusive, his hips thrusting into me.

He had no idea how to kiss.

# CHAPTER THIRTY-ONE

## TELANI

### WINTER 361 A.C.

I stayed in that detestable place for eight more days, until help started arriving and the most impatient guests began leaving.

Ida, or Gospa Ida, as she was called now, had acquired an escort of three gaudy ruffians who followed her like sinister shadows. She proved herself quite competent in dealing with the people who complained, protested or threatened, showing a surprisingly small amount of gratitude for their rescue. They were nervous like cats and mad like badgers and I understood them, but I was fed up with them. I was fed up with the lack of servants and Tinka, who charged her weight in gold for each day she remained in the castle. I was fed up with Gospa Elisya, who talked only of Myrit. I was fed up with watching over our supplies and with the snow that slowed the arrival of help and news. I was particularly fed up with Raden who, with wholehearted support from Gospa Elisya, started acting like the lord of the place.

And I was fed up with myself, old, heartsick, irritable and craving the southern sunshine.

On the eighth day, Raden marched to my desk wearing an expression that suggested he had more important things on his mind than counting the rotten apples in the pantry. Out of the corner of my eye, I noticed Ida sneaking in after him, quiet as a mouse.

"I want to talk with you," he said in his formal voice.

I looked him up and down, wondering why I had ever thought he looked anything like my lord. I took in his watery blue eyes, his hard voice, his complete lack of a sense of humour.

"I'm listening," I said as politely as I could, considering the circumstances.

"I am grateful for the help you gave me," he said without any gratitude in his voice, "but I do not want to detain you here. You must take extremely important news to Myrit."

"Abia," I said.

"No, Myrit," he corrected me. "You must take the news to the king about the death—"

"The only person I will take anything to is Gospa Liana in Abia. The king will have to be informed of the circumstances of Prince Amron's death by someone else, preferably you," I said with more hostility in my voice than was necessary.

He narrowed his eyes. "All right," he said. "Perhaps it's better that way. The last thing I need is your lies in his ears."

I refused to be baited.

"However," he went on, "I'm sure we will meet again soon, in Abia. Prince Amron died without an heir. The title of the Knez of Larion has returned to the Crown."

"I believe the king will confer it upon his younger son," I said.

"A boy who still plays with a wooden sword? I don't think so," he sneered. "I am sure he still wants me out of Leven. As I seem to be hard to kill, perhaps he will try another approach and compensate me if I forget my claim. It's wiser for him to bargain, now that he's lost the man who created and protected him."

The king had his reasons. He was preoccupied with negotiating, cajoling, making new friends. Perhaps he would sacrifice Larion to get rid of Raden's threat. But Gospa Liana was quite another beast. Prince Amron had been a kind man, bound by oaths, blood and tradition. She was none of that.

But I just said, "That's not for me to worry about."

"Indeed," he said. "Your task is only to get out of my way when I go south in the spring, after the wedding."

"The wedding?" I was surprised, but I should not have been. *Gospa* Ida stepped forward and took his hand. "Oh, I see," I said. "I am sure your bride's family will give you substantial support in winning the South to your side. What did you say, my lady, where do you come from?"

"I come from a small estate on the border of Elmar and Larion," she said. "You won't be familiar—"

"I was born on the border of Elmar and Larion, my lady," I replied. "I know every manor, village and farm in a hundred-mile radius. And I know every noble family."

"Well then, it seems that you and Gospodar Criscer have a lot in common. He will testify he knew my late father."

She did not as much as blink, I give her that. She just stared at me coolly, like I was a cockroach on her plate.

I regretted my words. If a competent girl like her wanted to marry a fool like Raden, I could only wish her luck.

"Congratulations," I said at last. "May you be happy." In some other circumstances, I would have liked her.

And so we parted.

It was winter dawn when I rode out of the castle, without entourage and without a farewell. I stole out like a thief while everyone upstairs was still sleeping. Only Tinka was awake in the kitchen, and she waved to me.

"Abia?" she asked.

"Yes."

"I'll stay a bit longer. With Gospa Ida."

"Clever."

The old hound we had seen on the first morning appeared from nowhere. He greeted me with a rusty growl, warming up for a proper howl, but Tinka booted him. "Shut up, you'll wake the mistress."

I was sure she didn't mean Gospa Elisya.

The forest path was still bad, full of potholes covered in snow, and the dawn was icy and grey, with dampness that crept into the bones, but those were just the usual drawbacks. They were nothing compared with the empty spot to my left, an absence so heavy it dragged me down. As long as I had remained in the castle, counting miracles and horrors, all the possibilities were still open. I had seen dead people come back to life. I myself had died, or almost died, and came back whole and unscathed. So long as that strange

309

story outside of time had lasted, I was able to believe—stubbornly, persistently—that it was not over. I could pretend I was waiting for him.

But once I rode out and left those cursed walls behind me, it was finished. I was just a lonely traveller on the road, an old soldier with no-one to call his own.

I should have protected him with my life. It was my most important duty and I failed.

Wrapped in such dark thoughts, I went deep into the forest, among the bare trees surrounded by untouched snow. Between them, through the fog that floated over the ground, the first rays of sun appeared. Drops of water in the air and the snow on the ground dispersed the light, intensifying it, until I found myself inside a brilliant cloud. I saw a flash of red, a fox disappearing into the bushes. Time stopped. A rush of panic mixed with hope filled my lungs.

There was a rustle of hooves in the snow, slow and ceremonious. The luminous cloud parted, and a huge apparition stepped forward: a magnificent, snow-white stag with royal antlers. And on its back, without a saddle or reins, *her*.

Not Morana, no. Another one.

I recognized her, although I had never seen her before. The stag, the bow and arrows. Lela, the goddess of the hunt, appeared before me in her human form. On that freezing morning, she wore a light gauzy tunic, green as the forest, tied with golden ribbons, cut wherever it could be cut without falling off her and transparent in all the other places. Female bodies had never aroused me, but I felt deeply embarrassed. I couldn't decide where to look: at the almost-nude body of a girl or into those terrible divine eyes, black with golden stardust in them. I turned towards the stag, although his stare was hardly any better.

"So?" she asked impatiently. "Done?"

She wasn't using her divine voice, the one that resonates in the head, but the silvery voice of a girl, as if she intended to be frivolous and remove all dignity from the meeting.

"My lady?" I asked carefully.

"Perun says it's done, but that old fool keeps forgetting things, so I have to check for myself. Our sister has gone too far, she gorged herself on lives until she was as full as a fat old spider. Perun worried she'd become too powerful once again, and then we would have to go to war and the earth would burn and everything would stretch into eternity."

She was talking about the Goddess of Death as if she were some insolent girl.

"Perun said, 'I'll go'," she continued, "'I'll disguise myself as a traveller, appear out of the blue.' But I said no, Morana would know right away, you cannot hide yourself from her and enter uninvited. She protected herself, find someone less obvious."

A thin, unpleasant smile hovered on her lips.

"I said, send Amron, he has nothing better to do than pester my daughter in Abia, let him play the hero once again, he's good at it, like all your offspring. Perun said, 'what if something happened to him?' and I said, don't worry, there were worse things he didn't survive."

I wished I could hurt her.

"In any case, Amron's done his duty and he's dead again. He's feasting in Perun's hall, with heroes, virgins and mead."

"Really?"

"No, but you mortals like to imagine it that way, don't you? Perun, that old fox, still has some plans for him. More unfinished jobs." A shadow crossed her face. "I worry about my daughter, though. She'll try to save him because she loves him, although I never understood what she sees in him. I thought she would tire of him, he would grow old, she would get fed up. But she'll have none of that, she refuses to let him go."

The goddess paused for a moment and frowned. Up to that point, she could have been mistaken for a dumb, chatty eighteen-year-old, but when she turned her eyes to me, I felt as if the whole universe suddenly raised the top of my skull and looked into my head.

"You're going to Abia, aren't you? Carrying the news to my daughter?"

All I managed to say was, "Yes, my lady."

"Tell her to stay out of it. Tell … tell my Liana, who refuses to speak with me, that it is high time she stopped resenting me for not thinking the role of a mother suited my divine status. Now that she is grown I would be glad to include her among my companions. Tell her she won't have any cares or obligations, that she won't have to worry about mortals and pretend to be wife to one of them. Tell her that here in the forest she can have anyone, or no-one, according to her wishes. Tell her to stop acting like an impudent child."

"I will tell her word for word, my lady. Perhaps she has already forgotten the prince."

I said it impulsively, angrily, without thinking, but it was too much. Even when they were not particularly clever, the gods felt irony like we feel hot iron on our skin. It was deadly to them.

"Are you mocking me?" she asked, and her voice was suddenly directly in my head. The illusion of a half-naked girl was still there, but it started to dissolve around the edges. I didn't want to see what was behind it. "You learned that from your master? Such spirit and resistance, and from whom? What are mortals? Just little bags of blood and bones that are easy to spoil and even easier to hurt. One stab and it's over, the life leaks out of you. I truly wonder sometimes where you get the courage to step out into the world when everything can kill you: stone, wood, metal, fire and water. Everything can kill you and it does kill you. You'll die soon, too: ten years or a hundred, it doesn't make any difference. Because I'll still be here."

I had nothing to say; I nodded in silence.

"Your prince is dead, mortal, because it was his time to die. Even Perun had to agree with that. And my daughter can be stubborn again and fight for a lost cause, or come to me, where she belongs. Tell her that."

She watched me furiously, but there was nothing else to say. She didn't bother with a farewell; she just clouded her appearance. A wisp of fog was all that remained of her.

I reached for the flask with a trembling hand, washed my mouth and spat out, feeling like somebody had fucked me against my will. Then I spurred the horse and rode on through the eerily silent forest until the narrow path led me to the main road. The sun penetrated the clouds, gilding the icy peaks of the White Mountains in the distance as I rode to the south-east, passing through Haragov Dol without stopping, without thinking about the map we held in our hands on the day the blizzard caught us. The winter landscape was barren, empty bar an occasional house with smoke coming out of its chimney, and a lonely hawk, circling high above.

I turned the goddess's words about unfinished jobs over in my head, about the plans Perun had for my lord, about the things Gospa Liana should stay out of. I asked myself what she would say to that.

I smiled for the first time in ten days.

She had no need for a secretary. But an assassin, even one as old and rusty as myself, might turn out to be useful.

# THE END

# ACKNOWLEDGEMENTS

Writing is a lonely process, but it takes a village to get a book published. I am immensely grateful to everyone who helped me on this long journey.

When this book was just a rough first draft, many kind writers on Scribophile helped me polish it. I will forever be grateful to Mari, James, Michael, Ann, Stephanie, Josephine, Sue and all the others who read and critiqued it.

I'm grateful to all the Codexians who encouraged me and read my work. Special thanks goes to Jess, for helping me with my query, and to Eleanor, for reading my first chapters. My Eastern European writers' group offered me friendship and support when I needed it, as did the writing community on Twitter.

I am grateful to editors who published my short stories, who worked with me and made me a better writer. Cat Rambo offered me her immense wisdom, experience and kindness. And Antonia Rachel Ward has been a true friend and the best editor I could wish for.

Lastly, my family has always been there for me. Mum and Dad never questioned my eccentric career choices. My daughter offered me her insight whenever I needed it. My husband has celebrated every victory with me. And my cat has done nothing special, but I'd feel guilty if I left her out.

*Jelena Dunato*
*April 2023*

# ABOUT THE AUTHOR

Jelena Dunato is an art historian, curator, speculative fiction writer and lover of all things ancient. She grew up in Croatia on a steady diet of adventure novels and then wandered the world for a decade, building a career in the arts.

Jelena's stories have been published in *Beneath Ceaseless Skies*, *The Dark*, *Future SF* and *Mermaids Monthly*, among others. She is a member of SFWA and Codex.

Jelena lives on an island in the Adriatic with her husband, daughter and cat.

You can find Jelena on her website jelenadunato.com and on Twitter @jelenawrites.

ALSO AVAILABLE
FROM GHOST ORCHID PRESS

ghostorchidpress.com

Printed in the USA
CPSIA information can be obtained
at www.ICGtesting.com
LVHW030324160923
756757LV00041B/348